DEATH BY CUPCAKE

There was a more somber toast to Leon, and then Ernie stepped forward. "Folks, there's desserts coming out now. Annabelle and Jeremy, we have plates over here for you with some food. And there's more drinks—I promise you, there's better champagne."

Everyone laughed, and Jeremy took the plate that Scooter offered him shyly. He bowed slightly and flashed his megawatt smile at her. She blushed and then went over to give Annabelle her plate.

Jeremy picked up one of the mini cupcakes from his plate and lifted it in the air. "If I've learned nothing else in life, it's eat desserts first, my friends."

He popped the cupcake into his mouth and made a surprised look as he chewed.

Seconds later, he fell over onto the floor . . .

Books by Julia Henry

PRUNING THE DEAD

TILLING THE TRUTH

DIGGING UP THE REMAINS

WREATHING HAVOC

Published by Kensington Publishing Corp.

WREATHING HAVOC

Julia Henry

KENSINGTON
PUBLISHING CORP.

www.kensingtonbooks.com

KENSINGTON BOOKS are published by

Kensington Publishing Corp.
119 West 40th Street
New York, NY 10018

All Kensington titles, imprints, and distributed lines are available at special quantity discounts for bulk purchases for sales promotion, premiums, fund-raising, and educational or institutional use.

Special book excerpts or customized printings can also be created to fit specific needs. For details, write or phone the office of the Kensington Sales Manager: Kensington Publishing Corp., 119 West 40th Street, New York, NY 10018. Attn. Sales Department. Phone: 1-800-221-2647.

The K logo is a trademark of Kensington Publishing Corp.

First Kensington Books Mass Market Paperback Printing: October 2021

ISBN-13: 978-1-4967-3309-2

ISBN-13: 978-1-4967-3311-5 (ebook)

10 9 8 7 6 5 4 3 2 1

Printed in the United States of America

To my favorite traveling companions, the Troisi sisters,
Stephanie and Marianna
Here's to many more adventures

CHAPTER 1

"I haven't seen the lot this full since the Goosebush Players did *The Full Monty*," Ernie Johnson said. He pulled into the parking lot carefully, creeping along behind three other cars whose drivers were hoping for enough room to sidle into a space.

The Stanley Theater had started its life as a large hardware store. In 1978, the store went out of business, mostly because it wasn't in the center of town, and most folks thought that if you needed to drive, you may as well drive over to Marshton and the then-new strip mall. The strip mall had been leveled years ago, but box stores had taken over the town and depleted it, many Goosebush residents felt, of its charm. Goosebush had a new hardware store, Bits, Bolts & Bulbs, which Ernie had run for the past fifteen years, and which was more in keeping with the town, strong on service and part of the community.

In 1981, Stanley Sayers, a local businessman, bought the old hardware store in order to turn it into a theater. There were doubters, some of whom wanted to see the space used differently, but in the years since, the Stanley, as it came to be known, became as much a part of the cultural life of Goosebush as any other building. In the early days, the level of the productions had been extraordinary. Now people came to the theater more to see friends than to be fed artistically.

"Well, I'm glad that dear Leon is a bigger attraction than the promise of naked men," Lilly Jayne said.

"We weren't naked," Ernie said. He was a member of the Goosebush Players and a frequent actor in their productions. "But you're right, the parking lot is packed. We should have asked Harry to help." Harry Lentz was a board member at the theater who was able to fit cars into the lot like a puzzle master.

"Ernie was naked onstage?" Delia Greenway piped up from the back seat.

"I wasn't naked. The show is about a group of men who are willing to dance—oh, never mind. It was a fun musical to do. Leon was terrific in it," Ernie said. He coughed gently and wiped away the tear that rolled down his face.

Lilly reached over and put her hand on his, giving it a squeeze. "Leon loved being in the Goosebush Players. He'd helped run the theater for years. But he didn't join the Players and start acting until after his wife passed."

"Why did he wait so long, do you think?" Delia asked. "He obviously loved it, and he was pretty good."

"One word. Betsy. His wife. Betsy Tompkin was a

lovely woman, mind you," Lilly said. "But she had a strict sense of propriety. Propriety as she defined it, and she was wound pretty tight. To Betsy, proper behavior meant no white after Labor Day, dues paid the first of the year for the yacht club, and no drawing attention to one-self in public forums. I suspect she may not have ap-proved. I remember my mother telling me how horrified Betsy was that her father had invested in a theater."

"She may have been a handful, but Leon never said a word against her," Ernie said. "He once told me that he was so lonely after Betsy died that he felt lost. He used to come into the theater and sit at the back and watch re-hearsals. At that point, he was the landlord for the Goose-bush Players; that was it. One day an actor was sick, and JJ asked him to stand in for the actor and read his lines. The actor didn't come back, so Leon took over the role."

"Do you think JJ invited him because of talent, or be-cause of potential donations?" Lilly asked. She glanced back and smiled. "Delia, don't look so shocked. James Jentry was a businessman first and foremost. In all the years he ran the company, he never put art before com-merce."

"Lilly, you speak truth. JJ was a friend, but he always kept his eye on the bottom line. But honestly? I think he was thrilled that Leon wanted to get involved. There's al-ways a dearth of middle-aged men. Leon adored perform-ing and loved being part of the theater community. He said no one was more surprised than he was that he took up acting, but he was hooked. He did say once, during the run of *Monty*, that Betsy wouldn't have approved."

"I don't think I ever met her," Delia said.

"She and I went to school together," Lilly said. "She

met Leon when she was on a trip with her parents and Leon was leading the tour. He was a few years older than we were. His seventieth birthday was three years ago. Betsy died fairly young. She's been gone ten years at least. Leon did adore her. Bless him. She tried most people's patience, but not Leon's."

"No kids?" Delia asked.

"One, Fred. They had given up on the idea of children, and then Fred came along. Leon doted on him. Fred decided to go to college in California, and then he stayed out there. I haven't seen him in a couple of years, though we exchange cards around the holidays. I did call him, of course. Poor Fred. He took the news hard."

"Fred wanted him to move out west when Betsy died, but Leon said no. Goosebush was home. The theater became his family," Ernie said. "As it does with many of us." He drove around toward the back of the theater and pulled the car in beside the dumpster.

"I can't believe that a week ago, Leon was at a budget meeting about the theater and the *Christmas Carol* drama. Now we're at his memorial service," Ernie said. "It's such a shock."

"It is," Lilly said. "All things said, I have to say that the service feels a bit rushed—"

"The show must go on," Delia said. Both Ernie and Lilly turned around and looked at her. "What? That's what everyone's been saying. That Leon wouldn't want his *Christmas Carol* reading to get canceled, and with Thanksgiving on Thursday and the decision to do new versions before Christmas, it's challenging enough. Someone said that the best memorial for Leon is a successful show. Do you agree?"

"I do. Leon would want us to go on. Though it won't be the same," Ernie said. "And it won't be nearly as much fun. Ah well, much as I dread this, we should we go in."

They went around to the front of the theater, and Ernie held the door open for them both. Delia walked into the lobby and went to the coat rack on her right. She wore so many layers that it would take a while for her. Lilly saw Tamara O'Connor across the lobby and walked over to her. The women gave each other a big hug.

"Oh, Lil. It's just so sad," Tamara said.

"It is, isn't it?" Lilly said, stepping back and looking at her friend. They'd known each other for over sixty years, and neither of them took the other, or their friendship, for granted. "He was a good man."

"A very good man," Tamara said.

"Where's Warwick?" Lilly asked, looking around for Tamara's husband.

"He really wanted to be here, but he's got a game."

"Of course. I suspect that Leon would approve his absence. He was such a fan of Goosebush football."

"He never missed a game, unless he was in a show. Warwick says he must have been quite the player back in the day, because he really understood the nuances of football," Tamara said.

"I can't remember if he played or not. Fred played; do you remember? He may have become an expert because of his son's interest. He was like that. Leon loved being one of the cheering parents."

"Betsy, not so much, if I remember correctly."

"She was never the tailgating type," Lilly said. The

women both smiled and shook their heads. "Delia was asking about her in the car on the way over."

"What did you say?"

"That Leon loved her very much. That's the nicest thing I could think of at the moment. Haven't come up with anything better in the few minutes since."

"He loved her almost as much as she loved herself," Tamara said. "Oh stop, don't look at me like that. You know it's true."

"Of course it's true. But we're here to celebrate Leon, and bless him, he loved her dearly." Lilly looked around. "Is Fred here?"

"Yes, he's in the theater with Delores. I tried to stop it from happening, I really did. But she was in full Delores mode. I didn't have a chance. The door's locked, so I can't rescue him."

"Oh dear." Lilly waved Ernie over to her. "Delores has Fred in the theater," she whispered.

"On it," he said, going over and using a key to open one of the doors to let himself in.

"Does Ernie have keys to everything in town?" Tamara asked.

"Pretty much. Hey, I'm going to hang up my coat," Lilly said.

"I'll stay near the door in case Ernie sends out an SOS," Tamara said.

Lilly smiled and handed Tamara her purse to hold. She walked over to the packed coat rack and found an empty hanger. After her scarf was safely in her sleeve, she managed to wrestle her coat onto the rack.

Turning around, Lilly paused and took it all in. People milled about, hugging, talking in small groups, looking at the displays of pictures strewn around the lobby. Some were of Leon and his family, but most were of Leon in shows. She'd look at them later. Someone walked over to hang up his coat, and Lilly smiled and stepped forward to make space. Hearing a deep baritone, she turned and saw her neighbor and friend, Roddy Lyden, talking to Stan Freeland, owner of the Star Café. Stan had agreed to cater the memorial service, and Roddy had volunteered to help him set up. Roddy looked over and waved. "Save me a seat," he mouthed, and Lilly nodded. She was going to do that even if he hadn't asked.

"Ladies and gentlemen, please come in and take a seat," Ernie said, opening the theater door wide and propping it open. Delia pulled open the other door and put the doorstop down to keep it in place. They both stood to each side, handing people programs as they walked in. After a couple of minutes, Scooter McGee hurried out of the box office and took the programs from Ernie, urging him to let her take over. Lilly wasn't surprised. Scooter lived to be useful and wouldn't be content as a guest while other people were working.

"Should we go in?" Tamara said.

"May as well," Lilly said. "Ernie told Delia and me about the plan for the service this morning over breakfast. I promised we'd sit close to the front and participate so that others would follow along."

"Participate? What does that mean?" Tamara said.

"Well, there will be some songs, some readings, and he wants to make sure that—"

Lilly noticed that Tamara was no longer paying attention to her, so she turned and looked over her shoulder.

She really couldn't blame her friend for losing focus. It wasn't every day that a movie star walked into the room. Especially in Goosebush.

"I've never been to a memorial service where people sang show tunes," Lilly said a while later when they were back in the lobby. Small groups were gathered, looking at pictures, swapping stories, both laughing and crying. Lilly looked around and saw a woman pouring herself some hot apple cider. She knew the face, but couldn't place her. She turned back toward her friends.

"Then you haven't lived," Ernie said. "I've been to many."

"I loved that song you sang," Delia said.

"'You Walk with Me.' From the aforementioned *Full Monty*. Leon loved that song. He'd stand in the wings every night to watch it—" Ernie took out his handkerchief and mopped his face. Tamara reached over and put her arm around his shoulders, giving him a squeeze and a kiss on his temple.

"A lovely service, Ernie," Roddy said. "I know that you had a great deal to do with putting it together."

"It really was wonderful," a younger man said. They all looked over and stepped apart a bit to make room for Fred Tompkin in their circle. "Dad would have loved it. Especially the Shakespeare." He gave Lilly a kiss on the cheek, and then stood next to Tamara, after bussing hers as well.

"Read by Jeremy Nolan, no less," Tamara said, taking Fred by the arm and holding him close. "I didn't know he was a friend of your dad's."

"Dad used to talk about him when I was a kid, but I

thought he was making up stories to impress me," Fred said. "Then a few years ago, I needed an internship in college, and Dad reached out to Jerry to ask."

"Jerry? Not Jeremy?" Tamara asked.

Fred leaned into the group. "Jeremy was a stage name. He prefers Jerry, but you have to wait till he tells you that."

"Jeremy it is, then. I doubt we'll be on a 'Jerry' basis, unless he decides to buy a house in Goosebush and choses me as his broker. Sorry, go on with your story. Leon connected you with his old friend—"

"And much to my surprise, I got an internship. I realized Dad wasn't just telling stories about the good old days."

"Is that why you stayed in California? Did Jerry—Jeremy—help you?" Lilly asked.

"Sort of. I worked for his production company the next year. I didn't get to know him that well at the time, but he took Dad and I out to lunch when Dad visited, and Jerry seemed to love catching up with him. They'd kept in touch. Dad was good like that. He kept in touch with a lot of people."

"Your father connected with people," Lilly said. "He was a wonderful, caring friend. I'll never forget the kindness he showed me during some very dark times. A lot of people loved him."

"I know," Fred said. "He was a good guy."

"The best," Tamara said. The silence was heavy with grief, but no one moved to fill the space right away.

"Jeremy Nolan got his start with the Goosebush Players, back when Mel John was the artistic director," Delia said, changing the subject. "I talked about him in one of my Goosebush stories."

"Goosebush stories?" Fred asked, turning toward the younger woman.

"Fred, this is Delia. Delia Greenway. She knows more facts about Goosebush than I do," Lilly said.

"Not really, Lilly, but I'm working on it. I volunteer a lot at the Historical Society, and I've been doing some research for your father. He asked me to pull some records, since the theater turns forty soon. Some members of the board want to publish a remembrance, so I've been doing some digging in old records. Leon was helping me, but he'd start telling me stories, and we'd get sidetracked. I loved listening to him. Fred, I'm very sorry for your loss. I liked your father a lot."

"Thank you, Delia. So did I. I'm going to miss our Sunday talks."

"We'll all miss our Leon talks," Ernie said.

Fred reached over and clasped Ernie on the shoulder. "Thanks for today, Ernie."

"The service was a joint effort—"

"But you've also kept Delores away from me," Fred said. "That was a real kindness."

"I've seen that determined Delores look before. She wants to talk about the theater, but I'm more than happy to help you avoid her. Especially today," Ernie said.

"She did say that she and my father had come to some sort of agreement about the lease, and they were going to make an announcement on Sunday. She even says she signed a contract, but I can't find it in his paperwork. Probably in a pile that made sense to him, but I'm still trying to figure out his filing system."

"An agreement about the theater?" Lilly asked.

"Yeah. Like Delia said, the theater turns forty next year. That's when it finally opened. And the Goosebush

Players turn one hundred. According to Delores, they were cooking something up, some huge event to celebrate both anniversaries."

"My conversations with your father didn't indicate that he was cooking anything up with Delores," Ernie said. "He was distracted lately, and we didn't talk about much except the *Christmas Carol* project he was producing. We were supposed to have dinner last week to talk. He said he'd been rereading your grandfather Stanley's papers, and they were giving him ideas. I know he wanted to go over some things while we had time to plan for the anniversary of the Stanley, partially to make sure folks remembered your grandfather, and all he did for Goosebush." Ernie wiped his eyes again.

"Dad was really focused on legacy, especially lately. When he found out he was sick last spring, he went into overdrive. Every week when we'd talk, he'd tell me he wasn't going to leave me with a mess. He started to question what he really wanted to do with his money. I know that the theater has a part of his heart, and he wanted to make sure it was taken care of. I really thought he'd have more time to hammer out the details."

"He was still working on them. We have a board meeting for the theater next week, and Leon planned to talk about some changes," Ernie said. "Unfortunately, I don't know what those plans were. I hope he left some instructions, or notes, so we can try and implement them."

"His house is a disaster of paperwork," Fred said. "We were planning on coming out for Thanksgiving to see him and help him sort things out, and I think his piles were in preparation of our visit. I wish we hadn't waited."

"There was no way to anticipate him having a heart attack," Lilly said. "I knew we didn't have much time, but I was hoping for more. Here's what I do know. We can all work on making his final wishes come true, so please let us know if you find out what they were."

"Delores is over talking to your wife," Ernie said to Fred. "Don't panic; I'll go rescue her."

"Thanks, Ernie. She can hold her own, but she and Dad were close. It's been a rough few days. Could you let her know I'll be with her in a few minutes? Thanks. Lilly, do you have a couple of minutes to talk?"

"Of course, Fred," Lilly said. Roddy gave her a wink, and she followed Fred.

Fred led Lilly back into the theater. They walked down the aisle. Fred looked around and gestured to a seat in the front row. He waited until she'd settled in and then sat down next to her.

"Lilly, I've got a huge favor to ask."

Lilly nodded. She'd learned long ago not to say "of course, anything" in these sorts of circumstances. "Of course, anything" could get you involved with things that were complicated at best. She was still dealing with Harmon Dane's estate, and would be for years, all because of an "of course, anything" one night over dinner, and Harmon passing away before he'd clarified his intentions. Not that it was his fault, since he was helped along, but still.

"Dad did leave a will, and he'd updated it recently. Several times. As I said, ever since he got sick, he started questioning how he wanted to leave things."

"That's good," Lilly said.

"I guess. Usually Dad had a plan and stuck to it, but

he'd been changing his will regularly. His lawyer said Dad called him two or three times a week. He'd decided instead of leaving the Stanley Theater to the Goosebush Players, he'd leave it to a trust, with very specific instructions about the use of the space. I didn't see the details; we were going to go over them when I came out. But I do know that his plan wasn't to give the Goosebush Players exclusive use of the space. At least, that wasn't the plan when we talked last week."

"I don't understand. He left the theater? Why did I think the town owned it, and he was only on the board?"

"Dad didn't like to make a big deal about it. My grandfather bought out the partners years ago, and then he left it to my father. The board is more of a front that Dad set up, a group of advisors. Yeah, Dad owned the theater. The thing is, Delores expected him to leave it to her outright. The trust is designed to run the theater, and there's also money for the Goosebush Players. But he was very nostalgic recently, thinking about what it was like when my grandfather was in charge of the theater. The amazing work that he helped produce. I wish I'd had the chance to know Stanley better. Anyway, Dad wanted to have more groups using the space. Shake things up a bit."

"I wasn't living here in the heyday of the Stanley, and didn't know your grandfather well, but my parents used to talk about those days with great fondness. It makes sense that Leon wanted the theater to reclaim its former glory."

"Not to Delores. Like I said, he was still formulating it all, but part of the plan he was working on created funding for a theater manager who was not Delores. He said he was going to talk to her, but she acted surprised when I brought it up. I bought some time and told her that we wouldn't be able to settle the estate for a while. That I needed to follow through with the other things he'd indicated in the will."

"That makes perfect sense to me."

"So, here's the favor, Lilly. I have to get back to California. I can do a lot from there, but I need someone in Goosebush to be my representative. Not an executor, really. But someone to help me make some decisions moving forward. Someone who knows Goosebush, and is able to weigh all the factors evenly. I'd like that someone to be you."

"There must be other people—"

"Dad wrote me a note that went with his most recent will. He told me he was going to ask you to help oversee the execution of his will. The trust idea wasn't fully formed, but he mentioned that you helped Harmon Dane take care of his birds—"

"Create a bird sanctuary. Harmon had laid it out in his will, so I'm only executing his wishes."

"He also said you were the most sensible person he knew, and you'd help me make the right decisions when the time came."

"Oh my. Well, then." Lilly looked down at her lap and reached into her purse for a tissue. She dabbed at her eyes and looked back at Fred. "Of course, I'll help however I can."

"Thank you, Lilly. That's a huge load off. I'll be in touch early in the new year to get the house on the market, and we can talk more then. His lawyer has asked that I keep his paperwork at the house for now, but I've been scanning and trying to sort. I'm still in a state of shock, to tell you the truth. I haven't been much good at focusing."

"I'd imagine you are," Lilly said, patting Fred's hand. "So, you'll sell the house then? You could keep it and rent it—"

"No, we'll sell. I couldn't bear the thought of renters. It needs some work, but it's too wonderful a place to let it sit empty most of the year. My wife and I are going through it now and having some pieces of furniture shipped to us. We'll finish getting rid of the rest of it later."

"I can help coordinate that, if you'd like. I know some people who can sort and sell or donate what you don't want."

"There won't be much. After my mother died, my father really pared down. He called it 'minimalist living.' He kept the artwork, photographs, things like that. But he already gave us the family china, her jewelry. Things from the Sayers side of the family."

"Well, that both makes it easier and harder, doesn't it? What's left are the things he really cared about," Lilly said, taking Fred's hand and giving it another squeeze.

Fred and Lilly were halfway down the aisle toward the lobby door when it opened and Jeremy Nolan walked in. "Oh, sorry to interrupt—" he said.

"No worries; we were just leaving," Fred said. "Taking a look at the old place?"

"I am, if that's all right," the actor said, walking up to Fred and giving him a brief hug. He turned to Lilly and smiled. "Sorry, we haven't had a chance to meet. I'm Jeremy Nolan." He held out his hand.

Lilly blushed and smiled back. She lost herself in his blue eyes for a second, and then she took his hand. "Lilly Jayne."

"Lilly of the old Jayne house?" he asked. "I used to drive by that place and wish I could see inside. It looked like a movie set for a haunted house, set back, huge, and imposing with wrought-iron gates, overgrown with ivy."

Lilly laughed. "When were you here? Back in the eighties? Windward—that's the name of the house—did look a little worn back then. She's in better shape now."

"Of course," Jeremy said. "Sorry, that was a lousy thing to say. Being back here has stirred up a lot more memories than I expected."

"Good memories?" Fred asked.

"Mostly. Yeah, mostly good," Jeremy said. "Great memories of the theater we did. Mel was a helluva direc-tor. Sorry, speaking in shorthand," he said to Lilly. "Mel John. He was the artistic director back in the day. We made some great work. He and Stanley were a great team. God, I miss those days." Jeremy Nolan smiled at them both, stepped a bit farther into the theater, and looked around.

"It was nice of you to come today, Jerry. Thank you. My father would have been thrilled. Doing the reading was so generous," Fred said.

"Your dad reached out to me a couple of months ago. He found out I was going to be in Boston working on a film, and he wondered if I'd be willing to talk to him about the theater. We had some great email exchanges. I'm just sorry we didn't have our meeting."

"Did you have something scheduled?" Lilly asked.

"For next Friday. The day after Thanksgiving. The

film is shut down for a few days, so I was going to come down and visit. I wish I'd have come earlier. We had a lot to discuss. More regrets. That's one of the challenges of getting older. Regrets. Listen, Fred, if you need anything, reach out, all right? Anything. Ms. Jayne, it was great to meet you." With that, Jeremy Nolan took one more look around the theater and left.

Lilly looked over at Fred. "That was interesting. Mel John? Do you remember Mel John?"

"Before my time, I'm afraid," Fred said. "Though my father mentioned him many times, mostly when he was talking about theater that impacted him." He looked around and turned back to Lilly.

"This place—it meant so much to Dad. I want to make sure I do right by it. By him."

"What sorts of documents have you found about the theater?" Lilly asked him.

"So far I've been focusing on trying to find all the notes he left for the trust. His lawyer had started that paperwork, but Dad hadn't given him all the details. He had been emailing us both a lot, so we feel like we can figure it out, though how much will hold up if anyone wants to contest the will, I don't know. That's probably another reason he wanted you involved, to help smooth things over."

"You said he'd been looking over your grandfather's papers?"

"He mentioned diaries, but I haven't been able to find them. As I said, it's a mess. He also has a file cabinet full of stuff about the theater. Mostly old records, pictures, call sheets from shows. My grandfather saved everything. I was going to donate it to the Historical Society."

"Why don't you let me go through them first? And, if you don't mind, forward me the emails he sent Jeremy Nolan if you find them."

"Is something wrong, Lilly?"

"No, nothing's wrong. I'm only wondering what it was that your father wanted to talk to Jeremy Nolan about. And if I can help Leon fulfill that wish in any way."

CHAPTER 2

At the end of Lilly's driveway, there was a large gate. She'd been tempted to remove it, but then she became a focus of the Goosebush gossip mill and decided that she liked her privacy and to keep others at bay. For people living in the house, there was a password to open the gate. Visitors needed to text to be let in, because the intercom was broken. And strangers? Strangers parked in the shipyard parking lot across the street and came up the front walk, where Lilly would decide whether or not she'd open the door. Lilly liked it that way.

She was mid–pie crust on the Wednesday before Thanksgiving when her phone began to jump across the kitchen counter, indicating an incoming text. She dribbled cold vodka into the mixer with the dough and pulsed twice before she wiped her hands. The text was from

Bash. She texted back, buzzed the gate open, and opened the kitchen door. She counted to ten, and then she buzzed the gate closed again.

Lilly went back to the crust. She took it out of the food processor and piled it onto the marble board. She drizzled the last of the liquid and moved it around until all of the dry bits were incorporated. She quickly divided the crust into thirds and molded each into balls that she flattened slightly and wrapped up. She added the disks to the stack in the refrigerator and turned to say hello to Bash.

Sebastian Haywood was the chief of police in Goosebush. He'd been growing into the role with the help of his mentor, the previous chief, Ray Mancini. Bash also had his secret weapon, Lilly Jayne. At the beginning of his career, he'd run things by Lilly to get her perspective and make sure he was seeing all angles. These days, he usually waited until he was stumped to talk to her.

"Bash, how are you? There's some coffee in the pot. I'm afraid you're going to have to help yourself. I'm up to my eyes in mini pies and need to make my apple filling before I can stop for a moment."

"Man, I love your apple pie. Do you need help peeling? I enjoy peeling and chopping."

"Bless you. Because there are a lot of apples." She took her floury hand and pointed to the bushel basket on the kitchen table. It was full of apples. Mostly Granny Smiths, but a few others for variety.

"That is a lot of apples," Bash said. "But this is my secret skill. Point me to the utensils."

After a few minutes of getting Bash set up and double-checking the size of the apples he cut, they were on a roll.

Lilly made two more batches of pie crust and sighed. "Those are finally done."

"How many crusts did you make?"

"Eight double crusts. I know, it's a lot. But running out of pie on Thanksgiving is an idea that haunts me. The crusts need to chill for an hour."

"Is that your secret crust? I always love your pies," Bash said, picking up another apple and quickly peeling it. He hadn't been boasting about his skills.

"I use cold vodka and water, and a bit of shortening in addition to butter. The combination makes the crust have that wonderful shortbread texture. I'll give you the recipe if you'd like. It was my father's."

"That would be great. Though it's easier to come by and eat yours."

Lilly laughed. "Let me help you, and we'll get these on the stove for a few minutes to cook a bit. And then we'll have some lunch. Delia made a wonderful roast last night, so I can put together some open-faced sandwiches."

"Sounds perfect," Bash said. He was focusing on peeling a single strip and didn't look up when Lilly sat down at the table and picked up an apple.

"To what do I owe this visit?" she asked as she started to peel. Lilly always let Bash work his way into the reason he stopped by, but he'd usually started talking by now.

"Leon's service was nice, wasn't it?" Bash asked, discarding the core into the bowl Lilly had put on the table to keep the compostable materials separate.

"It was, very. I still can't believe he's gone," she said. "I thought we'd have more time."

"So did his doctor," Bash said. "Leon was sick, but the tumor didn't affect his heart."

"I wondered about that. Maybe the stress got to him?" Lilly stopped peeling and looked over at Bash.

"His heart didn't show any signs of damage. It just stopped. I'd let that go, but then there's the coffee." Bash picked up another apple and started to peel it vigorously.

"The coffee? What coffee?"

"He died in his car. Hard to know if he was coming or going. He didn't have anything on his calendar. Maybe he went out for breakfast?" Bash mumbled.

"Bash, slow down. I'm not understanding. What coffee?"

"The coffee. Right. He had coffee in his system. But his coffee maker broke a couple of days ago, and he didn't have instant. No coffee cups had been used. There wasn't a to-go cup in his car. Nothing tossed in the trash. I checked the usual haunts, but no one saw him that morning. So, where did he get the coffee?"

"He could have had a visitor?"

"Maybe. He got the coffee somewhere. Like I said, it was in his system. The only thing he'd eaten recently."

"Bash, do you think the coffee had something to do with his death?" Lilly said, putting down her apple and looking at him.

"I don't know," Bash said, looking up. He shook his head and then used the corer again. "I've asked the medical examiner to run some more tests."

"I hate to think, but of course it did occur to me. I'd hoped . . ." Lilly handed her peeled apple to Bash to core and took a deep breath. "I'd heard he died at home. I didn't realize he was in his car. Who found him?"

"His housekeeper. At nine o'clock. His newspaper was delivered at six-thirty, and it was inside and opened. He had a habit of putting sections into the recycling bin as he read them, and the front page and metro section were recycled."

"Maybe that's when he had his coffee?"

"Apparently, Leon didn't eat before noon, according to his housekeeper. He'd wake up, take his medications, read the paper, and go for a walk or work out. A man of routine. As I said, the only thing in his system was the coffee. Which was an eggnog latte, though he didn't have any eggnog at his house, either. It was one of his favorite drinks."

"Did anyone—"

"Order an eggnog latte? I'm checking that in the places that sell them. I checked in with Stan, and the Star sells them. Dozens every day, so not a lot of help there. I've been looking at other places, but no leads." Bash picked up another apple and began to peel.

"I hate to think that something happened, but it is odd. Does anyone know that you're looking into this?" Lilly asked.

"A couple of people at the station. And the medical examiner, since she's running the tests."

"What does she think?"

"After she talked to his doctor, she thinks it may be worth looking into."

"Oh, Bash," Lilly said. "I'd wondered, but I convinced myself that I was just expecting the worst, given what's happened here over the past few months. Then I didn't hear anything, and Fred didn't seem worried, so I let myself believe that he died of natural causes."

"That's still likely the case, Lilly," Bash said with concern.

"Let's hope so. In any event, that's a heavy burden for you to bear alone all this time. What can I do to help?"

"You don't think I'm making a big deal out of this? For all I know, he got a craving, so he drove over to Marshton and had a coffee, then he drove home and had a heart attack. I keep telling myself that's more likely than foul play."

"It is," Lilly said, chopping the last of the apples and putting them into the bowl. She looked over at Bash and smiled. "But I'm glad you're double-checking. Leon wasn't himself these past few weeks, but that's understandable given his diagnosis. Wanting to understand why his time was even shorter than expected is a kindness to his memory, I should think. He was a dear man. I'll keep this news close to the vest, of course. But please keep me posted."

"Thanks, Lilly. I will. Phew. I feel better talking it through. I'm sure it's nothing."

"So am I," Lilly said, hoping she or Bash would be convinced. "You're taking care of Leon, and I appreciate that," Lilly said, smiling at the young man. She felt a heaviness in her heart, but she forced herself to sound upbeat. "Now, how about that sandwich? Do you have time?"

"Sure. How about if I get the meat carved while you put the apples on the stove? How many apple pies are you making?"

"Two or three dozen. But that's not all. I'm making all sorts of mini pies. Apple. Cherry. Pumpkin. Pecan. Mincemeat. Chocolate cream—"

"Whoa. How many people are coming for Thanksgiving dinner?"

"Well, Tamara and Warwick, and their entire family. Their new kitchen isn't finished, and they always have Thanksgiving at their house. Roddy's daughter is going to her in-laws, so he'll be here. Stan Freeland is coming over. And Ernie and Delia, of course." Lilly brought the apples over to the stove and put them in the pot. She tossed in cinnamon, sugar, boiled apple cider, nutmeg, and butter and stirred it all together.

"Of course. I keep forgetting that Ernie's moved in. I guess it's good his house sold so quickly, but that was a quick turnaround putting his stuff in storage. How long do you think he'll stay?" Bash had found the roast, and taken out the leftover gravy and some mustard. Lilly pointed him to the frying pan, and he put the gravy in it.

"Poor Ernie; it was a bit of a blur. Two weeks to pass the papers and move out. Thank heaven for moving companies and storage units. He's got one of the larger rooms on the second floor with a sitting room, so he has some of his things with him, and he's settled in well. He'll be here for a while, since the clear-out of the Preston house is taking longer than he expected. Mostly because of the family treasures he's finding on Albert's side of the family. He's looking for relatives who might be interested, but so far, he's only found distant cousins. It's quite a project, and he's been so busy with the plans for the Garden Sculpture and Lights event."

"Ernie's one of the busiest people in Goosebush these days, that's for sure. Are you entering a garden sculpture of some sort?" Bash asked.

"I'm not inspired, but I'm trying to come up with an idea. Creating a large-scale sculpture out of plant materials that also lights up sounds complicated to me."

"Me too, but Stella's asked me to help her with one."

"That's what big brothers do, isn't it? Help their little sisters with projects?"

"Stella's always got projects, that's for sure. As long as folks can pull it off, it could be a great way to light up Alden Park for the holidays while giving Goosebush a fun community project."

"'As long as folks can pull it off' being the key part of that sentence," Lilly said. "Heaven help us all with people getting ideas for public projects from reality television shows."

"There's a show that makes garden sculptures that light up?" Bash asked.

"Not exactly, but these timed events seem to be all the rage. Since the park has been cleared, I suppose it will be nice to decorate it in some way. Lights and twigs to help Goosebush get in the holiday spirit."

"Yeah, that's one way to do it. Ernie's working on the *Christmas Carol* readings as well, right?" Bash layered the sliced roast into the gravy and stirred it around.

"He is, especially now. They were Leon's special project, so Ernie's stepped in to help."

"They're turning into a pretty big deal," Bash said, putting gravy in the frying pan.

"Theater isn't my world," Lilly said. "But doing updated versions of *A Christmas Carol* sounds interesting." Lilly took a spoon and sampled the sauce of the apples. She added more nutmeg, set the timer for ten minutes, and kept stirring.

"There's some wicked famous playwright doing one of the pieces, right?"

"Mitchell Layton. Carolyn Kegan and Dorothy Christie are the other two playwrights. I only know this because Ernie talks about the readings all the time. It's an ambitious project that Leon had been planning for months. Now Ernie's in charge, but he's recruited Delia to help with scheduling."

"That's a good move. But why isn't Delores helping?" Bash asked, layering slices of roast beef on the hot gravy to warm it up a bit but not cook them.

"As I said, this was Leon's baby," Lilly said. "From what I understand, Leon specifically did not want her involved. There's much palace intrigue around the whole thing, but as I said, theater isn't my world." She took out two plates and put them on the counter next to Bash. She laid a slice of bread on each plate and then stood back to let Bash do his work. Another stir of the apples, and then she turned off the heat. She'd let them cool and then start putting the pies together after she ate lunch.

"I should ask Ernie about the project," Bash said. "I didn't realize that Leon was so involved with it. Anyway, thanks for the lunch invite, Lilly. My mother used to make open-faced sandwiches all the time. I miss her, both of them, especially this time of year."

"Bash, you know you're welcome to come over tomorrow," Lilly said. She got two glasses out of the cabinet and brought them over to the refrigerator for ice and water.

"Thanks, Lilly. We're going to try and cook a turkey dinner. Again. Stella found Mom's old recipe cards, and she's determined that she's going to pull it off this year. But maybe we can come by for mini pies?"

"Please do. After all that peeling, you deserve an apple pie."

"You aren't going to believe this," Delia said, storming into the kitchen a couple of hours later.

Lilly barely looked up. She was in the zone of making fluted pie crusts and didn't want to lose steam. The apple pies were all in the oven, so now it was on to the rest. "Good afternoon, Delia. What won't I believe?"

"This video."

"I'm covered in pie crust. Hold the phone out a bit; I have the wrong glasses on." Delia did what Lilly said, patiently moving the phone in and out until Lilly nodded. Delia hit play, and Delores's face filled the screen. She started talking about the upcoming hundredth birthday of the Goosebush Players, mainly focusing on her tenure.

"The video is well done," Lilly said. "Very artsy."

"She got a video intern this semester," Delia said, sighing. "But did you hear what she said? She got half of the history wrong. The other half's forgotten. She didn't talk about the theater at all. Without the space, the Players would have fallen apart years ago. I feel like Leon is rolling over in his grave."

"That's not a good feeling," Lilly said, looking over at Delia. "Play it again. I'll pay more attention."

Delia did what she was told. Afterwards, Lilly looked at Delia and nodded. "I see what you're saying. Put on the tea kettle, will you? What do you think Delores is up to with that video? There wasn't a 'come see our holiday show' or 'donate today' or even a 'thank you for being part of the theater' message. Seems like a bit of a lost opportunity the day before Thanksgiving, but then what do I know?"

"Right?" Delia said. "I've just joined the board of the theater, so I'm learning how that works. I'm not involved with the Players, and I know that's a complicated relationship."

"Is it? I had no idea that Leon owned the Stanley, did you? Of course, I'm not as much a part of that world as you and Ernie are."

"I didn't understand how separate they were until I started helping Leon with the anniversary project. But he never said a word against Delores."

"She's a piece of work, isn't she?"

"As Ernie would say, she sits on my last nerve. I mean, listen to what she said in that video. She's trying to hog all of the credit for the work of a lot of people. Including Leon. When I first hit play, I thought it was going to be some sort of tribute to him. He certainly deserved one."

"Ah, Leon. I've been thinking about him a lot today," Lilly said. "Tell you what. Tomorrow's Thanksgiving. Let's be grateful we had Leon in our lives, and that Delores isn't coming to dinner. Don't giggle, Delia. The rest of Goosebush is showing up, or seems to be. Not that I mind, especially since I'm only worrying about desserts. But I do have to get a move on with these pies."

"Let me wash my hands, and I'll help. I can smell the apple pie filling. Is that left over?" she asked, gesturing to the pot on the counter.

"Yes, I wanted to get the rest of the pies made, and then if there's extra crust, I'll make more apple pies."

"Can I try a spoonful?" Lilly took a spoon out of the silverware drawer and handed it to Delia, who dipped it into the pot, scraping the sides for extra sauce. "Delicious, as always. You're right, Lilly, we've got a lot to be grateful for this year. Even if these past couple of weeks have been extra sad. Maybe I'll work on my own tribute to Leon."

"That sounds like a lovely idea," Lilly said, going back to her fluting and thinking about Leon.

CHAPTER 3

"More wine, Auntie Lil?"

"A half a glass, thank you, Tyrone," Lilly said. She smiled up at her godson as he poured her some more white wine. She suspected it wasn't the same wine as was already in her glass, but no matter. Thanksgiving Day had been full of happy accidents; maybe a new wine blend was another.

"How about you, Mom?" he asked, holding the bottle up for Tamara to look at. "I'm the designated driver, in case that has you worried."

"Well then, I'll have a bit more, thank you, son," Tamara said, nodding at her youngest as he poured more wine into her glass. He put the cork back in the bottle and then set it on the table. "How's the cleanup going?"

"All under control. Bash and Ernie are washing some of the serving dishes, and I'm helping put things away.

They're thinking about waiting for another half hour or so for dessert."

"At least," Tamara said. "That was an amazing meal. I'm still stuffed."

"And to think, you were afraid there wasn't going to be enough food," Ty said. He sat down on the edge of a chair and smiled at his mother.

"Given that our entire family was going to descend, being worried about enough food is always a legitimate concern."

"Ty, that's our mutual nightmare, your mother's and mine. Not enough food. Our mothers would both haunt us if that ever came to pass."

"Would they ever," Tamara said. "I think of them so often on days like this. They would have gotten a kick out of the next generation, don't you think? Speaking of which, it seems pretty quiet in the house. Are your nieces and nephews behaving? They're leaving that poor cat alone, I hope."

"Roddy and Dad took everyone over to Roddy's house to burn off energy. They were going to run around Aunt Lil's gardens, but Roddy suggested they run around his backyard, since it's so open, and Dad thought it would be good to add a little structured play to the day."

"Why don't you go over and join them, Ty. Do your sisters a favor and tire out your nieces and nephews, will you? You're good at that. They were all very well-behaved at dinner, which means there's some pent-up energy that needs to be let go."

"New people at the table helped," Ty said. "They felt like they had to use their company manners. 'Course, I may have threatened them."

"Ty—"

"I told them that we wouldn't play video games if they made you upset," Ty said.

"When the fun uncle says something, it has weight, I suppose," Tamara said. "I'm really glad that Bash and Stella came over, even if it was because their turkey didn't turn out."

"It will eventually defrost, and they'll have a nice meal tomorrow," Lilly said. "We've all made that mistake, though this is Stella's third failed attempt at Thanksgiving dinner. I'm going to suggest she try again in January when there's less pressure. Selfishly, I'm just as glad. Their contributions to the sides were wonderful. I will admit, I'm a traditionalist for Thanksgiving. But those roasted vegetables and corn soufflé were wonderful."

"You aren't that traditional, Lil," Tamara said. "We've been adding Jamaican dishes to the menu for years. And Delia's coleslaw is hardly traditional."

"But those are all family recipes," Lilly said. "Tried and true. Anyway, it was a lovely meal. I certainly hope that Ernie is packing up leftovers for people to take. We can't possibly eat all that food."

"They're sending some stuff back with my sisters, but the rest you're keeping here. Come on, Auntie Lil. You know we'll end up eating here, anyway. I'm going to head back into the kitchen and help. Then I'm going next door to wear out the young'uns, unless you need something else?"

"No thanks, sweetie. We're good." Both women watched Tyrone leave the room, then turned to each other and smiled.

"Do you remember how scared I was when I found out

I was pregnant with him?" Tamara asked quietly. "I had just turned forty; the girls were all in middle school. I couldn't believe it."

"He is such a blessing to us all," Lilly said.

"Yeah, well, there were those high school years, which weren't as much of a blessing. I was so worried about him, and about us, back then. Ty was so lost, and we couldn't get through to him. Then Alan took him under his wing. Ty mentioned being interested in archaeology, and next thing you know, Alan's got him sitting in on lectures and visiting sites. The next year, Ty was interested in filmmaking, and Alan found him new classes and people to talk to."

"Alan loved that Ty's curious about so many things," Lilly said, remembering the joy her late husband had in introducing Ty to new ideas and fostering his interest. "Alan was the same way as a young man. He loved Ty very, very much."

"And Ty sure loved his uncle Alan." Tamara wiped the tear that slid down her cheek. "Sorry, Lil, don't mean to be maudlin. There's something about the holidays."

"Especially this holiday. Alan really loved it. He focused the day on gratitude, family, and food, in that order. I was making the pies yesterday, and felt him over my shoulder, critiquing the apple filling, reminding me to chill the vodka for the crust, suggesting a better topping for the cherry pies."

"He'd be really happy today, with this houseful. Don't you think?"

"I do, I really do. I will say this, Tamara. For the first time since he passed, I've enjoyed a holiday without feeling as if my heart was breaking again. It's not that I don't miss him—"

"Of course you miss him. We all do. But this was nice, adding new people to the mix. That helped, for sure. I'm so glad Roddy was able to join us. I thought he was going to be with his daughter."

Lilly felt herself blush a bit. She looked over at the new gas fireplace in the corner of the porch, mesmerized by the dancing blue flames and grateful for the heat it threw off. "She went to her in-laws, but his ex-wife is there, as well. He's spending Christmas with her."

"I wonder what his ex-wife is like?" Tamara asked.

"He's got three of them, you know," Lilly said. "He's told me that they are all lovely women, but he was a terrible husband, working all the time and taking them for granted."

"He doesn't seem the type to take people for granted, does he? He's been attentive to all of us."

"He has, though he's retired, and that likely helps," Lilly said. "Heaven knows he's got a million projects going at once. It's hard to believe that he's only lived here for six months."

"I wonder what he did, back in his working life?" Tamara asked. "I thought he was in business, but then he mentioned some legal work—"

"And he's mentioned working for the government, as well. He's never been too specific. He'll tell us when he's ready, I'd imagine."

"You know me, I'm just being curious, is all. Roddy's a puzzle, and I'm just trying to figure out the missing pieces." When Lilly didn't say anything else, Tamara went on. "Speaking of curious. Did I tell you Nicole's newest idea for getting involved with Goosebush?" Nicole Shaw worked with Warwick as the assistant coach, and had been trying to meet more people, primarily the young, male, and marriageable sort.

"What's she doing now?"

"She's volunteering in the box office for these *Christmas Carol* readings."

"I didn't know she liked theater."

"I'm not sure she does, but she likes people. She started volunteering for the Goosebush Players, helping in their box office, but she didn't understand Delores's business practices, so she quit."

"Didn't understand, or didn't agree with them?"

"Both, I think. She was new to selling tickets, so she thought it may have been her. She asked Warwick about them, and he encouraged her to leave. Bless her heart, she's a nice young woman, but she doesn't read people very well. Anyway, Warwick drafted her to help him with the *Christmas Carol* ticketing last week. Leon had asked him to help out a couple of months ago."

"Why Warwick?"

"He's set up a lot of ticketing in his day, mostly for sporting events and fundraisers."

"Your husband is a man of many talents," Lilly said.

"Helping people feel like part of the community is one of them. Like I said, Nicole doesn't know many people, so she keeps volunteering. She knew that Delores wasn't teaching her the right way to run a box office, and Scooter McGee was useless, since she does what Delores tells her to do. Don't look at me like that. You and I both know Scooter would forget to breathe if someone didn't remind her. Anyway, Nicole talked to Warwick, and he told her he'd be glad to have her help with the first reading. He'd offered to help Delores with ticketing a while back, and have the Goosebush Players use the ticketing system the school had invested in, but so far she's not bit-ing."

"If the Goosebush Players ever get audited . . ." Lilly shivered. The Goosebush Players never made enough money for people to pay attention, but still. "Good for Warwick. Where is Nicole, by the way?"

"Texas, visiting her family. She'll be back for the read-ing on Sunday."

"What sort of things was Delores doing that made Nicole nervous?"

"The Goosebush Players tickets are the old-fashioned kind. Printed. She'd ask Nicole to put seats aside as com-plimentary under different names, but then Nicole saw a check come in for four of them. She asked Delores about it, and was told not to worry about it, they'd reconcile the books later."

"That does sound like a problem. Bless Nicole for try-ing. I wouldn't have," Lilly said. She paused and lowered her voice. "You know, Tam, I'm only going to say this to you."

"I won't tell anyone," Tamara said, miming crossing her heart and giving Lilly the Girl Scout salute.

"I feel petty saying this, but I can't believe they didn't postpone the readings for another week, given that Leon passed. Every time I hear Delia and Ernie talk about the project, I want to scream."

"Thanksgiving is so late this year, there's not much time between now and the new year—"

"I know, I know. The show must go on. There's a read-ing a week. Blah, blah, blah. I see how hard Ernie is working on it, and I'd hate for his work to be for naught. I wish that Leon's passing mattered more to people, is all."

"Oh, Lil, his passing mattered to a lot of people. I'm sure we weren't the only group sending him a prayer at dinner today. Ernie said the board is going to vote on dedicating the rest of the Goosebush Players season to him, and he's going to mention him before the reading on Sunday."

"Has Delores blessed that?" Lilly asked.

"She has final say, but he was a huge donor and a member, so I can't imagine there will be a problem. Delores doesn't have anything to do with the readings," Tamara said. "The theater is producing them, not the Goosebush Players. She's working on the holiday extravaganza she's got planned."

"I was surprised that she canceled the Players' *Christmas Carol*. It was already cast and everything."

"From what Ernie told me, she insisted that members of her cast couldn't also do Leon's projects, thinking that would stop them from happening. Then the cast decided they'd rather do the readings, so they all quit."

"But tickets had been sold—" Lilly said.

"Not many, from what I understand. I think that people were pretty sick of the same old Delores special. I hear the extravaganza is selling well, but that's from Delores."

"Why do you call it the extravaganza? What's it called?"

"I don't remember, honestly. She's using her face in the marketing, so I don't read the details."

"Tamara—"

"Don't you 'Tamara' me. The woman's a menace. You know that's true."

"She is pretty awful," Lilly said. "Apparently, she was haranguing Fred before the funeral about some sort of paperwork Leon apparently had. Something about the theater and an announcement."

"What sort of announcement? I'd been talking to Leon about zoning for the theater, and he never mentioned anything to me."

"Would he have?"

"His father-in-law and my father were good friends. My dad owned part of the theater at one point."

"How did I not know your father was a theater guy?"

"Years ago, my father was on a business council for Goosebush. It wasn't an official group, mind you. More an ad hoc group of concerned citizens who understood the importance of supporting small business for Goosebush."

"Like the garden squad, except we worry about plants."

"A lot like the garden squad, actually. Friends who work together for the good of the town. Anyway, forty, almost fifty, years ago, they put a lot of effort into getting a huge lot zoned for business. It took years; you know how that goes. Once it passed, a lot of folks were interested, but the group had plans. They sought out what they hoped was the perfect store for the site, something Goosebush needed. A hardware store."

"I keep forgetting that was what the theater used to be," Lilly said. "I'm not sure I ever went there."

"The owner made some bad decisions about the way he treated other businesses in town. Ticked off the wrong people. Before anyone knew what happened, there was an unofficial boycott of the store, which closed. The group was beside themselves. Leon's father-in-law, Stanley Sayers, bought the building and the site, and the group started to think about other viable options."

"There must have been a few, like another hardware store," Lilly said.

"By then, folks had gotten used to going over to

Marshton. And then, at a town meeting, the board of selectmen decided the lot had to be used for cultural purposes."

"How could that be decided in a town meeting?"

"The lot had been owned by the town, and there were
two options put forward. One for the store, one for a museum. The store won, because the town was hoping for
tax revenue. When the store went belly-up, the culture
warriors stepped in and said they wanted to have a run at
the space. There was a group that had been formed when
the zoning was happening—they still wanted to make it a
museum. But Stanley got it in his head that he wanted to
start a theater company."

"So, the museum people lost out. Town government
can be so petty sometimes," Lilly said.

"Sure can. Anyway, it took a while to convert the
space. Then the first theater company failed. Leon tried to
produce shows for a couple of years—"

"Leon? Where was I? How can I not remember this?"

"This was almost forty years ago. You were in grad
school. In London."

"Ah, right. Go on; what happened next?"

"Stanley was a supporter of the Goosebush Players for
years. They were mostly a community theater, but he
started to offer them serious financial support so they
could hire artistic staff. Then he rented them the theater.
He made some sort of deal where the Players used it during the year, and then another theater company came in
during the summer. It was pretty successful for a while,
but then he died." The two women paused, and Tamara
shook her head. "After Stanley died, the plans changed.
The Players eventually got a long-term lease on the
space."

"The zoning board mustn't be thrilled. The space isn't the income stream the town hoped for."

"The restaurants and other businesses do well when there are shows. Plus, all of the educational programs the Players do are a real benefit to the town. I think that the theater had been a success to a degree."

"Held back by Delores, I'll bet."

Tamara laughed. "True. Man, she's a piece of work. Do you know why the readings aren't being done in the theater? Because Delores said no."

"And she could do that?"

"She could, and did. She almost didn't let Leon's memorial service be held there. But Ernie pointed out that it wouldn't look good for her to say no to that one."

"Why are they doing the readings, anyway?"

"The theater doesn't have a mortgage, so the rent the Players pays is what covers all the expenses. They're trying to raise money for new seating and other improvements. But I think it may be more than that. Leon thought this was his last Christmas, and he wanted to do a *Christmas Carol* that he was remembered for. Then he decided to commission three new versions, so that he'd be part of creating future productions if any of them are any good. I hope he gets that dream."

"Ernie's very excited about them," Lilly said. "He may have mentioned how refreshing it is not to have to live in Delores's world. Every day for the past month."

"I've heard the same thing from Portia Asher," Tamara said. "The last couple of years, Delores has moved from running the group to directing everything herself and choosing all the plays. Not her strength. The board has been pulling their hair out, but since the Goosebush Players is a for-profit organization, they didn't have much say."

"I didn't realize that," Lilly said.

"The education program? That's its own non-profit. Delores couldn't care less about that work, though it pays the bills. Honestly, the work those kids do is better than what Delores produced."

"Remember that musical she directed last summer?" Both women looked at each other and shook their heads at the same time. Some things were never mentioned aloud in order not to hurt the feelings of friends. Ernie had been miserable in the show, and they'd all agreed never to talk about it.

"I know, it's been a mess. But here's a fun fact. The Goosebush Players' lease is up at the end of the year. I heard from PJ Frank that Leon was talking to folks about bids for a new theater or other use of the lot. I know he'd been talking to me about zoning hearings and how to schedule them. I think Leon may have been considering kicking Delores out."

"Could he do that? Put something else on the lot?"

"As long as part of the use was cultural, yes. It would have had to go through approval processes, but Leon was a popular person," Tamara said.

"Fred mentioned that his father was working on how he wanted things left and kept changing his mind. It sounds like this could get messy."

"He'd made it clear that a theater was part of any plans going forward. PJ said he and Leon were supposed to meet next week. If he wanted to kick Delores out, I wonder what his plans were."

"I wonder if Bash knows about Leon's exploratory meetings."

"Knows about—Alan, what are you doing out here? Where's your diaper, young man?" Tamara went running after her youngest grandson as he pealed with laughter and ran down the hall.

Lilly got up and walked towards the kitchen, bringing their glasses with them. She wanted to talk to Bash. If Leon was killed, she may have found a reason.

CHAPTER 4

Lilly went into the kitchen and looked around. The large coffeepot was perking, and a few of the "better at room temperature" desserts were on the kitchen table, still wrapped. The dishwasher was going, and the next load was waiting on the counter by the sink. She walked back out and meandered down the hall, looking in the rooms. The only other living being was Luna, the tortoise kitten that Delia had adopted last month. Luna looked up from her perch on the ottoman next to the fireplace, flicked her tail hello, and put her head back down. Lilly walked over and rubbed her head.

"Do you want me to take you upstairs, sweetheart?" she asked the cat gently. Luna didn't move, so Lilly let her be. The children and the kitten had played hard before dinner, so she was tuckered out. A rarity for her. Lilly rubbed her head again and stood up when she heard foot-steps.

"Auntie Lil, Mum's upstairs rocking Alan. He proba-bly won't take a nap, but they're both resting," Rose said. Rose was Tamara's youngest daughter and looked just like her mother. Lilly smiled every time she saw her.

"Rose, where's everyone else?"

"Over at Roddy's house. He's got some games set up, and everyone's hanging out until dessert time. Alan needed a diaper change, so I brought him back."

"Still? It must be cold—"

"Roddy's got a fire pit cranking. It's pretty fabulous, let me tell you. I'm going to walk back over and enjoy it now that I don't have to chase a toddler around for a bit."

"Where's Gordon?" Gordon doted on Rose, and was usually a very hands-on father. Which was a good thing, because Alan was a very energetic baby.

"He's playing with the nieces and nephews. They're all having a great time. Want to come over?"

"Sure, I'd love to. I should go up and tell Tamara—"

"I already told her that I'd take you with me."

"Let's go out the back and through the gate," Lilly said. "My coat is back in my library."

Lilly put her heavy wool coat over her Thanksgiving dress. The gray didn't exactly match the fall leaves that floated all over her A-line dress, but that didn't matter to Lilly. What mattered was being warm. She slipped on her short boots and pulled on her gloves. She looked up to see Rose smiling.

"I know I must look a sight," Lilly said.

"I was just thinking that you looked pretty hip," Rose

said. "You've got flair, Auntie Lil. Always did. Always will."

"You have to say that because I'm your godmother," Lilly said, smiling at Rose.

"Nah, wouldn't say it if it wasn't true. Thanks, by the way, for hosting today. I haven't enjoyed Thanksgiving this much in years."

Rose held the back door open and closed it behind her. Lilly linked her arm with Rose's as they made their way slowly through the gardens. November was not a blooming month, but there was still great beauty in Lilly's backyard, and Rose took her time looking it all over.

"It was a lovely day, wasn't it?" Lilly said. "I take no credit for the meal, though."

"The meal was great, but it was the company that made it fun."

"I agree," Lilly said. "I think having new people at the table made it much more special."

"Mum and Dad were so relaxed. They wouldn't have been at their house."

"It's not really ready for company, is it?"

"I don't know about that. They could have pulled it off. But then they'd be in entertaining mode, which is always a little stressful for them. Pitching in at your house is their happy place."

"I'm always happy to host," Lilly said. "This house is much happier with people in it. And what a wonderful gift to have all of you here. Usually one or two of you are at your in-laws."

"I'm so glad it worked out this way," Rose said. "I love spending time with my sisters. And Ty, of course, even though he is spoiled rotten."

"He's not spoiled—"

"Don't even start with me, Auntie Lil. He's spoiled. A great guy, but spoiled. Comes from being the youngest."

"Maybe a little spoiled." The women walked through the back gate, and Lilly stopped to take it in. "My, look at this."

Lilly's house was built on a triple lot, but the house and the gardens filled it up. Roddy's house was built on a double lot, with the house closer to the street, which was in keeping with the rest of the neighborhood. His back-yard was enormous. He'd spent weeks planning and prepping the ground to bring back the gardens next spring. He'd also had some hardscapes put in at the last minute, and Lilly hadn't seen the final project completed. Roddy had taken pity on a contractor whose client had changed her mind the day before installation of a project, leaving flats of turned cobblestones that couldn't be re-turned. Ernie had introduced them, and together they'd designed some patio areas, paths, and seats.

"Turned out well, didn't it?" Roddy asked, jogging up to Lilly and Rose.

"Throw the ball, Uncle Roddy!" a young voice called out. Roddy looked down at the football in his hands and turned. Before he could toss it back, Rose grabbed it from him and ran towards the mass of children and adults, all of whom welcomed her back with cheers.

"Don't let me keep you," Lilly said.

"Honestly, I could use the break," Roddy said. "I filled in when Bash took a time-out. I only played for a few minutes, and I'm already done in. So, what do you think?"

"I love it," Lilly said. "And you had them put lights in. That's a lot of decision making in short order."

"I would have dithered on the decisions, given a

choice. The entire lot was part of the package that they offered me. I may make some tweaks next spring, but for now, I'm delighted. I hadn't planned on benches and as many paths, but it will work."

"It will definitely work," Lilly said. "There are lots of interesting gardening nooks along the side now. And I love the way the paths highlight the original Winslow garden design. I see you also got a fire pit?"

"Bought it from Bits, Bolts and Bulbs. I always like to give Ernie business when I can."

"So do I," Lilly said. "He does so much for this town, but doesn't get nearly the credit he deserves. This week, I noticed a few people posting on Instagram about the materials they bought over in Marshton for the wreath contest. Honestly, it made me so mad. Why not go to the Triple B and post about that?"

Roddy laughed. "Perhaps you'll need to show them how it's done," he said.

"What's that over there?" Lilly asked, pointing to a wire fence around a patch on the other side of Roddy's yard.

"You have an eagle eye, Lilly," Roddy said. "I've decided to try my hand at growing garlic."

"Growing garlic?"

"I was talking to the landscaper, and he told me how easy it was. And now's the time to plant. I put some cloves in and mulched the top so that they'd be warm this winter. I've got to gussy up the fencing, but I think I'm going to put a vegetable garden in next spring, and that seemed like a good place to start."

"That's wonderful on all fronts," Lilly said. "I've always wanted to have a vegetable garden, but not enough to give up space. Please plan on using the greenhouse this winter to start some seedlings."

"Thank you; that would be perfect. I've got so much space back here; feel free to consider some of it yours next spring. Here, have a seat by the fire. I'm going to get a few more pieces of wood."

Lilly walked over to the fire pit and put her hand on Bash's shoulder. "Sitting the game out?" she asked.

"I got a call, so I stepped out. Then another call came in. Just finished, and enjoying the fire."

"Everything okay?" Lilly asked.

"Yes, fine. It's Steph Polleys' first shift that she's in charge of, and she wanted to check on a few things. Most everything's quiet right now. Though things typically kick up a bit in the evening, after folks have been drinking for a few hours."

"Your job is never quiet, is it?" Lilly said.

"No. Thought it would be, when I first took it. Didn't understand all that goes on in every town under the surface. But that's enough about that. Thanks again, Lilly, for having us over at the last minute. What a great meal."

"I'm so glad that you and Stella came. And don't forget about dessert. There's an embarrassment of riches."

"I never forget about desserts. This break in between is great, though. What a gorgeous day. Remember last year, and the snow? Glad that didn't happen this year."

"So am I," Lilly said. She stretched her feet out towards the fire and sighed. "I think I could fall asleep out here. I've never seen one of these before. It's really rather lovely, isn't it?"

"It is," Bash said. "'Course, you have to make sure the

fire isn't too close to the house, and that there's water nearby."

"Yes, of course," Lilly said. She took note of the bucket on the corner of the patio and wondered if Roddy had put it there or if Bash had.

"Bash, I hate to bring this up—"

"Is it about Leon?" Bash said, lowering his voice.

"Well, sort of. I was speaking with Tamara earlier. Do you know about the theater and the rules around its use?"

"Sort of. Leon was in charge, so I looked into it. The town has a say into its use, and it needs to stay a theater was what I gathered."

"I just learned two things that throw a different light on that. One, that a new building could be built as long as a theater is part of it."

"That's a good-sized parcel of land. I wonder if—"

Lilly looked up and saw Delia heading towards them, so she spoke quickly. "The other interesting fact is that the Goosebush Players have a long rental agreement—"

"Right—"

"That's up at the end of the year," Lilly said.

"Huh. That's interesting."

Lilly nodded at Bash. "I thought so, too," she said.

"Also, interesting that no one's mentioned it to me," he said.

"No one thinks Leon didn't die of natural causes."

"True—"

"Bash, would you take my place in the game?" Delia ran over, panting. "I want to go over and start getting the desserts out."

"Do you need help?" Bash asked, nodding at Lilly and putting his phone in his jacket pocket.

"Stan asked me that, too. No, there isn't much daylight left, so everyone should enjoy the game."

"I'll come over and help," Lilly said, reluctantly getting up from her chair. She looked around and saw that Roddy and Warwick were over by the woodpile, talking. "Bash, I'll text you when we're ready."

"Thanks for the talk, Lilly. Keep in touch on that, will you?"

"Well, that looks stunning," Lilly said, surveying the dining room table. There were plates of mini pies, cookies, and homemade candies. Stella Haywood's cheesecake sat in the center of the table, alongside Stan Freeland's chocolate mousse. Tamara had brought a large fruit salad along with her mother's signature Jell-O mold. Lilly couldn't wait until someone broke into that—a frozen combination of raspberry Jell-O, walnuts, cranberry sauce, whipped cream, and cream cheese that transformed into nirvana, at least to Lilly. She half hoped that no one else would like it, but knew that wasn't possible. It was a holiday favorite.

Delia snapped a few more pictures, turned to Lilly, and smiled. "It really does. I'm so happy that Ernie made fudge. He makes the best fudge I've ever had."

"You know he uses Fluff in it, right?" Lilly said.

"Fluff? Really?" Lilly smiled as she watched Delia go through the ingredients of Fluff in her brain. Delia's food philosophy was if you couldn't pronounce it, you shouldn't eat it, and corn syrup was to be avoided. Fluff may not pass the test. "Oh well, who cares? I love it. I've already had a piece."

"You're having a nice day?" Lilly asked, taking a pile of napkins from Delia and putting them on the sideboard next to the dishes and silverware. Desserts were going to be buffet-style, so Delia walked over with the pile of plastic plates that were reserved for the grandchildren and the clumsier adults.

"A great day; why do you ask?"

"You've been working so hard this semester. I know that a quiet holiday might have been nice for you, especially this year."

"No way," Delia said. "I know I'm an introvert, but I love being around lots of people at the holidays. It's so not what I had growing up. I'm grateful to be part of this family now." Delia walked over to the china cabinet to take out the coffee cups and saucers.

The first time Lilly met Delia, her late husband Alan had introduced her as the best graduate assistant he ever had. Later, he'd told Lilly that Delia was a talented student driven by loneliness and self-doubt as much as anything. He asked if Lilly would mind her coming to Thanksgiving, and of course, Lilly said yes. Soon, Delia was at most holidays. When Alan got sick, she came every day, eventually moving in to help him finish his work. Lilly never knew the details of her estrangement with her family, but Alan had known, and was very protective of Delia. Not for the first time, Lilly was grateful that Alan had brought Delia into her life. She couldn't imagine what the past three years would have been like without her.

"I'm glad you're part of the family, as well," Lilly said. Delia blushed and turned back toward the table. "What do you think, are we ready? Should we text Bash?"

"May as well. It may take them a while to wrap up the game, but it is getting dark." She took out her phone, and her thumbs flew over the screen. She smiled and showed Lilly a picture that Stan had sent her of Ernie celebrating a touchdown with a leap in the air. "Who knew that Ernie was a great touch football player? Did you know that?"

"I had no idea. Though that's not the sort of thing that comes up in everyday conversation, is it?"

"No, I guess not. Thanks, Lilly, by the way. For worrying about me. I'll grant you, I'm looking forward to winter break. Though I've got projects lined up. I'll be working on Fritz's house."

"Still?"

"Still." Delia nodded. "And the Historical Society is a mess regarding volunteers, so I promised Meg I'd help straighten things out there."

"I'll reach out to Meg. I'm happy to make my volunteering there more official."

"You know, if you wouldn't mind being the point person on the theater project, that would be great. I want to give that priority over the Goosebush Players project, but they both have anniversaries coming up. Sorting through the project and deciding who gets what is a huge task. There's a lot of overlap."

"Why not give them both copies of the same things?"

"Delores wants them to be unique—"

"Tell you what, Delia. How about if I deal with Delores? She seems to cause you and a lot of other people a great deal of stress."

"Are you sure, Lilly? She can be a handful—"

"That's my specialty. We can talk more about the project tomorrow. I think I hear footsteps on the back porch, so let's get the cider out and the tea water on."

CHAPTER 5

"You aren't going to believe this," Delia said to Lilly the next morning as the older woman walked into the kitchen. Lilly looked at her young friend for a moment, and then walked over to the coffeepot, poured herself a huge cup, and made her way to the kitchen table, where she sat down heavily.

"How can you be so chipper this early in the morning?" Lilly asked, blowing carefully and taking a sip of the dark brew.

"It's not that early," Delia said.

"It is for the day after Thanksgiving," Lilly said. "I didn't even do much, and I'm exhausted."

"You did a ton," Delia said. "You were the hostess of the day."

"That's not much," Lilly said. "That's what I do."

"But you do it so well. You kept conversations flowing, made sure everyone felt welcome, figured out the timing for everything. Not everyone can do that, Lilly. Stan and I were talking about it. It's your special skill. One of them."

"You're very kind," Lilly said. She took another sip and felt more human. "Now, what is it I won't believe?"

"Warwick just called me. The reading for Sunday is completely sold out."

"The theater space at the Star seats what, a hundred people for this type of event? That's very impressive."

"It's because there's a movie star in the cast."

"A movie star?"

"Jeremy Nolan. And his ex, Annabelle Keys."

"Annabelle Keys. She's a lovely actress. I haven't seen her in anything for years. You know, I saw someone who looked familiar at Leon's service, but I couldn't place her. When did that casting coup occur?"

"Mitchell Layton—"

"The playwright. I've heard his name so often, it was nice to finally meet him."

"He's interesting. Talented, but a handful. He had Thanksgiving dinner with Jeremy and Annabelle, and they volunteered to do it."

"Ah, so that's why he didn't come to dinner."

"Who?"

"Mitchell. Ernie had invited him. That's neither here nor there. So how did you find out?"

"It was supposed to be a secret, but of course it leaked out, so the tickets sold out. Warwick is trying to find a bigger space."

"Why Warwick?"

"Ernie asked him to see what he can do. Ernie'd do it, but he's busy. Day after Thanksgiving. Retail."

Lilly nodded. She was glad to hear it was busy at his store, but still worried that it might not be busy enough for her friend. "Isn't the reading on Sunday? That's two days from now. Seems pretty late to be looking for a new space."

"It is last minute, but come on. We could reach all of the revenue goals in one weekend with more seats."

"Wasn't this supposed to be a low-key reading for the playwrights to hear the work? Ernie explained the whole thing to me. Develop the work this year with a possible production next year. Will a bigger audience be a good thing?"

"Actors like audiences," Delia said.

"Don't actors usually like rehearsals, as well?" Lilly asked. "Ernie said Mitchell's canceled most of the ones that were scheduled." Ernie had explained that the deadline of a rehearsal brought on a creative fever in Mitchell, so he'd use the rehearsal time to make large changes instead. Lilly sensed that it stressed Ernie out, but whenever she asked, he'd made excuses for his new friend Mitch—Ernie called him Mitch—and Mitch's creative process. The other two readings were in better shape, but Mitchell was a better-known playwright, so Ernie said that also caused stress.

Lilly thought Mitchell/Mitch was temperamental and selfish. Not that her opinion mattered much. She didn't understand why anyone would put themselves through what Ernie went through to get a show open. According to Ernie, she didn't get the joy of the theatrical process. Lilly told him that they defined joy very differently.

"The no-rehearsal idea has been nixed as of this morning."

"That's good," Lilly said.

"So, um, I have a favor to ask. It's a big one, so feel free to say no."

"Go ahead."

"Can we have a couple of rehearsals here at the house?"

"We?"

"Ernie sucked me in. I've been drafted to be the stage manager. Jimmy was going to do it and run the lights, but now he's nervous about doing too much, given, you know, the movie star angle."

"Sure, I suppose? Is the house big enough?" Lilly looked around and tried to imagine ten actors standing in her kitchen with scripts in their hands. She couldn't see it.

Delia laughed. "Are you kidding me? This place is huge. And we're not going to be moving around, just reading. I'm wondering if the dining room makes sense, or if we should use the living room? If that's okay?"

"It's all good. Whatever you need to do, do it. I'll stay out of your way," Lilly said. "What time?"

"Six. Come to think of it, we need food if it's at six."

"We have plenty of leftovers," Lilly said. "Unless the movie stars have special diets."

"I hadn't thought of that . . ."

Lilly laughed. "I'm sure it will be fine, Delia. You said that Warwick's looking for a bigger space?"

"Trying. The schools are all closed for the weekend, and he doesn't want the facility folks to have to come back early. I've got a call in to see if the space in the library is free."

"That's not that many more seats than the Star, and the stage is very small," Lilly said. "You know where it has to be, don't you? The Stanley."

"Delores has already ruled that out. She says she's got a rehearsal in the theater that night."

"Which can take place at the Star. It makes the most sense, doesn't it? The theater seats four hundred people—"

"Three seventy-seven—" Delia said automatically.

"Three seventy-seven. Which is much more than one hundred. It's either that or the church—"

"The churches aren't available. Warwick checked."

"If you want it to be in Goosebush, then it has to be the Stanley."

"Delores will never go for it."

"Why don't you check in with whoever decides these things, and if they think it's a good idea. I'll ask her," Lilly said.

"You'll ask Delores to give us the theater? What makes you think she'll say yes?"

"Fred asked me to help arrange Leon's affairs. That may inspire Delores to be on my good side."

Delia nodded and smiled. "You're something else, Lilly. Okay, I'll see what people think."

Lilly's breakfast was comprised of two mini pies, one apple and one cherry. She watched as Delia bounced between her computer and her phone, texting, messaging, emailing, and whatever other communication techniques people used in lieu of calling one another. Luna came into the kitchen, stretching and yawning. She looked at her dish plaintively and meowed at Lilly.

"She's eaten," Delia said.

"But she's hungry," Lilly said. "Look at her. Maybe a bit more kibble?"

"She's had a bit more kibble, as well," Delia said. "Seriously, Lilly, you spoil her. I wouldn't be surprised if you didn't start cooking for her."

Lilly was going to make a retort but stopped. If Luna needed her to cook, she probably would. It still amazed her how quickly this tiny bundle of fur had become a part of their lives. She picked the kitten up and held her close, rubbing her head and whispering to her.

"Delia won't let me feed you anymore. I know, I agree. If it were up to me, I would. Tell you what, I'll feed you a big dinner tonight, okay?" She gently put the kitten down and got up to take her plate to the sink.

"You know, Lilly, you shouldn't pit Luna against me. I'm just trying to make sure she stays healthy."

"Um, Delia, she can't understand what I'm saying."

Delia looked up from her phone and gave Lilly a look that could fry ice in February, as her father used to say. "Do you know that for a fact?"

Lilly shrugged and assessed the kitchen. Some dishes left over from last night were waiting. She loaded the dishwasher, starting it. If there was going to be company, they needed to be ahead of things. Moving slowly, she went upstairs to prepare for the day. She came back downstairs a few minutes later, a quick flick of mascara and a dash of lipstick making her look somewhat presentable. In the hallway, Lilly zipped up her black boots and took a look in the mirror. Not bad. Today her dress had a cosmic theme. Her earrings were dangling white flowers that looked like stars. She wore leggings under the dress and added a cardigan over the top of it. Functional, but still appropriate for a meeting.

She walked down to the kitchen and looked inside. The room was empty. She crossed the hall to what used to be the breakfast room and poked her head inside.

She'd turned the room over to Delia this fall and was always surprised at the transformation. The room only had one small window because of the back-porch addition and the greenhouse on the side of the building. There was a French door that led out to the porch, but Delia had put curtains up on it for privacy. The large space, with its built-in cabinets and shelves, suited Delia, who had different areas set up to serve different purposes. She taught online, and had the lighting setup and sheet draped in front of the door so that her background looked neutral. She had a movable white board that she drafted notes on and that the Garden Squad used while in the middle of cases. There was a small couch that Delia used for resting and the occasional nap. The three bookcases she'd brought in were all overflowing. Her desk was a large table with enough monitors on it to resemble a NASA station. Each area had a cat pillow, bed, climbing station, or scratching post.

Delia was sitting on the couch with her feet up. She was typing on her laptop, and Luna had fallen asleep on her legs.

"Anything new?" Lilly asked.

"Everyone thinks the theater would be great. But a couple of people asked that you really, really let Delores know that she has nothing to do with the event."

"I'll make that clear."

"Really clear."

"Got it. She's difficult."

"Yes, that. And apparently one of Mitchell's stipulations when he agreed to letting his work be read was that Delores could have nothing to do with it."

"Interesting."

"Yup," Delia said. She looked up. "It's all so exhausting, the drama. I'm really grateful that you're taking care of it, Lilly. Thanks."

"No worries," Lilly said. "Just keep your phone handy in case I need to ask you any questions."

Lilly loved where she lived. She loved Windward, the old family house that she'd inherited and renovated. She loved the town of Goosebush and its proximity to the ocean, small-town charm, and easy access to Boston. She loved her street, Washington Street, the road that connected the center of town to the beaches by way of a couple of rotaries. And she loved that she could walk to the Wheel, the central rotary where many businesses, including the Star, were located.

The Star stood for Stan's Theater and Restaurant. It was housed in an old Woolworth store that had somehow survived the '90s wrecking balls that had replaced the old A&P, gas station, and garden center with a prefabbed block of buildings that looked like they had weathered exteriors but were actually made of plastic. Lilly always did her best to avoid that part of the rotary, which was to her right. Instead, she walked to the left and headed to the Star.

She walked by the Cupcake Castle, pleased to see that it was packed with patient people waiting and hoping that the cupcakes wouldn't run out before they got to the front of the line. Lilly was always amazed at the magic Kitty Bouchard could do with cake, syrup, and different fillings, all topped with a sublime buttercream. Who knew that such an unpleasant person could create such bliss?

Lilly had fallen under the spell of those cupcakes over the past month and was just as happy that she had errands that prevented her from joining the line.

A couple of doors down, and she was at the Star. She approached the door carefully, letting her eyes adjust a bit before she went in. Stan had arranged heavy, dark curtains around the door as a barrier to the winter blasts, and more than once she'd surprised someone who was leaving, blinded by sunlight and not expecting to run into someone, quite literally, on their way in. Inevitably it lead to an awkward dance Lilly would just as soon avoid this Friday morning.

Lilly went through the curtains and smiled while she paused and got her bearings. The entire place was buzzing. The coffee bar on her right had a line, and the tables on her left were all taken. There were many browsers in the bookstore, and the cash register there also had a line. Lilly looked over at the coffee bar and waited until Stella Haywood looked up.

"Stan?" she mouthed.

Stella smiled and pointed toward the stairs. Stan was up in the theater.

Lilly walked up the old wooden stairs slowly, remembering the years she ran up and down them as a child fascinated by the tropical fish or in search of a specific color yarn on the second floor of Woolworths. The change in the space always delighted her. Downstairs the bones of the old store were still evident. Upstairs, there was no sign of hardware, yarn or pet supplies. Stan had completely transformed the space into a performance venue.

"Hello, Stan," Lilly said, unbuttoning her coat and taking off her gloves.

"Lilly, hello!" Stan came around from behind the counter and gave her a kiss on the cheek. "Thanks again for a wonderful day yesterday. I haven't had that much fun in ages."

"Thank you for being there," Lilly said. "It's been a long time since I've enjoyed a holiday as much."

"Now that I know you're a master pie baker, I may need to hire you to help with desserts."

"Oh, you," Lilly said, pleased. The food at the Star, both in the restaurant and coffee bar, was of the highest caliber. "How's it going today?"

"Busy, really busy. Too busy. We have shows up here this weekend, and I don't know how I'm going to pull it off. We're down on staffing, and my regulars are all working on the reading or the Players' event."

"The extravaganza—"

"The Delores debacle, from what I've been hearing."

"Oh dear—"

"Yeah. You know, I started the theater on a lark, because I had friends who were looking for space to perform. But now it's taking off, and I'm having trouble adding another business to the mix. The whole situation has me thinking."

Lilly had offered to help Stan with a business plan for the Star, and they'd had a couple of meetings to talk about it. She'd asked Stan to think about his capacity and what he could do without hiring more staff. He'd emailed a couple of times to ask some questions, but Lilly didn't know where things stood.

"What have you been thinking about?" she asked quietly. Stan was a complicated man with a vision. She never could have imagined the old five-and-dime being a vibrant space that included a restaurant, theater, coffee shop, and bookstore, but here she was, sitting in a theater lobby that used to be the fabric section of Woolworth.

"I love having the theater space, but I need help running it. There's this woman, Virginia Blossom. She's from New York, but her folks had a summer house here, and she's winterizing it, planning on relocating."

The name struck a chord with Lilly. She tried to think of where the house could be, and who her parents were, but nothing came readily to mind. She didn't dwell. Stan was still talking.

"She's looking to produce some cabaret shows, and came to me to see about renting the space. I resisted at first. I have control issues."

"I never would have guessed," Lilly said, smiling at Stan. To pull off what he had with the Star, he'd have to have control issues.

"Now I think it may be a good option. I can carve out time for the spoken word events and the comedy shows, so my regulars would still have a space to perform. But she'd run the box office, take care of the schedules, hire the staff. She'd get it running at a higher level. She's offered me a pretty good deal to take over."

"Hold on. Virginia Blossom? Now I know how I know the name. Didn't she put in a proposal to open a jazz club or something like that last year? Or earlier this year?"

"You have a good memory, Lilly. Yes, and she got shot down. There are only two entertainment venues in Goosebush, aside from the schools and the churches. The Star and the Stanley."

"And no outsider can come in and build another one," Lilly said.

"Yeah, she got a lesson in Goosebush 101. Let people

get to know you first. Get a few folks on your side. And then go before the town meeting. Anyway, I'm thinking about taking her up on her proposal. It's just that I need to—" Stan trailed off and looked around the lobby.

"Be sure it's the right move. This is your baby, Stan. Of course you want to make sure it's taken care of. If you want a sounding board, I'm happy to listen. You said she gave you a proposal? We could run a couple of models, and maybe work on a counterproposal, if that would make you feel more comfortable."

"That would be awesome, Lilly. I don't suppose you have time next week—"

"Of course. If not in person, we could meet online—"

"Listen to you. High-tech meeting options."

Lilly smiled. "Delia has been showing me how some of these programs work, and I'll confess, they make it a lot easier to get some meetings going when people don't have a lot of time. I know that you're busy, so whatever works."

"I'll figure out a couple of times and text you to see what works for you. Thanks so much. Whew. I feel much better. Now, sorry, you didn't come here to hear my business musings. What can I do for you?"

"You know that the reading is sold out for Sunday night."

"Do I ever. I've got people crawling out of the woodwork begging me for tickets. Get Jeremy Nolan to play Scrooge, and the whole world wants to be there."

"They've been trying to figure out a bigger space to move it."

"I know; Warwick and I talked earlier. All of my suggestions weren't available," Stan said. "Holiday weekends are tough."

"I'm going to ask Delores if they can use the theater."

Stan whistled softly. "You are a brave woman," he said.

"Why is that the reaction of everyone? I know Delores can be difficult—"

"That's one word for it. It's more than that. She's taken it as a personal affront that she wasn't asked to be part of this reading series. As a director or actor. Anything. Instead, she was cut out of it."

"Whose decision was that? I can't imagine Leon not trying to make everyone happy."

"I heard that Leon told her, but it was a committee decision. He'd created a group of advisors, and they felt that it was important to separate the theater and the Goosebush Players for this. Now that I know how sick Leon was, it makes sense."

"It does—"

"Problem is, someone also mentioned that they wanted to raise the caliber of the event."

"Who said that?" Lilly asked. No wonder Delores was upset.

"I have no idea. Someone took a picture of an email, blacked out the sender, and forwarded it to Delores. She's been quoting it ever since. Very dramatically. Usually ending with her dabbing her eyes and taking a dramatic breath."

Lilly laughed. His Delores imitation was excellent. "That's good to know before I talk to her. If I get her to say yes, can she use the Star for rehearsal?"

Stan looked pained for a moment, but then he nodded. "Just tell her that the tap dancing has to be practiced in street shoes, because my floors can't take it. And that she can't rehearse with live animals."

"Tap dancing and live animals? What exactly is this show?" Lilly asked.

"She's being coy and has sworn people to secrecy. But I hear that she's seen the Rockettes one too many times. She's been looking for a camel."

Lilly laughed, and Stan joined her. "Maybe she'll settle for a llama," she said.

"Don't give her any ideas," Stan said, chuckling some more. "Oh, hey, one more thing before I say yes. Would you get me some tickets to the reading?"

"Absolutely," Lilly said. "Thanks, Stan. I look forward to talking to you next week."

CHAPTER 6

Lilly parked in the theater parking lot and walked over to the front doors. They were open, so she let herself in. She looked over to her left and saw Scooter McGee sitting in the box office window, reading a book.

Scooter had been christened Elizabeth, but her only other sibling, a brother twelve years her senior, had nicknamed her Scooter. She volunteered for the Beautification Committee in addition to the Goosebush Players and a dozen other groups around town. She'd been both blessed by significant family fortune and cursed with a lack of ambition, so Scooter's fifty-some-odd years hadn't contributed much to the world. She was the type of volunteer who took on any project, however, which Lilly appreciated. She was also a person with unflagging good cheer.

"Scooter, I didn't know you worked in the box office,"

Lilly said through the glass window. Scooter turned on the microphone so Lilly could hear her.

"I don't usually. But people are away for the holiday weekend, so I told Delores I'd help out. My brother and his family are visiting, so I'm just as glad to be out of the house."

Lilly laughed. "How many children does Bucky have?"

"Five. And three grandchildren, if you can believe it. They're all there. It's fine, but a lot. They're coming back for the Garden Sculpture and Lights show."

"Are you helping out with that?" Lilly asked.

"Ernie asked me to go and help figure out the grid system for Alden Park so they can work on the electrics set up. So yes, I am. I'm also going to work on a piece, if I come up with an idea."

"My mind is blank on that one, as well," Lilly said. "Is the box office busy?"

"It would be if we were running *A Christmas Carol*," Scooter said, smiling. "The phone is ringing off the hook for tickets. I changed the message, and I'm letting the calls go to voice mail."

"Well, the new Scrooge is probably the reason why," Lilly said. She didn't think not answering the phone was a good box office tactic, but this wasn't her theater.

"New Scrooge? What happened to Ernie?"

"Nothing; he's still in it. But Jeremy Nolan agreed to play the role. Annabelle Keys is going to be in it, too."

"Jeremy Nolan?" Scooter said. "Wowzah. You know, he worked here at the theater years and years ago. I knew him . . . wow. I saw him at Leon's funeral, but he didn't remember me. I was so hoping he would—"

"You must have been very young," Lilly said.

"In high school. He was my first great crush," she said.

Scooter blushed again and looked down at the book she was reading.

"Ah, well. I hope this isn't too awkward, but you'll see him again on Sunday if I can talk Delores into letting me use the theater," Lilly said.

"Wow. At least I have time to prepare this time. I hope for your sake she says yes. But I wouldn't count on it. What time is it? Three? She should be on break. If she's not in the theater, she'll be in her office. I'll buzz you in."

"Wish me luck," Lilly said, turning and pulling on the door once she heard the buzzing sound.

A stampede of tap dancing feet blasted through the theater doors. She looked over and saw several people huddled in the corner of the lobby. Walking over, she hoped to recognize someone. No such luck.

"Is Delores still in rehearsal?" she asked to the group in general.

"They were supposed to be finished a half hour ago," one of the women said. She swayed back and forth, holding a sleeping baby in her arms. "I hope they finish soon. I have an afternoon of errands to run."

"Sherry, I can drive Lizzie home for you—" another woman said. The music stopped, and Lilly heard a loud clapping sound, and then Delores's voice screaming "again!" Everyone winced, and the music started again.

"Who's in there?" Lilly asked.

"The mice," a man said.

"The mice?" Lilly asked again.

"The mice for the Nutcracker dance," the woman named Sherry said. "They've been rehearsing for two hours. It was supposed to be an hour."

"How old are they?" Lilly asked.

"Four."

Lilly didn't know much about children, but two hours of a dance rehearsal seemed like a lot for four-year-olds. "Have you asked her how much longer—"

"She kicked us out," Sherry said.

"Huh. How about if I go in and see if I can get this wrapped up?" Lilly said.

"That would be great—"

"I'd appreciate it—"

"You're a brave person—"

Lilly smiled and walked over to the theater doors. She waited until the music stopped and then let herself into the theater.

"I'm sorry for interrupting rehearsal," Lilly said to Delores after the last of the children had left the theater.

"I should thank you. They were abysmal. A waste of my time. I may have to cut the number."

Lilly thought back to the little dancers she'd seen on stage, obviously exhausted and eager to please. She shook her head and forced a smile back on her face. She'd talk to Ernie about rehearsal protocol later.

"What can I do for you, Lilly?" Delores said. She took the corner of her scarf and threw it back over her shoulder. Today she was in rehearsal mode. Ernie had described it. Black tights, a long shirt, character shoes, and pashminas layered and tied over her body, depending on the temperature. Today her cat's-eye glasses were black with rhinestones, and her white hair had a purple streak down the middle.

"I have a favor to ask," Lilly said.

Delores's eyebrows shot up, and she pursed her very red lips. "You're asking me for a favor?"

"Well, yes. Sort of. I'm asking on behalf of the theater," Lilly said, gesturing to the room.

"The theater? I don't understand. *I am the theater*."

"Well, you're actually the Goosebush Players. I'm asking on behalf of the Stanley Theater. Leon's theater."

"What have you got to do with the Stanley?"

"Leon's son, Fred, asked me to help out with his father's estate."

Lilly let that statement hang in the air for a bit, and she watched Delores react to the news. To her credit, the reaction was barely a flicker. Once Lilly felt sure that Delores had processed the information, she went on.

"You know that they're doing this series of readings—"

"Of adaptations of *A Christmas Carol*. Yes. That's why I had to cancel our annual production of Mr. Dickens's masterpiece, in order to not overshadow these works in progress. How dare they—"

"Well, I wouldn't know how they dare," Lilly said. "Theater making isn't my forte. But I do know some things. First, that the readings are to benefit the theater itself. Something about upgraded seating."

"Long overdue, I'll grant you."

"Second, that the first reading is sold out. I'm not sure if you've heard, but Jeremy Nolan has agreed to play Scrooge—"

"Stunt casting. How lazy. A truly great script doesn't require stunt casting. But I'm not surprised. The poor man probably felt the call of the stage when he was here last weekend. He sent a lovely donation to the Goosebush Players, in memory of Leon. Yes, the theater calls us all back."

"Again, not my area of expertise," Lilly said. "The demand for tickets is high, so I've come by to ask you to let the reading take place here, at the Stanley."

"Impossible. I've got a rehearsal—"

"Which can be moved to the Star." Lilly decided she'd mention the restrictions on tap dancing and animals later.

"Not optimal—"

"But sufficient, surely?"

"You have no right to ask me—"

"I know I don't have a right. But here's the last thing I know. These readings meant a lot to Leon, and Leon was my friend. I'd imagine the theater, and the future use of the theater, will be part of the conversations I'll be having with Fred. Letting this first reading happen at the Stanley is definitely something I'll share with him."

Delores looked at Lilly, who didn't blink. She'd negotiated with people a lot tougher than Delores and knew that silence was her best tool.

"Leon was a good man," Delores said. "And a good friend to the Goosebush Players. His donations helped us put on the quality productions we've come to enjoy."

"He loved the theater," Lilly said. "Again, I'm not an expert, but I always thought he was a pretty good actor."

"He was. He always insisted on auditioning and being cast for his talent, not his money, which I admired. Not every actor would have made sure the playing field was level, let me tell you. I'll miss him, both onstage and off." Delores dabbed at her eyes, but Lilly didn't see any tears. Maybe the tint of the glasses obscured them. She thought about Stan's impression of Delores and bit the inside of her cheek to keep from laughing.

"I didn't know he owned the theater," Lilly said. "I knew he was on the board, of course."

"He was on both boards. The Stanley and the Goose-bush Players. They're both on the cusp of anniversaries, and we had big plans for the next year."

"Plans?" Lilly asked.

"We'd come to an agreement giving the Goosebush Players another ten-year rental agreement for the space."

"You had?" Lilly said.

"Yes. Alas, the letter we signed seems to have gone missing."

"You don't have a copy?"

"No, Leon took it. He was going to have it notarized. I realize that should have happened at the time of signing, but it was a mere formality. His intent was clear. Poor, dear Leon." This time, the tear was real, and Delores didn't bother to wipe it away.

"Maybe there's an email—"

"No. We'd met about it the day before he had his heart attack. Up until then, the negotiations weren't going terribly well, if I'm going to be honest. Two old friends pushing each other's buttons. Forgetting what was truly important. The work. Our shared history. Finally, we sat down over a bowl of smoking bishop, as it were. We came up with the agreement, and Leon went home and drew up the letter of agreement."

"I wonder what happened to the letter?" Lilly asked.

"Well, it's obvious, isn't it?"

"Not to me."

"Someone else wants to get hold of the theater," Delores said. "You know, Leon was getting offers to buy the place all the time. He'd resisted, but lately another offer had him tempted."

"What offer?"

"I don't know. Probably that awful Blossom woman. She's been nosing around enough, trying to rent the space from me on nights when the theater was dark."

"Did you agree to do that?"

"We weren't allowed to sublet the space, so I sent her to Leon. Apparently, she put a bug in his ear. Leon, bless him, wasn't immune to the charms of a young woman with designs on him. Or, in this case, on his theater."

"Did Leon talk to you about letting her use the space?"

"He did, and I said no. That was, and is, my right."

"Was that going to change with the new lease?"

Delores paused. "Those details were still being hammered out. But yes, I did agree to give him access to the space on occasion."

"In the future, you would have let the readings happen here?" Lilly asked.

"Perhaps, but—"

"How about doing it this Sunday? The rest of the readings can be at the Star, as planned. But this Sunday's reading would benefit from being here."

"I supposed I could host it—"

"No, Delores. You don't want to confuse people, just in case it doesn't go well. Don't you think? It would be gracious of you to let them use the space, in Leon's memory. I'll be sure and let Fred know."

"Well, I suppose I could make the sacrifice. For Leon."

"Thank you, Delores. I'll let Stan know that you'll use the Star that evening?"

"No, only during the day. I think I'll plan on attending the reading. Would you be sure that they hold a ticket for me?"

Lilly forced herself to smile. She held out her hand, and Delores shook it. "It's a deal."

＊　　＊　　＊

"I still can't believe you were able to pull the space switch off," Warwick said. He was sitting on Lilly's back porch with her, typing on his laptop. "Nice touch getting it in writing, by the way."

"I was about to leave, and she started listing things I needed to be aware of, so I suggested we write things down to make sure we were both on the same page. I put it all in an email that I sent to us both, and I made her reply with a yes while I was still there. I hope that I covered everything they need."

"And more," Warwick said. "Getting the space starting at noon was great thinking."

"Delia suggested they might want to do a tech rehearsal, whatever that means." Lilly looked up from her knitting and smiled at Warwick. She was proud of herself for thinking about the letter of agreement, and appreciated Warwick's compliment.

Warwick laughed. "I had to ask, too. It's a rehearsal to make sure the lights and sound cues are all set. Normally that's done for a show, not a reading. They're spiffing it up a bit." Warwick clicked on a few more keys and then hit enter. "This moving tickets from one theater to another is a little complicated. Thanks for letting me hang out here to work on it. I wanted to be near Delia and Ernie in case I had any questions. Good thing, because I've already had a few. There are a lot of politics around who sits where in a theater. Who knew?"

"I thought it was general admission."

"With a few VIP seats reserved. Leon's idea. Have a few folks pay a bit more, get VIP seating, and then get invited to a reception later. When we got more seats, I

raised the price of the VIP tickets and ad
They've already sold out."

"I heard that Leon drafted you to help
asked. She was knitting a shawl and had to c⸻
row count with the pattern. Darn it, she had knit too many
mesh rows. Ah well. Imperfection was charming in hand-
made gifts. Her knitting projects were always very
charming.

Warwick looked up and smiled. "Leon was always
there to lend a hand when I needed it. I asked so many favors over the years. The man never said no. I was, am,
more than happy to help out."

"What kind of favors?" Lilly asked.

"He was one of those parents who kept supporting the
team long after his kid graduated. His support was behind
the scenes, but he was my go-to guy when I wanted to get
special shirts, or extra promo materials. He also thought it
was terrible that the town had decided to make parents
pay participation fees, so he set up a fund and got people
to donate. He helped the theater department out, as well.
He always said that sports and the arts were where lost
kids could find a home."

"He was a good guy."

"The best," Warwick said quietly. "I knew he was sick,
but I was counting on having him around for a while
longer."

"I wonder if he made arrangements to continue his
support," Lilly said.

Warwick shrugged and shook his head. "No idea. He
never talked about that stuff. You know, the school isn't
the only place that Leon supported behind the scenes. His
clandestine philanthropy rivals yours, my friend."

"I have no idea what you—"

"Lil, it's me. I know you."

"Yes, yes you do." Lilly paused, and then she started knitting again. "Listen, if you hear of any projects that need particular support now that Leon's gone, make sure to let me—"

"Is it okay if I open some wine?" Delia said, bursting onto the back porch. She was carrying Luna in one hand, and the kitten's eyes were huge.

Lilly put her knitting in a bag and zipped it up. She'd learned the hard way that knitting and Luna did not coexist well. "Hand me the kitten, Delia. Yes, of course you can open some wine."

Delia looked down at Luna, and then she handed her to Lilly. "I meant to bring her upstairs. I'm a little nervous, I guess. I hope tonight goes well."

"So do I," Lilly said, petting Luna gently. The kitten closed her eyes and leaned into Lilly's hands. She stood up and put the kitten on her chair. "What can I do to help? Did you put the food out?"

"I did. It was really nice of you to let folks come early and have a meal."

"Please, you and Ernie both live here, too."

"Are you going to join us?" Delia said.

"Oh, heavens no. I'll eat my food out on the porch."

"Warwick?"

"I'm going to join Lilly. Tamara's got a dinner meeting over in Marshton, so I'm hanging here."

"Would you both mind helping me move some of the furniture in the living room?"

"Move furniture?" Lilly asked skeptically.

"I'll show you."

* * *

After Warwick and Lilly helped Delia move the furniture into a semicircle, they helped her set up a few extra chairs. When they finished, they went back to the kitchen to look at the buffet of leftovers Delia had laid out. Though there was plenty of food, Lilly was a bit concerned and was going to suggest ordering some pizzas. She needn't have worried. The kitchen door opened, and Ernie came in, carrying a few bags.

"Where's the kitten?" he asked quickly.

"She's locked up on the porch," Delia said. "I opened the door to the breakfast room, so she thinks she's getting away with something." Luna made at least one attempt to escape a day, and Ernie was always on guard. It would be one thing to get out into the backyard, but escaping into the driveway would be a disaster.

"What have you got there?" Warwick asked Ernie.

"I bought some more beverages. There's a case of beer in the car if you don't mind—"

"No worries—" Warwick said, heading toward the kitchen door.

"And some chips," Ernie said to his retreating back. "I know there's plenty of leftovers, but I wanted to make sure. I bought a large salad from the deli, a plate of cold cuts, and some more rolls."

"Excellent," Lilly said. "Salad is a wonderful idea, just in case the movie stars eat like birds."

"Exactly," Ernie said. "I told Mitch to text me and park in the driveway. He's bringing Jeremy and Annabelle with him. Everyone else is going to park in the shipyard lot and walk over."

"They could probably all park in the driveway," Lilly said.

"Mitch is worried about crashers," Ernie said. "Apparently there are some reporters skulking about."

"Skulking?" Delia said. "Have you been watching old movies again?"

"That's enough out of you," Ernie said, smiling at Delia. "Is that the front doorbell? Already?"

The next few minutes were a bit chaotic, with the doorbell ringing and then the gate being buzzed open and shut. Delia manned the front door, and Warwick and Lilly took turns taking coats and getting drinks. By six-fifteen, everyone had arrived, and they were all standing in the living room awkwardly. Lilly looked over at Mitchell, who was standing near the piano conferring with Delia on some notes.

"Should we get started?" Jeremy Nolan asked. Lilly had watched one of his movies this afternoon. She'd fallen asleep, but that was more about being tired than being bored. He was a good actor. And a very handsome man, both onscreen and off. "There are some notes I made on the script—"

"Notes you made?" Mitchell said. "Your text this morning said it was brilliant."

"And it is. Just needs a bit of a polish. That first scene when Scrooge is sitting at his desk. I think he should enter instead. Maybe—"

"This is a reading, not a full—"

"Delia and Ernie have put together a meal for all of you," Lilly interrupted the two men. She put on her hostess smile. "Now, you're all welcome to bring a plate back in here. Or you can come into the dining room and eat." When no one moved, Lilly went on. "I don't know how these things go, but I'd imagine the process would be a lot easier if you spent a few minutes getting to know each other, wouldn't it? Portia, what do you think?"

Portia Asher looked at Lilly and smiled. "I think that would be an excellent idea. I've been looking forward to this project all week, as much to catch up with folks than the reading itself. Seems like we haven't had a second to say hello ever since Leon died."

"Dear Leon," Annabelle Keys said. "Leon is why we're here, isn't he, Jerry?" She walked over to Jeremy Nolan and put her hand on his arm.

He looked over at Annabelle and smiled. "You're right, sweetheart. He's why we're here. I think the dining room sounds terrific. What do you think, Mitchie?"

"Warwick, show people to the kitchen, won't you?" Lilly said. She hung back and looked at Mitchell and Delia. Delia looked worried, and Mitchell looked angry.

"I never should have—this might have been a bad idea," Mitchell said. "We had a lot of wine at Thanksgiving; that's my excuse for thinking this would work. I wonder what the changes are? Delia, sit next to me. We'll need to take notes. The star has opinions. He always has, damn him."

Delia and Lilly watched Mitchell leave the room and turn left towards the kitchen.

"Lilly, please tell me you'll have dinner with us," Delia said. "I don't know what happened this afternoon, but Mitch is wound pretty tight. I need you to keep the conversation civil."

CHAPTER 7

The next morning, Lilly was hiding in her library. She didn't like to admit it, since it went against her hosting instincts, but it was true. All of the other spaces on the first floor had been taken over by theater people, and so Lilly hid.

Her library had been larger, but the kitchen renovation cut into the space. Still, it was more than enough for Lilly. Shelves held a few books but mostly treasures from her travels with Alan. The fireplace had a gas insert that let her be cozy with the flick of a remote. Her desk had everything she needed, and the locking cabinets helped her keep her privacy. Her mother, Viola, had always warned her not to keep things out for prying eyes.

Of course, her mother didn't just say "don't leave your business laying out for anyone to see." Instead, she'd told Lilly a long, winding story about a third cousin who had come to visit, and seen her grandfather's latest will lying out in an envelope. He took it out and realized he'd been cut out of the will, and so he'd stolen it. The theft was almost undiscovered, but the old man was a bit spiteful and, on his deathbed, asked to see the will one last time. He'd found a few blank pages in the envelope instead. Apparently, the fury he felt had helped him rally for a few extra weeks while he did his best to investigate what had happened, and write a new will. Well, the third cousin's wife, who never liked her husband much, told the old man what had happened and returned the original document. The third cousin and the entire branch of his family were all disinherited. The third cousin's wife divorced her husband and moved in with Lilly's great-grandmother after the old man passed away.

Lilly loved her mother's stories. They always had a point, told you a bit about family history, and stayed with you. Lilly looked around the room and smiled. Viola would have loved this room and the way Lilly was using it. She picked up the remote for the fireplace and turned it up a notch. She needed to talk to Mary Mancini and see if anything could be done to help with the draft from the porch that seeped in from the French doors that opened up to it. This part of the porch wasn't enclosed, so the sunlight and view were unfiltered. Lilly looked out of the window and then sat back in her chair. Blast. There were still people out there.

The reading rehearsal went late last night, and it didn't go particularly well, at least from what Lilly could ascertain. Once they'd started to discuss Jeremy's notes, Mitchell had agreed to make some changes, and it opened the floodgates. They'd decided to hold another rehearsal on Saturday, so Lilly had woken up to coffee brewing, a

large delivery of food from Stan, and apologies from both
Delia and Ernie. Lilly had told them not to worry, that
people should make themselves at home.

The problem was that everyone *had* made themselves
at home, and they were wandering about. Lilly had tried
to sit on the porch, but Jeremy, who insisted on being
called Jerry, smoked and had to go out to the back patio to
indulge. Since he was Jerry, either Annabelle or Mitchell,
now Mitch, always went with him. Delia had taken great
care to set him up with an ashtray, so there was no concern about cigarette butts or ashes in the garden. Lilly's
only concern was the strangers in her space.

It also turned out that actors eat a lot of food. More of
a constant grazing, so Lilly couldn't sit in the kitchen, either. She didn't want to hide in her room, so to the library
she went. She paid a few bills, charged her e-reader, and
took out her watercolors. She was at sixes and sevens.
Nothing to do, and no one to talk to. She'd texted Roddy
to see if he was home, but she hadn't heard back from
him.

"Knock, knock," Lilly heard someone say as they let
themselves in. "'Tis I—"

"Portia, come in, come in," she said. "How's rehearsal
going?"

Portia turned and made sure the door was closed, and
then she sat down in the other club chair in the office.
"Pretty well," she said. She leaned back and closed her
eyes. "I needed to get away for a minute. I hope you don't
mind."

"Not at all," Lilly said. "How goes it with the Ghost of
Christmas Present?"

"That was last week," Portia said. "Before Annabelle
came on board."

"I would have thought she'd be Mrs. Cratchit."

"Didn't want the role. Probably saw that Janice wasn't going to give up the part easily. Anyway, Present is a good role. Annabelle's going to be great in it."

"I'm sorry, Portia," Lilly said. "You must be disappointed."

"I was, but it's fine. Now I'm playing six other characters and having a great time chewing up the scenery. Six parts are a lot at my age, not going to lie. I don't know if I could do it without a script in front of me. Especially with all the changes."

"Changes?"

"Yes. Mitch keeps making script changes. Every time we have a break, he and Delia get the new pages printed out. The entire process has been like that, but now the pressure's on. He constantly takes breaks to fix or polish."

"That's why everyone's—"

"Milling about? Taking over your house? Yes, that's it. It's going to be a long damn day."

"I may go out for a few hours—"

"I would. The drama is contagious."

"Drama? Like Mitch and Jerry arguing?"

"That, and more. They all worked together, you know, back in the eighties. When Mel John had taken over as the artistic director of the Goosebush Players, he was producing his own work in the summers. They were here from Memorial Day to Labor Day for years. Sometimes they'd come in for special projects during the year, as well. Those were good years, Lilly. The work was great."

"Were you involved then, too?"

"I've been involved with the Goosebush Players for my entire life. Which is almost as old as the group itself."

Lilly laughed. "Not true. Do you remember all of them?"

"Of course. Mostly from the summer work. Mitch was young, and not a very good actor. Turns out he was learning to be a playwright. He worked closely with Mel those days."

"Did Mel write plays?"

"Yes and no. He adapted plays for the Players, but kept it fairly standard fare. He pushed, but not too hard. But after Memorial Day? That was Mel's time. Stanley let him do whatever he wanted, and it was extraordinary. I think Mitch's first playwriting credit was one of those summers."

"Annabelle was there—"

"She was a pretty young thing. Talented, but nothing special. She's really come into her own now. Age and life are working for her. She's always been more of a character actor."

"And Jeremy?"

"Ah, Jerry. I used to joke with my husband that I'd consider leaving him for Jeremy Nolan. He was handsome and charming and talented, and not above flirting with a forty-year-old mother of four. Lord, he was something. He always had that extra thing; you know what I mean?"

"That thing?"

"That star quality that draws your eye right to him. He did a *Hamlet* that took my breath away. I still think about it all these years later. Those five summers when Mel was running the theater? It rose above what it was and is now. It was a company of actors doing great work. I was proud to be part of it."

"Did they all remember you?" Lilly asked gently. If they didn't, she'd tell Ernie to remind them.

"I brought in some old albums, and once they saw me in a picture, they did. I think I look the same, but it has been a lot of years. I was old to them then. Now they're older than I was. Crazy to think about."

"Do you have the albums? I'd love to see them."

"They're looking at them now, telling stories. I'll show them to you later if you'd like. I wanted to take a break and come talk to you, Lilly. I'm worried about something and thought you could help me figure it out."

"What are you worried about?" Lilly asked.

"This," Portia said, taking out her phone and clicking a few buttons. She handed Lilly the phone.

Lilly held it close and then moved it away so that she could understand what she was looking at. She finally gave up.

"What am I looking at?"

"Sheila keeps posting updates on her wreath entry."

The wreath contest was a library fundraiser that had been going on for years and years. People chose a title of a book out of a hat, and created a wreath that evoked the novel in some way. The entries were all hung around the library, and people voted on the best one, and then bid on them at a holiday party.

"What's her book?" Lilly asked. All she could see were piles of shopping bags and a wreath form on a table.

"Who knows? It will be subpar, as usual."

"Portia!"

"Don't 'Portia' me! You know she's a gasbag. Anyway, I meant look at the bags. All from the big box store over in Marshton."

"Ah, I see. I saw someone else post pictures from a box store the other day. Like that was something to be proud of."

"I think we should amend the rules. Tell people that everything for their wreath has to be sourced here in Goosebush."

"I don't think we can do that—"

"Hogwash. Of course we can. It's not much, true. But if you're going to show off how much shopping you're doing, may as well show off that you're supporting Goosebush businesses."

"Like Ernie," Lilly said.

"Like Ernie. And that gift shop on the Wheel, the new one that no one goes in? Turns out she's got some cute stuff, and she also sells the work of local craftspeople."

"I haven't been in there—"

"Then there's the Star. The stores by the supermarket. The market itself, for heaven sake. We're all in trouble if he closes down."

"Do you think that will happen?" Lilly hated that idea. She loved the mid-sized grocery store and was friends with the owner. They stocked what she liked, and she knew where everything was. The thought of having to leave Goosebush for groceries made her shudder.

"I don't think so as long as we start supporting the businesses in town."

"You're right, of course," Lilly said. "Let's talk about changing the wreath rule for next year. But maybe the garden sculptures for Alden Park pieces could all be locally sourced?"

Alden Park was a jewel in Goosebush that had been neglected for years. Finally, after a few fits and starts, plans were being approved to bring it back next spring. But this winter, the space was going to be used as a holiday mart for a couple of weekends. Someone had come up with the idea of creating over-the-top sculptures out of used and organic materials. The pieces all had to include a light source, since it got dark so early. Lilly wasn't on the committee that came up with the idea, but Portia was.

"Interesting idea," Portia said. "Some people have started on them already, but we can still ask them to go local. Not that many people have signed up yet, which is a shame. I was looking at the list this morning, but I didn't see your name."

"To tell you the truth, I have no idea what I'd do. A large garden arrangement? That I understand. But sculptures?"

"The meeting where we were deciding how to decorate Alden Park for the holidays got out of hand. I still don't know what happened. We were talking about how to make it a space where everyone felt included. Then one of the kids said he'd make a lightning bolt, and someone else said they'd make a hammer. My grandson explained that they were talking about Thor. Anyway, everyone started talking about it and decided it would be fun to try and create a piece that meant something to them. One of the goals was to get more young people involved. Chase tells me they'll sign up next week when they're back from Thanksgiving break. I'll admit, I had to come around to the whole idea, but Chase and I are having fun working on our entry."

"What is it?"

"I'm not going to tell you. But, to quote Chase, it's going to be wicked awesome. Listen, I'm going to remind you about that wreath rule change for next year. But remind me if I forget."

"You know what, Portia? Maybe we could try shaming people into doing that now."

"What do you mean?"

"We could talk about our own projects, and how we bought things here."

"Great idea. I can get my grandson to help me figure out the social media. Chase can do that hashtag watchamacallit."

"Well, when he figures it out, let me know, and I'll let Delia know. And then it will become a thing."

"Excellent! Let's make Goosebush a thing."

There was a knock on the door, and Delia stuck her head in. "Portia, they're going to run the party scene again. Do you need more time?"

"No, I'm ready to go," Portia said. "What do you have in that bag? Are those my scrapbooks?"

"They are. I have a huge favor to ask of you, and to ask of Lilly. First you. Can I borrow these for a while? You have pictures and programs that I haven't been able to find. I'd love to scan them."

"Yes, of course. I'd give them to you, but I still like going through them sometimes. I'll leave them to the Historical Society in my will, though."

"Thanks, Portia. I love how organized you are. Names on pictures, chronological order, dates, and shows."

"Well, you should see the diaries I have."

"You keep a diary?"

"For every show. I'll show them to you whenever you'd like. All right, I'm going to go and grab some tea. I do four voices in this scene. Gotta go warm up the old pipes."

Lilly nodded at Delia, who understood and closed the door quietly. "How's she doing?" she asked.

"She's fine," Delia said.

"Because this feels like a lot of pressure for someone her age—"

"No, Lilly, she's great. Mitch thinks that she's one of the best actors in the show. She seems to be having a wonderful time."

"She is," Lilly said. "Phew. I'm glad to hear it. This whole thing seems to have taken on a lot more—"

"Pressure."

"I was thinking polish, but pressure, too. How are you holding up?"

"I'm okay. So much for a quiet weekend, though. I've got another favor to ask you."

"What is it?" Lilly said.

"I marked some of the pictures in the albums. I'd like to get them scanned and give Mitch, Annabelle, and Jerry a copy."

"Mitch and Jerry. I still can't believe we're calling Jeremy Nolan 'Jerry.'"

"I can't believe a lot of things this weekend. Anyway, there are a couple of dozen photos. Would you take them down to the Historical Society and scan and print them? You remember how to do that, right?"

"I think so—"

"Roddy will be there, so he can probably help. He's really good at the computer stuff."

"Why is he there?"

"He's been volunteering on Saturday mornings. He's helping us install the new scanner system that you donated."

"An anonymous person donated."

"Yes, whatever. He's trying it out this afternoon. I was supposed to be with him, but this rehearsal was called."

"Tell you what. I'll go and scan, print, and help Roddy. How does that sound?"

"Perfect; thanks, Lilly. Rehearsal may go pretty late today—"

"Don't worry. I won't hurry back."

CHAPTER 8

"What's all this?" Lilly asked as she walked into the Historical Society. The Historical Society was founded several years ago, when a few Goosebush citizens had decided that the important town history really needed to live in one place. Not the legal documents. Those were all in the town hall. The police records were in storage or online. No, these important records included the letters, the pictures, the newsletters. The gossip. The history of what happened in Goosebush that didn't make it into the official documents.

No one could imagine how many donations would come in over the years. More than once, those documents had helped explain a property line, shone light on an unexpected branch of a family tree, or helped people remember why groups were founded and by whom. Of late, more people had been dropping off boxes while clearing out family homes, without even looking inside. Which is why Meg Mancini (the head volunteer) and Delia had instituted a "sweep first, list later" policy. They'd decided to spot-check donations to determine if they were appropriate for the archives. Anything that wasn't would be given back to the donor or sent to the local thrift store. Delia wanted to make sure that the Historical Society didn't become a dumping ground.

While Lilly agreed with the policy, she was a bit wary of the editorial control of two people, so a small committee had been formed. Any questionable documents would be brought before the group, and majority ruled. Though loathe to join another committee, Lilly had made sure to be part of this one. She always erred on the "sunshine is a disinfectant" side of letting people see the truth, warts and all, of Goosebush.

For a long while, the large room in the basement of the library was sufficient, but no longer. There was a brief hope of a house being left to the group, but the probate on that was going to be tied up for a while. There was a new push to digitize and organize the records and store some of them offsite. An investment had been made into software and hardware in order to start the project. Lilly was all for hiring an expert to do the work, but Meg and Delia wanted to see what was involved first.

Fortunately for the project, Roddy had volunteered to work on the tech and write up some procedures. Meg had put together a box for him to scan and organize as a test case to see how the software worked. The committee was going to decide on the right path for the project from there. Unfortunately for Roddy, he'd run into some issues and was up against a deadline of the committee meeting on Wednesday.

Lilly had parked in the back of the library and taken the elevator right down to the basement. Usually, she parked in front and wound her way down, saying hello to people and peeking her head into the Alan Macmillan Room. She'd funded the space in her late husband's name, and she'd overseen every detail from the furnishings to the AV equipment. The Mac, as it was nicknamed, was a large conference-style room that was used for poetry readings, meetings, and small events. She'd also donated a few of Alan's favorite paintings and part of his scholarly library. The room was well used, and Lilly loved seeing people in it.

But today, she had a bag full of pictures to scan. And she'd gotten an SOS text from Roddy as she parked.

"You got here fast," Roddy said to her. "I only just sent the text."

"I was already on my way over to borrow the scan machine thing."

"The scan machine thing?" Roddy smiled at her, and she smiled back.

"Delia told me you were here, so I thought maybe you'd help."

"Of course."

"But first, what's the SOS about? And what in heaven's name is this?" Lilly gestured to the plastic bins piled in the corner.

"That's the reason for the SOS. This whirling dervish from the library came in this morning and dumped them here. I tried to dissuade her, but to no avail."

"Donations?"

"No, not unless the Historical Society is going to archive fake holiday greenery and rather large and somewhat garish plastic ornaments."

Lilly put her bag on a chair by the table and looked more closely at the bins. She looked at Roddy and shook her head.

"This isn't a storage dump," she said.

"No, it isn't. But the woman suggested that the library would need to use this space for a short time. She seemed to have some sort of authority, or at least acted as if she did. Honestly, after our conversation, I wasn't sure which end was what."

Lilly barked a short laugh. Authority? To use the Historical Society as storage? The society paid the library a more than fair stipend for rent every year, and Lilly knew well that the library depended on the income. Lilly took her phone out of her pocket and pulled up the contact number for the head of the library, Dot Robie. She punched it, and not surprisingly, her call was answered on the second ring. Lilly tended to have that effect on people. After a short conversation, she turned to Roddy and smiled.

"The boxes will be removed shortly," Lilly said.

"Lilly, it's a good thing that I'm on your right side," Roddy said. "You can be, if you'll excuse the phrase, a bit scary."

"Oh, Roddy, you have no idea. You should have seen me in my early days, when I was in business. Right after my divorce, I prided myself on being what Delia would probably have called a fierce force. But then I changed."

"What changed you?" he asked.

"Meeting Alan and becoming a professor's wife. I had to be nice to people. Then we moved back to Goosebush, and my mother got me involved with the town. Business stayed business, but I became the soft, sweet person you see right now." Lilly watched Roddy's face contort, and she laughed. "Put it this way. I don't pull out the full Lilly unless a circumstance requires it."

"But Dot didn't bring the bins down—"

"She'd obviously sanctioned it, though. And given the person with the boxes keys to the space. Keys that are supposed to be emergency use only."

"Minh Vann was her name. She's the new librarian. Just started this past week. She only moved to Goosebush last week, but she was happy to start right away. Or so she said."

"Did you ask her what she did for Thanksgiving?" Lilly asked.

"No, and she didn't volunteer it. She speaks in a sort of stream of consciousness that is mesmerizing. She started the minute she let herself in and didn't stop until she was done."

"Speaking of which, we should get this place re-keyed," Lilly said, fingers flying over her phone's keyboard.

"Rekeyed? Isn't that a bit much?"

"Not at all. There are some real treasures in here. We should have done it sooner. Who knows who has keys at this point—oh, good, Ernie's said he'll get someone over here this afternoon." Lilly put her phone in her pocket and looked around. "Now, which boxes belong here and which don't?"

Roddy and Lilly spent the next half hour sorting boxes, bins, and bags. She'd volunteered a few times recently, but it was obvious there had been several piles of things added since she was last here. She rifled through a couple and then looked up at Roddy. "Why are there so many bits of theater memorabilia?" she asked.

"Delia asked people to bring what they had as part of the project she's working on. Do you see the sheet clipped to each item? Who donated it, their connections to the theater or to the Players, whether or not they wanted to donate it or if they'd like it back, who's in any pictures, that sort of thing. There's actually some method to the madness there."

"She asked me to help with that project," Lilly said. "But this place is a mess."

"Well, the volunteer base has dwindled significantly over the past few months," Roddy said, raising an eyebrow at Lilly.

"For good reasons," Lilly said, thinking of two volunteers in particular. The organization needed a better vetting system.

"Nevertheless, we need to sort things and get a game plan. I do think the tech will help, but hiring someone who knows how to do this—" He was interrupted by a knock on the door, which he answered.

"Ms. Vann," he said, stepping aside to let the new librarian in. She was pulling a dolly behind her.

"I am so sorry; I didn't realize that I'd mistaken the storage room. Of course, I should have known. I mean, what would you be doing in a storage room. It's just that I get so focused. Don't worry. I'm here to move the things—"

"I don't think you mistook anything. You just got bad directions," Roddy said.

"Well, nevertheless. Let me get the bins out of here. I guess tomorrow is decorating day at the library. I jumped the gun a bit. I tend to do that. Jump the gun. Get ahead of myself. Wait, I'm sorry. There's a new person here. Hello. I haven't introduced myself. I'm Minh Vann. You must be Lilly Jayne."

"I am, indeed. I'm afraid my reputation has preceded me."

"It's a wonderful reputation. I've been looking forward to meeting you. You're exactly as you look in pictures. I saw a few pictures when I was doing my research on the library. Before I decided to move here. Nice to meet you. I look forward to chatting in the future. But now, let me get to work." She turned back to the bins and started piling them on the flatbed of the dolly. Roddy helped, and he walked with her down the hall, holding the top of the bins. He was back in a few minutes.

"She's organizing the storage room."

"Still talking?" Lilly asked.

"I find her charming," Roddy said. "All right, let me see what this scanning project you brought is. It will be a good test drive for the equipment."

Lilly took out one of Portia's scrapbooks and turned the pages gently until she got to the Post-it that Delia had put in the book.

"Here's one. Delia wants to scan the pictures for Jerry, Annabelle, and Mitch as a thank-you for the reading."

"Jerry? Mitch?"

"I've had a bunch of actors move in for the weekend—"

"Not really—"

"No, but they may as well have. Rehearsals till all hours last night and starting this morning. People milling about, discussing motivation, and going over lines. It's quite a scene. I will say, this reading is going to be something."

"I'm surprised they haven't drafted you into playing a part," Roddy said.

"Don't start. I have no skills in the acting arena. I'm excellent at being an audience member. They'd hand you a script in a second, though. English accent, deep voice. Mitch keeps saying they're short on men."

"Ernie's called me twice already to ask me to join." Assured that all of the equipment was on and functioning, Roddy took the picture out of the scrapbook and turned it over. He started to type in some information. "This is a great test case. They are lovely, professional photos, so the quality is excellent. Portia's named everyone on the back."

"Ernie's asked you to be in the reading?" Lilly said. "Why didn't you say yes?"

"It's been years since I've done anything like that," Roddy said. "I may have been tempted, but now that professional actors are involved, I don't think so."

"Well, come over tonight and meet Jerry. He's actually quite nice, for a movie star."

Roddy laughed. "I think I'll be here for a few more hours, then we'll see. Let me show you what I'm doing." He showed Lilly how the software database could be filled out with details of the picture, using certain keywords and descriptors that would help later. Then he scanned the picture and printed a copy. It looked just like the original. "Now, of course, these pictures can be touched up. But this is exactly why we need to hire someone who knows what they're doing."

"What do you mean? It all looks wonderful to me," Lilly said. "Could you print out three more copies?"

"Of course, though why don't I scan them all first. You may want to bring them to a copy shop for better quality prints. I can put them on a memory stick."

"Maybe I can make the copy shop make them into a scrapbook," Lilly said. "Here's the next photo. Now show me again what you're doing."

Roddy walked Lilly through the steps he took as he recorded and scanned the photo. "The reason we need to hire someone is to decide what the parameters are for keywords and categories. If Delia was available, she could do it. She's got the brain. But until then, I'd hate to get started without making sure we're doing what will work best for the archives."

"That's a smart approach," Minh said from the doorway. "Sorry, didn't mean to eavesdrop, but I was waiting until you finished. I agree, that's the best way to approach the project. Understand the scope and set the parameters. Oh, look at this. State of the art. Once you've got a system, you'll be able to do a hackathon to get it all done in good order."

"A what?" Lilly asked.

"A hackathon. Get several computers going at once. You can feed people, but not while they're working. It's a good way to get a few shifts going, though. Food, breaks. Some prizes for who gets done first, who uses the most keywords, that sort of thing. They work really well—"

"But there's only one scanner," Lilly said. Another

scanner would use up a lot of the budget, never mind space, she thought.

"True, but it's the data entry that takes the most time. You'll need to spot check for accuracy, but people should be fine after a bit of training."

"You sound as though you know what you're doing," Roddy said.

"I've worked on several projects like this back home. As part of the volunteer work I did as part of my master's."

"Where's home?" Lilly asked.

"Oh, I did say home, didn't I?" Minh said. She was a few years younger than Lilly and a head shorter. Her black hair was cut in a stylish bob, and she had a streak of gray in the front. "I meant California. Here's home now. Though I haven't been here long, so I'm not sure it feels like home yet, if you know what I mean."

"Did the library job bring you here?" Lilly asked. She doubted it. The position didn't pay a great deal and was only part-time.

"Yes and no," Minh said. She sighed and looked at Roddy and Lilly. "It's sort of a long story, but I've been doing some family history research, and I've found some interesting leads in this area. My youngest is studying abroad this year, and my other two are in college, and so I decided it was time for a bit of an adventure. Bad divorce, so no one else to worry about. I was looking at Massachusetts and the coast. And, well, the job came up, so I decided that it was all meant to be." She took a deep breath and let it out.

"Welcome," Lilly said. The story made it quite clear that Minh wasn't from New England. No New Englander shared that much personal information within ten minutes of meeting someone. "Goosebush is lucky to have you."

"I love the library, and I've enjoyed meeting people. I'm renting an apartment over in what was the old middle school? At least that's what they told me. Feels like an old school. I do love that."

"Love what?"

"That they made apartments out of the old school rather than tear it down."

"Truth to tell, that was a bit of a compromise. They couldn't agree on how else to use the space. It's a beautiful location."

"It is," Minh said. "I'm renting it from someone who uses it in the summer, so I was lucky that it was available. You know, I'd be happy to help with this project, whatever it is. I've got a lot of time on my hands—"

"Thank you very much, Ms. Vann, but we're not sure—"

"Tell you what, talk to Ms. Robie and ask for references. It's only fair. I'll ask her to send you my resumé as well; how's that sound. I love this sort of thing, helping people get organized and get online. It's my jam, if you'll pardon the expression. Are you going to the reading tomorrow night? I'm going to try and go. I'm a huge Jeremy Nolan fan, but then who isn't, am I right? He's swoony. Anyway, I'll see you later."

With that, she left the room, closing the door behind her.

Roddy and Lilly looked at each other, and both laughed.

"What was that?" Lilly said.

"A bundle of energy," Roddy said. "Rather charming, really. We should follow up to see if she's up to the job.

That energy could get this project sorted quickly. Why are you looking at me like that?"

"Charming, huh?" Lilly said. "Let's scan these other pictures, shall we?" She made a mental note to do some research on Minh Vann herself. What was her real reason for being in Goosebush? Something made Lilly doubt it was a part-time job in the library.

CHAPTER 9

"Lilly, you're up," Ernie said, dragging himself into the kitchen.

"I am," Lilly said. "And so are you. Shouldn't you be sleeping in a bit? You were all still rehearsing when I got home last night."

"I wanted to clean up. But I see you've done that already." Ernie sat down on one of the kitchen chairs heavily. "I'm so sorry that we've been kicking you out of your own home. I didn't even hear you come in last night."

"Roddy and I worked at the Historical Society for a while, then I worked on a project for Delia. We went to the Star for dinner, which was lovely but surprisingly busy for a holiday weekend. When I got home, you were all mid-rehearsal, so I didn't want to interrupt. How's it going?"

Ernie shook his head and sighed. He had bags under

his eyes and looked tired. "It's a lot. I mean, I knew this project was going to be a lot of work. But I thought Leon would be around to help. And I didn't think we'd have movie stars in the mix."

"Do you want some coffee?" Ernie shook his head, so Lilly didn't get up. "I did listen in a bit before I went upstairs. Jerry sounded good, and people were laughing and having a good time—"

"He's very charming," Ernie said. "And a lot of fun. But I don't think that laughing during *A Christmas Carol* was what Mitch had in mind. He's a very serious playwright, you know. Leon put a lot of effort in getting him to allow his work to be part of this project."

"You like him, don't you?" Lilly asked gently.

"Who? What? Me? Mitch? Of course; he's very nice. A bit temperamental these past few days, but a very nice man."

"And quite good-looking," Lilly said, smiling.

"Well, yes, I suppose he is," Ernie said. He was tapping his fingers on the table, focused on the rhythm.

Lilly and Ernie had both lost their husbands to long illnesses. And both of them were very single. But Lilly had noticed that her friend lit up when he talked about Mitch. She did wonder if Ernie had noticed it as well, though.

"Any more rehearsals?" Lilly asked.

"No, no. We're going to be doing a bit of a tech at the theater, but that's it. We've got the space at—"

"Noon."

"Noon. Right. And that's—"

"Over four hours from now. Ernie, go back to sleep for a couple of hours. You look exhausted, and you've got a big day ahead of you."

"There's so much to do—"

"And it will get done. But in the meantime, go get some more sleep."

"What are you doing today?" Lilly said as soon as Tamara picked up her phone.

"Why, good morning, Lilly. I agree, it's nice to hear your voice, as well."

"Tamara, don't start. I made the mistake of asking Ernie and Delia what I could do to help tonight, and I have a list a mile long. I need help."

"Warwick was just saying the same thing. Let me put you on speakerphone."

"Warwick, I thought you'd be at the theater by now—"

"Happy to say Nicole came back last night, so she's helping me figure out the ticketing. There's a bunch of other stuff that required changing due to the venue switch, so I'm working on those."

"Like tables for the food at the reception?" Lilly asked.

"Yeah, like that. Delia asked me to figure that out, so I'm heading over to the high school now—"

"Ernie asked me to do the same thing. Good thing I called. Here's what's on my list. Maybe there's some more duplication." Lilly read her list slowly, and then Warwick read his. There was, sadly, little duplication. But with Tamara's help, there was a redistribution of some of the work.

"Warwick and I will head over to the school to get some tables, the AV system for speeches after the show, a few chairs, some music stands, and all the rest of the equipment. You're sure that the theater doesn't have any of this stuff?" Tamara asked.

"I'm sure no one wants to ask Delores for a favor," Warwick said. "When Delia went by last night to get the keys, everything was locked up, which is why she called me."

"The reception was going to be at the Star, and Stan was going to provide the plates and glasses. But that's not going to happen now, which is why Ernie wants me to go over to Marshton to the party store. I'm also going to pick up the programs, the picture books, and some flowers," Lilly said. She'd been following Tamara's line of thinking and was rewriting the list by clumping like activities together. The list was still long but it felt a bit less daunting.

"Are you sure Stan doesn't have any paper goods?" Tamara asked.

"Not enough," Lilly said. "No worries. I'll buy cloth tablecloths and donate them to the school afterwards. I should be able to get all of this done in a few hours."

"Get Roddy to help," Tamara said. "I'll go with Warwick. Meet you there at four?"

"At the latest," Warwick said. "The house opens at six; the reading starts at seven."

"I'll get there as soon as I can. Is the catering all set?" Lilly asked.

"Stan's on it," Warwick said.

"Who knew a reading would be this much work?" Lilly said.

"Leon knew," Warwick said. "He'd been talking to me about the volunteers we'd need day of, but we never finished the conversation."

The three friends paused. It was only a week ago that they were all together celebrating Leon's life. Two weeks ago, they'd seen him in person. The grief was still raw.

"Well," Lilly started to say. She cleared her throat and started again. "Well, let's hope that Leon guides us to making good decisions today. I have no doubt that between all of us, and with Delia in charge, it will all come together."

They all hung up, promising regular check-ins. Lilly hit another one of her speed dial numbers. When Roddy picked up, she immediately asked him what his plans were for the day.

What might have been a chore alone was much more fun with Roddy in tow. He made sure they had a good lunch, and made her laugh in the party store as they explored the color-coded and theme-driven aisles. She stayed away from the holiday decorations, choosing to purchase supplies that could be used year-round. She concentrated on black, white, and silver.

After they went to the printer, she and Roddy stopped and bought several bouquets of flowers. Lilly planned on doing some cuttings in her greenhouse and garden to add to the arrangements. Arrangements she could do. But a sculpture? She sighed. She felt as though she lacked imagination and didn't like the feeling.

They both hurried home to dress. Lilly checked on Luna and made sure her food and water were fresh. Luna seemed delighted to have the run of the house again, and happily bounded back to the breakfast room after sampling her dinner and rubbing Lilly's ankles. Lilly stopped and listened. For the first time in several days, there wasn't a din of voices rattling around the house. She was glad for a moment, but then she felt lonely.

She would have liked to take a nap, but there wasn't time. Instead, she put on a black velvet dress. She knew that her pumps would have been the best choice, but instead she pulled out a pair of red booties she'd just bought. They were cute, but more importantly, they were comfortable. Her rhinestone poinsettia earrings were enough jewelry for the evening. She stepped back from the mirror and smiled. Even she had to admit she cleaned up well.

Roddy met her by the back porch. He looked dapper, with a well-fit gray suit and a red tie.

"You look lovely, Lilly," he said.

"As do you," she said.

"Are these all coming with us?" He pointed to the bundles of branches and greens that she'd left on the back steps.

"Yes. I put a box of vases in the back of the car already. I think we have everything."

"I'm quite sure we do. Here, let me get those. Shall we?"

Lilly texted Tamara as she left, and when they got to the theater, there were half a dozen volunteers waiting. Lilly and Roddy explained what each package or box was as they handed them out. She handed the vases to Scooter, who had called Ernie and volunteered for the event. She could be trusted to arrange the flowers appropriately.

Roddy took the last of the packages in, and Lilly went to park the car. Per Ernie's instructions, she left it by the stage door. She touched up her lipstick one last time and then made her way to the front door. She was met by a flurry of activity. The tables had been set up, and they were being covered with the linens Lilly had bought. The coverings went to the floor, all the better to hide supplies, food, and personal belongings under the tables during the event. She took a look over at the flowers where a small group of people were tackling the arrangements. Scooter had it well in hand. She walked over to Warwick, who was sitting with Nicole, sorting through pieces of paper.

"Warwick, can I help?" she asked.

"Lilly, I am so glad to see you. Yes! We've got some ticketing issues that need to be handled."

"Delores just handed us a list of people who need to be accommodated," Nicole said. "We don't have enough room—"

Lilly smiled and held out her hand, so Nicole gave her the list. A quick count indicated thirty people. "Did any of these people buy tickets?" Lilly asked.

"No. I think they all tried, but it's been sold out—" Nicole sounded a bit panicked, so Lilly reached out and touched her hand gently.

"Of course it has been," Lilly said. She took out her phone, took a picture of the list, and then folded it in thirds. "Where's Delores? I'll talk to her."

"We may have some seats open up—" Warwick said.

"And if that happens, we'll start a waiting list. Do you have her tickets?"

"They're right here." Warwick handed Lilly an envelope that had Delores's name on it. She looked inside and saw that there were six tickets.

"She's not sitting near me, is she?" Lilly whispered.

"Other side of the theater," Warwick said.

"You're a good man, Warwick O'Connor. Now, let me go and talk to Delores, and then I'll be back to help."

Delores Stevens had moved over to the flower group and had taken over the arrangements. She was dramatically talking about height and volume, taking out the flowers and tossing them back on the table. Lilly walked over and touched her elbow.

"Delores, Scooter does a wonderful job of arranging flowers. She'll get it done, and it will be lovely. Would you come with me for a moment? I'd like to have a word."

Delores tossed the rest of the bouquet on the table and turned and stomped toward her office, which was right behind the box office and across from the ladies' room. Lilly winked at the volunteers, and Scooter started to sort the flowers and greens again.

Lilly followed Delores into her office and closed the door.

"Delores, here are your tickets for this evening. They put six aside for you."

"That's wonderful," Delores said, opening the envelope and looking at the tickets. "Fourth row? But certainly, I should be closer—"

"They wanted to make sure you had good sight lines," Lilly said, making it up on the spot. More likely, they didn't want the actors to be able to see her, though her red turban would make not seeing her very difficult.

"Ah, well."

"Here's the list you gave the box office. Your six seats

can be used for those people." Lilly turned away and went to open the door.

"But I need more tickets—"

"Delores, our agreement didn't indicate that you'd get more than two tickets. We gave you six. The rest of the people on the list can go on the waiting list, though it's very doubtful they'll get in at this point."

"You can't . . . this is my theater."

"No, it's not," Lilly said. "You are a tenant. As I mentioned, it was very nice of you to move your rehearsal. But you agreed that you wouldn't interfere with the reading, and I'm going to hold you to that. Do you understand?"

Delores's face went from red to purple, then finally turned pink before she spoke again.

"There aren't any more tickets? Even for purchase?" she finally asked.

"Any tickets would only be available for purchase," Lilly said. "I will let you know. They are sorting lists now, but I'm going to tell them that your requests will go through me." Lilly paused, but Delores just glared, so she plastered on her most obsequious smile and left Delores to fume.

Lilly and Roddy climbed upstairs minutes before the show started. They'd given up their seats downstairs to help accommodate the problems that Delores had created. The folding chairs they'd been given were in the upper gallery, where there were usually lighting instruments and technicians. Lilly looked over to her left and saw that Tamara was on the other side of the gallery.

Scooter had volunteered to sit with the tickets so that Warwick could watch the show, but he was still handling ticketing issues. There were benefits to being the football coach, not the least of which was that he was tough to intimidate.

"Did you know that Delores had charged people for those tickets," Roddy whispered.

"I thought maybe she had," Lilly said.

"A pretty penny, from what I understand," Roddy said. "That's why Warwick was trying to accommodate them all. Thankfully, Bash was here. There were several ticketing scrapes he had to help with."

"Like?"

"Tickets being sold online that didn't exist. Scalpers."

"For a reading?"

"A Jeremy Nolan and Annabelle Keys reunion event. They've both got a fan base."

"Of course. We should have anticipated this, I suppose."

"It was hard to anticipate how fraught it would get. That Virginia Blossom woman? The singer? She was making all sorts of snide comments about the lack of professionalism. Bash finally took her aside and spoke to her," Roddy said.

"Lack of professionalism? Who does she think she is?" Lilly asked.

"She thinks she's quite something, from what I could see. Honestly, why do people not understand how a small town works? There were a number of people who were quite rude. I'm glad Warwick was there with Nicole, and Scooter was a help. That's why we're up here. Attempts to make people happy took some creativity."

"Delores is a piece of work," Lilly said. She watched as the red turban climbed over audience members in the fourth row. Her seat was in the middle of the row, and there wasn't a great deal of room for her to wiggle by. Lilly was glad she had a picture of the list. She'd text it to Ernie so he could make some calls in the morning to find out how large the donation Delores needed to make to the Stanley was. "I'm glad it all got sorted out. I was afraid there was going to be a brawl for a moment."

"Yes, well. Adding a row of folding chairs here, moving people there. It was actually a fun puzzle. I am sorry that I suggested we'd be willing to move up here. I didn't expect it to be quite so dusty."

"No worries," Lilly said. "We'll miss some expressions, but I'm so nervous for everyone that I don't think I would have enjoyed sitting down there anyway."

The lights went down, and the actors all filed out holding their black binders, which they put on their music stands as they took their places. Lilly looked around and finally found Delia in the stage management booth, wearing a headset and talking into it. The applause was loud and kept going, but the actors didn't break. After a few seconds, Ernie stepped forward, and the crowd hushed.

"The thing to remember is, Marley was dead. Dead as a doornail. If you don't remember that, you'll miss the magic of what happened on Christmas Eve, not that long ago."

CHAPTER 10

Ninety minutes later, the audience was on their feet, cheering the cast, all of whom were beaming. Annabelle and Jeremy took separate bows, and then Jeremy took one on his own. After a couple more minutes the actors filed out, and the lights came up.

Lilly looked down and saw Delores fighting to get out of her row and then start down the aisle. Before she got there, Ernie had come back out to address the audience.

"Thank you all for being here tonight for this first of three readings. As you all know, this series was set up as a fundraiser to help support some renovations to the Stanley, as this wonderful space is known. Your generous support will go a long way to getting that work started. Now, if you'll give us a couple of minutes, we'll be out in the lobby to join you in a toast."

The crowd clapped lightly and then began gathering their things and heading out.

"What an interesting take on *A Christmas Carol*," Roddy said, standing up and then holding out his hand to Lilly to help her up. "I quite enjoyed it."

"It was a little dark, don't you think?" Lilly asked.

"A little? My dear Lilly, it was very dark. Perhaps that's why I liked it so much. I hate the cloying versions we so often see. Dickens's tale was dark, and all about the redemption of the human spirit. This captured that in a modern context."

"True, but yikes. Bob Cratchit being arrested for embezzlement? And still being in jail at the end of the play?"

"I suppose that was supposed to indicate that Scrooge had a lot of cleaning up to do in order to redeem himself. But I agree, that was a bit much. Especially with Mrs. Cratchit and the children wailing as the curtain came down. Shall we head downstairs?"

Roddy offered his arm, and Lilly took it. She shook her head, trying to get rid of some of the darker messages of the piece. She could only hope that Mitch wouldn't ask what she thought. Because honestly, she wasn't sure.

By the time Lilly and Roddy made their way down to the lobby, the reception was in full bloom. Jeremy and Annabelle were at a table near Delores's office, signing autographs. Most people left afterwards. The line was going very quickly, since Scooter was there moving it along.

Roddy walked over to the bar area to get them both a glass of wine. Lilly looked over at the tables of food.

They looked as if they were getting empty. She hoped that someone had thought to save some for Delia and Jimmy and the rest of the people who were in the theater cleaning up.

"That was unexpected," a voice beside her said. Lilly looked over, and the woman held out her hand. "I don't think we've met. I'm Virginia Blossom."

Lilly looked her up and down and finally put out her hand to shake.

"Lilly Jayne."

"Yes, I know. I've heard that you're the person to meet if I want to get things done around here."

"Who told you that?" Lilly asked.

"You know, Goosebush could benefit from more work being done like tonight rather than the usual, um, fare that this theater produces."

"Tonight was very interesting," Lilly said. "You know, I've always thought it a good idea to know to whom I was speaking before casting aspersions on the work of others. I could, for instance, be on the board of the Goosebush Players—"

"But you aren't."

"Or be friends with Delores Stevens."

Virginia looked to her right, where Delores was loudly holding court. "Doubtful," she said. "She moved away from you when you came downstairs. You were friends with Leon Tompkin, though. He and I had been having some really interesting talks about the future of the theater."

"Leon was a lovely and patient man," Lilly said, looking around for Roddy.

"We were planning on doing some work together," Virginia said.

Lilly looked to her left and saw Tamara and Warwick. Finally. "I'm surprised you were willing to compromise your professional standards," Lilly said. "A word to the wise, Ms. Blossom. Being nice to volunteers is a good practice. Especially in a small town."

Lilly turned away and walked over toward Warwick and Tamara, who were hanging back a bit.

"Warwick, congratulations on dealing with that ticketing fiasco," Lilly said. "You kept your cool under very challenging circumstances."

"From the outside, yes. But jeez, that wasn't fun. Thanks for being willing to give up your seats. What were you and Miss Sunshine talking about?"

"I may have mentioned that doing unto others was a good idea in Goosebush."

"She looks like she may be sick, so you must have made your point," Warwick said. He smiled and took a sip of his wine.

"She was telling me that she and Leon had planned on working together."

"Lil, you've got some dust on your dress," Tamara said. "Want me to help you brush off?"

"Great, I talked to Miss Blossom covered in dust. Ah well, I'm not surprised. There were dust bunnies bigger than Luna up there." She and Tamara brushed, and then Lilly did a quick twirl. Tamara gave her a nod. True friends didn't let each other go through life covered in dust.

"I enjoyed seeing the show from up there," Tamara said.

"You enjoyed it because you could make those faces during the show," Warwick whispered.

"Which faces?" Lilly whispered back.

"My 'what the hell just happened' faces," Tamara said.

"Combined with the 'wow, that was brutal' look?" Lilly said quietly. "My face may have had the same twitches."

"Seriously, that ending? Bob's in jail?"

"But Scrooge feels badly, so maybe the charges will get dropped," Lilly said.

"But poor Bob has to answer the 'have you ever been arrested' question with a yes, which means the poor man is stuck working for Scrooge forever," Tamara said.

"Unless Mrs. Cratchit gets a better job so that he can quit. Maybe go out on his own?" Lilly said.

"And do what? Bob has limited skills, thanks to working for Scrooge all those years. I doubt old Scrooge provided Bob with professional development opportunities," Tamara said.

Warwick had started laughing, and then he looked around. "Both of you, just stop. People are around."

"You're right, of course," Lilly said, doing her best to look admonished. "But you two are the only people I can have this conversation with. Honestly, I'd love to read the play. Maybe that would help me understand it better."

Roddy walked over to Lilly and handed her a glass of red wine. "I saw the three of you laughing over here," Roddy said. "Are you going to let me in on the joke?"

"Roddy, don't get them started again. They can be drama critics later," Warwick said.

"Ah, I see. Well, you're not the only critics. While I was waiting in line, there was much buzz about the play."

"Good buzz?" Lilly asked.

"Yes and no. The consensus seemed to be that the play needs some work, but that the playwright's take was an interesting one. Most people thought the darker tone speaks to today. There's great excitement about next week's reading."

"Even without a movie star?" Tamara asked. The four of them looked over at the autograph table, which was finally empty. Virginia Blossom had sidled up to Jeremy, and they were chatting.

"You know, I think that of the two of them, Annabelle was the star this evening," Roddy said. "My, she doesn't look pleased, does she? Oh, Jeremy has met Ms. Blossom. Perhaps someone should rescue him?" Lilly watched as Ernie did just that.

"Funny, he doesn't look pleased at the interruption. Lacking taste, obviously," Roddy said, looking over Lilly's shoulder toward Annabelle. "Apparently we missed some movie star mugging by Jeremy Nolan from our vantage point."

"Movie star mugging?" Lilly said. She watched Jeremy walk over to Annabelle, offering her his arm. She pushed it away and started to furiously whisper to Jeremy, poking him in the chest to make her point. Jeremy looked around and noticed that people were watching. He leaned down and said something quietly to Annabelle, who paled and stepped back.

"What does a man need to do to get a drink around this place?" Jeremy said to the crowd.

"Permit me," Mitch said. He walked over to the bar, grabbed a glass of champagne, and then handed it to Jeremy. "You like bubbles, if I remember correctly. I wanted to make sure that we had some on hand," he said.

"Back in the day, we couldn't afford good bubbly," Jeremy said. He took a sip and winced. "I see that you still can't, Mitch."

"Ah, Jeremy, not all of us went on to fame and fortune," Mitch said. "Some of us stayed in the theater and tended to the art, and kept the past close."

The two of them stared at each other for a few seconds. Finally, Annabelle stepped between them.

"Well I, for one, had a wonderful time. It's been a very long time since I've been on a stage, and I'm afraid that showed a bit. Thank you to everyone who helped me tonight," she said. The murmurs of protest started to bubble up from the other actors.

Annabelle took Jeremy by the elbow and steered him away from Virginia Blossom. "You know, this theater is where Jeremy, Mitch, and I worked so many years ago. I can't tell you how grateful I am to remember those wonderful halcyon days. I'd like to toast my dear friend, Mitchell Layton, the reason for this gathering of old friends and wonderful memories. You have a wonderful play on your hands, my dear friend. I hope this reading gave you what you needed artistically. I know that it fulfilled me both artistically and emotionally. Friends, could we all raise a glass to Mitchell Layton." Everyone cheered and raised a glass.

"And, if I may?" Delores said, stepping forward. "Another toast, to our dear friend Leon Tompkin. I can't help but think he was with us in spirit this evening. He is, actually, truly the reason we are gathered."

There was a more somber toast to Leon, and then Ernie stepped forward. "Folks, the desserts are coming out now. Annabelle and Jeremy, we have plates over here for you with some food. And there's more drinks—I promise you, there's better champagne."

Everyone laughed, and Jeremy took the plate that Scooter offered him shyly. He bowed slightly and flashed his megawatt smile at her. She blushed and then went over to give Annabelle her plate.

Jeremy picked up one of the mini cupcakes from his plate and lifted it in the air. "If I've learned nothing else in life, it's eat desserts first, my friends." He popped the cupcake into his mouth and made a surprised look as he chewed. Seconds later, he fell over onto the floor, his body convulsing, food strewn around him. Annabelle screamed and dropped her own plate, then knelt down next to Jeremy, cradling his head in her lap.

CHAPTER 11

The ambulance got there quickly, but Annabelle wasn't allowed to go with Jeremy. Bash called in for reinforcements. While he was waiting, he asked Warwick, Ernie, and Roddy to guard the exit doors. Lilly and Tamara stood in front of the theater doors to prevent people from leaving through the house.

"Folks, if I could have your attention!" Bash said loudly. "I'll let you go as soon as possible, but I need to get brief statements first. I'm also going to ask you all to email me any video or photos you took this evening. Oh good, Officer Polleys is here. She'll stay here and take photographs. People, I'll need to ask you to leave your bags, plates, and glasses exactly where you are. Thanks for your patience."

"Is he—" someone asked.

"We're not sure of his condition," Bash said. "Thank you all for helping us figure out what happened."

Bash walked over to Lilly, who had been filming the scene after the initial shock wore off and she thought to get her phone out. "How much of that did you get?" he asked her.

"Nothing until after it happened," Lilly said. "But I'm sure others did."

"Yeah, the video is already on social media."

"How awful! That's a terrible way for his family to learn about what happened. Do you think it was a heart attack or a stroke?"

"I have no idea, but what I do know is that he took a bite of food and keeled over. I need to treat this as suspicious."

"Of course. Do you know how he is?"

"Not good," Bash said. "That's why I want to get the investigation started. Because if he dies? I don't even want to think about that."

"What can I do to help?" Lilly asked.

"Annabelle Keys is back in her dressing room with Delia. She's pretty upset. I'll need to get her statement, but maybe I can do it later, at your house?"

"Of course. Let me know when Roddy and I can leave, and we'll take her with us."

"I may need Roddy to stay put for a while. And Delia. There are going to be a lot of questions about who was where, and when. There are more officers coming, but I don't want people to leave until we get details sorted out."

Lilly watched Bash's face contort, and he put his finger on the earpiece he was wearing. "Roger that," he said.

"Roger what?"

"The state police just arrived. They're taking over."

"You have this under control," Lilly said.

"Jeremy Nolan is a movie star," Bash said. "We need to get this right, just in case—you know. I work well with the staties when I need to."

Bash walked over to one of the officers who had just arrived. They conferred for a few seconds, and then Bash turned to the crowd, raising his voice again. "Folks, if you'll all come into the theater after checking in with one of the officers, we'll get you processed as soon as possible. Again, leave your food and drink where they are. We will need to check your bags."

"You can't force us to do anything," Virginia Blossom said.

"Well, actually, he can," a trooper said. She stepped forward and addressed the crowd. "I'm Trooper Elizabeth Harris. I'm sorry to tell you all that I just got word that Mr. Nolan died on his way to the hospital."

Lilly stood where she was until she was cleared to go into the theater. She watched as Trooper Harris walked over to Virginia and spoke with her for a few seconds before having another officer come over to take a statement. Lilly saw Delores say something to Scooter, who turned and stormed off. Delores tried to pick up a plate, but another officer stopped her.

"Ma'am, have you been helped?" Trooper Harris asked Lilly. The younger woman turned away from Lilly to follow her gaze into the crowd.

"Chief Haywood asked me to take Ms. Keys home with me," Lilly said, turning back after a moment.

"He did, did he?" the trooper said. She walked over to confer with Bash and then walked back to Lilly.

"She's stage left," Trooper Harris said, walking to the left of the lobby.

"That's on the right-hand side," Lilly said. The younger woman nodded and walked back to Lilly, holding the door open for her. Lilly wasn't sure exactly how to get backstage, and she was relieved when the door on the right-hand side of the stage was open. The lights weren't on all the way, but Lilly hugged the wall and kept moving forward. She heard weeping coming from down the hall, and they found Delia and Annabelle Keys in the last dressing room.

"You've heard," Trooper Harris said.

"Mitch just called. It's on the Internet," Annabelle said. "It's just so awful."

"May I speak with you alone for a moment?" the state police officer asked. "Miss, would you mind leaving us?"

"We'll be right outside," Delia said to Annabelle. She left and closed the door behind her.

"Delia, are you all right?" Lilly asked, opening her arms wide. Delia stepped in and held on. Lilly felt a shudder rip through Delia, and then she heard the aching sob. She rocked her back and forth until she stopped crying. When Trooper Harris came out, Delia stepped back and wiped her eyes.

"You all right, Miss—sorry, didn't catch your name."

"Delia Greenway," Lilly said. "She was the stage manager this evening."

"Delia Greenway," Trooper Harris said, writing the name down. "Where were you when Mr. Nolan—when he convulsed."

"I was still backstage," Delia said. "Cleaning up."

"Anyone with you?"

"Yes. Well, yes and no. There were a few of us in charge of getting the theater back the way we found it." Delia listed some names, spelling them all out.

"And they're all still here?"

"Yes. Out in the house, sitting in the corner. I asked them to stay put after I heard what happened. I knew someone would want to talk to them just in case."

"Just in case?"

"In case it wasn't natural causes," Delia said without emotion.

"Do you usually assume things may be foul play?" the officer asked. Trooper Harris was tall and looked as if central casting had sent her in. Her face was emotionless; her eyes were directly focused on whomever she was speaking to while seeming to roam the area at the same time. Lilly couldn't guess how old she was or much more about her other than she seemed in excellent shape, had short brown hair, and had light freckles sprinkled across her light brown skin.

"Trooper Harris, Delia and I have run into a couple of unfortunate events in the past few months—"

"The murders. Ah, you are *that* Lilly. Bash has talked about you."

"He has?" Lilly felt a blush rise up. "Hopefully with kind words."

"He thinks a great deal of you," Trooper Harris said. "We've been in a couple of training classes recently, and he's mentioned how you've helped him see the forest through the trees at times. It explains why he suggested you get Ms. Keys out of here. He trusts you to make sure she's taken care of, and to listen. He suggested that you could bring her to your home, and we could follow up with her there."

"Of course. My house is a few minutes away. Ms. Keys could stay the night if she'd like to."

"She mentioned getting a hotel room, but your place would be preferable. We could assign security if you think that's needed."

Lilly shook her head and smiled. "We'll close the drapes at the front of the house. If we need help, I'll let Bash know, but I think it will be fine. Can Ms. Greenway come home with me?"

The trooper shook her head. "We'll need her here for a while to track who did what when."

"Well, Ernie can bring her home with him. They both live with me, you see."

"Ernie is—"

"Ernie Johnson," Delia said. "He was in the play."

Trooper Harris made another note, and at that moment, the dressing room door opened, and Annabelle Keys stood on the threshold, balancing a makeup case, tote bag, purse, and small suitcase.

"Have you decided what you want to do with me?" she asked wearily.

"Ms.—"

"Jayne," Lilly reminded her.

"Jayne," Trooper Harris said, making another note. "Ms. Jayne has offered to bring you to her house, and we can question you there."

"You're welcome to spend the night, as well," Lilly said. "We've got more than enough room."

"You're very kind. That would be nice, thank you. I'm exhausted. It was such a wonderful night, and now. And now. Thank you, Trooper Harris, for being so accommodating. I know this whole celebrity thing is ridiculous, but I am grateful that I can try to come to terms with Jerry's death with some privacy." She took a deep breath and put down some of the bags so she could wipe her eyes.

"Of course—"

"And you will let me know when I can . . . I'll want to make arrangements for Jerry."

"Are you the next of kin?" Trooper Harris asked.

"His ex-wife. But we've stayed each other's ICE."

"Ice?" Lilly asked.

"In case of emergency. We actually talked about this last month, updated our wills and the like. Until someone else steps in, we agreed to take care of the details for each other. It's so odd. We just talked about it again last week, after Leon's funeral."

"Leon?"

"Leon Tompkin. He was an old friend. We worked together years ago."

Trooper Harris made another note. "All right, Ms. Jayne and Ms. Keys, let me check your bags; that's routine for tonight. Then you can go and get your car."

"I actually parked out back, since I was early. I think there's a door we can access back here," Lilly said.

"There is," Delia said. "Down the hall a bit. See the exit sign? It's across from the costume shop."

Lilly nodded and then looked back at the dressing room door. Annabelle's dressing room was the last one before the exit.

Trooper Harris went back into the dressing room with Annabelle to look through her bags.

"You'll be all right?" Lilly whispered to Delia.

"I will, but I can't wait to go home. Feed Luna, please."

"Of course."

"And don't forget to lock the garden gate door to Roddy's house."

"Why?"

"We had photographers trying to sneak back here before the show. If they figure out she's at your house, they may start sneaking through your garden."

Lilly shuddered. "Make sure you let Roddy know."

"Do you think Jerry had a heart attack?" Delia whispered.

"I have no idea," Lilly said. "One minute he was talking, then he popped a cupcake in his mouth, and next thing he was on the ground."

"It's so sad," Delia said, tears starting again. "He was very nice—"

They stopped talking when Trooper Harris came out and asked for Lilly's handbag. She handed it to her, grateful that she'd elected to bring the keys/lipstick/ID/money small purse. The search was thorough but quick.

"Excellent. Ms. Greenway, could you make sure the lights are on everywhere, including backstage? Let's get you ladies out of here."

"Trooper Harris, I haven't given a statement. Should I make some notes when I get home?" Lilly asked.

"That would be very helpful, Ms. Jayne. Include anything else that you noticed, will you?" Trooper Harris gave Lilly a nod, and then she picked up most of Annabelle's bags and headed toward the backstage entrance.

CHAPTER 12

The back of the building had been blocked off, so Lilly and Annabelle were able to get in the car unseen. Trooper Harris walked in front of them as they moved out in order to okay their exit. She paused and held up a hand.

"Reporters have descended," Trooper Harris said. "I'm going to suggest that Ms. Keys prepare herself."

Lilly was appalled by the chaos outside the theater. She'd parked next to the dumpster again, so the car was hidden. When she stepped out into the driveway, a flurry of lights flashed, and voices raised. How was she going to navigate through that?

"We'll get you through," Trooper Harris said, as if reading Lilly's mind. "Brace yourself, though. Ms. Keys is going to draw attention."

"How about if I hid in the back of the car?" Annabelle

said. "Wouldn't be the first time I've done that to escape from the press."

Lilly waited while Annabelle lifted the hatch on the back of the Jeep. She climbed in, and Trooper Harris took one of the beach towels out of a bag and laid it over her. Not for the first time, Lilly was grateful that she lived with Delia. Neat, orderly Delia kept the car they shared clean and prepared for any situation. Even though it was November, they often went to the beach and on occasion sat out if the sun was warm enough.

Lilly buckled her seat belt and started the car. She wiped her hands on her dress. She realized she'd left her coat, but it was too late. She'd text Ernie and Delia and ask them to bring it home. She backed the car up slowly and turned it toward the front entrance.

Trooper Harris walked in front of the car, talking into her radio all the while. A couple of other troopers were at the barricade that had been set up. One of them lifted the end to make room for Lilly. The other joined Trooper Harris and cleared a column of egress so Lilly could leave. She was blinded for a moment when camera lights turned toward the car, but she blinked and trusted that the people would get out of her way. A state trooper held people back as they surged toward her.

Taking a right would get Lilly home faster, but she decided to go left instead. It was a good call, as she saw a few people run toward their cars, which were parked all over the side of the street.

"Annabelle, hold on for a few minutes. We've got a couple of cars following us, and I want to lose them."

"I'm fine, so do what you need to do," Annabelle said.

Few people knew Goosebush as well as Lilly Jayne.

She'd driven, ridden her bicycle, or walked every inch of the town many times over in her sixty-five years. Lilly twisted and turned, finally losing the third car when she pulled behind a privet hedge and turned off her lights.

When they finally pulled into the Windward driveway, Lilly looked around before she hit the remote to open the gate. She drove a few feet, then waited until the gate closed before she wound her way down toward the garage. She pulled the remote out again and opened the garage door while turning on the lights in the backyard.

Lilly's garage was an optical illusion. It looked like a three-story cottage, but the first two floors were the garage itself. When you drove in, you drove up a rise, so that any flooding down the driveway wouldn't damage the cars. The garage could hold three cars, but until Ernie moved in, they'd used the other two spaces for a snow-blower, Vespas, and bicycles. From inside the garage, you walked up a short flight toward the second floor, which was on the same level as Lilly's backyard. It was complicated; the idea was that no one could access the backyard from the driveway because of the incline. Privacy and security had been part of the design of the house from the very beginning, an idea that Lilly grew more grateful for all the time. She loved that visitors couldn't pop in the back door and that her gardens were a sanctuary.

Lilly and Annabelle made their way to the backyard, and Lilly went and opened the back door to the porch, standing back to let Annabelle into the house. Once that door was closed, she opened the back door. Luna came flying out and stopped short when she saw Annabelle.

"I hope you're not allergic to cats?" Lilly asked, bending down and scooping Luna up. She waited until Annabelle was in the house proper and she'd closed the back door to let the kitten down again.

"No, not at all. What a sweetie. Where was she while we were rehearsing?"

"Locked up. She likes to think she's an outdoor cat, so we put her in Delia's office when we have company. Tell you what, why don't you have a seat in my library while I go and close curtains and lock the gate door."

"I'm so sorry you have to go through all of this for me—"

"Please, don't give it another thought. I had my own flash of celebrity a few weeks back, and people peering into the front of the house was awful. In fact, I've been exploring film to put on the windows so people can't see inside. Here's the room, and let me turn on the fire. Before I tend to things, can I get you something to drink? I can put on water for tea, or wine, or—?"

"Do you have brandy?" Annabelle asked, settling into the chair that faced the fireplace. She slipped her feet out of her shoes and put her feet up on the ottoman.

"Of course I do," Lilly said. She handed Annabelle a lap blanket and went into the kitchen. As part of the renovation of the space, she'd had a bar area added, which included a wine cooler, small sink, glassware, and a full bar. Lilly took a brandy snifter and pulled out a bottle of what her mother used to call "mother's comfort": a bracing, smooth brandy that warmed up your insides. Lilly poured a bit, and then she thought about what had happened. She poured a bit more.

She walked in and handed the glass to Annabelle. Luna had settled in her nap, and she was petting the kitten gently and staring at the fire.

"Back in a few," Lilly said.

Lilly went back to the kitchen and put her keys in the cupboard where everyone kept them. She took the key to the garden gate and went out to the backyard. It had taken a great deal of effort to get that gate open, and it hadn't been closed in the few weeks since. Windward had been built by an old sea captain, and he'd built the house next door for his daughter. After a falling out, the garden gate had been shut and locked, but Lilly preferred it open again now that they'd found the key. Likely that was because Roddy lived next door. She couldn't remember another neighbor who warranted an open gate.

Lilly locked the back gate but kept the lights on for Delia and Ernie. Moving to the front of the house, she closed the drapes quickly and then went upstairs to make sure the guest room was in good order, which it was. She was in the habit of keeping the bed made for when Tamara and Warwick stayed, so the linens were fresh and the bathroom was sparkling.

After she'd changed into a more comfortable dress, Lilly texted Ernie and Delia and asked them to bring her coat home with them. She took her time going down the stairs. The night was catching up to her, and she was tired. But there was work to be done.

She peeked into the library and saw that Annabelle hadn't moved. Rather than disturb her, she went into the kitchen to put together a tray of food. She included some of the ham and turkey leftovers. Because of the rehearsals over the past couple of days, there was more of a palette pleasing selection than ever, so Lilly made an assorted tray of finger foods. She picked out a bottle of wine and set it beside the tray. She put short wine glasses in each of her pockets.

Luna came bounding in, and Lilly looked down and

smiled. "Sorry, Luna, I'd forgotten. You had your wet food already, but here's some dry. I'm giving you extra; don't tell Delia."

Luna fed, Lilly tucked the bottle of wine under her arm and picked up the tray. She left through the hall door and walked to the library. It would have been faster to go through the kitchen door, but she didn't want to startle Annabelle.

"I thought you might want something to nibble on," she said to Annabelle as she came into the library.

"I'm not very hungry."

"I know you're not," Lilly said. "But try and eat something. It will make you feel better."

Annabelle smiled weakly and sat up a bit straighter. "What is that?" she asked, pointing to a stack of waffles.

"Delia makes them," Lilly said. "She takes stuffing, and adds all sorts of things to make a wet dough, and then she puts them in the waffle press. I should warn you, when I say she adds all sorts of things, I mean just that. They never taste the same. Most of the time they are fine. Sometimes they are wonderful. But there are other times when they aren't as delicious."

"Intriguing," Annabelle said. She picked up one of the waffles and tore off a piece. She nibbled it and then tore off a bigger piece. "That is wonderful. It tastes like Thanksgiving dinner."

"Even better with some turkey or ham. There's cheese as well," Lilly said, handing her a plate and napkin. She took the forks and spoons and put them in various places near the food so that Annabelle could make a plate. Which she did. Lilly poured herself a glass of wine and then followed suit.

The women ate in silence for a few minutes. Lilly

couldn't imagine what Annabelle was going through, no
matter what had happened to Jeremy. From the little
she'd seen them together, it was evident that they were
close. Though she did wonder what the argument had
been about right before he died. Was she jealous of Virginia? Or was there something more?

If Jeremy didn't die of natural causes, would Annabelle be a suspect? Of course she would. Lilly would also
do well to remind herself that Annabelle was an actor, so
she could be faking the pain on her face.

"Would you like more brandy?" Lilly asked.

"No, thanks, that was perfect. Maybe some wine? Did
you bring that glass for me?"

"I did," Lilly said, handing it to her. She passed
Annabelle the bottle.

"Thank you so much for opening your house this entire weekend," Annabelle said, pouring a small glass and
taking a sip before adding more. "You made the rehearsal
process much more bearable by giving us the comfort and
space of your home."

"Are rehearsals that difficult?" Lilly asked.

"Rehearsals are usually my favorite part of the process, but this one brought up some old ghosts I thought
were long buried," Annabelle said. She looked down at
her glass and then back up at Lilly. "Can you believe
Leon's memorial service was only a week ago? He was
such a lovely man. He was so good at keeping in touch.
Sent me a note on my birthday, and a New Year's card
every January. He'd add a note, and always include a
quote or a phrase that was just what I needed at the time.
I loved getting those cards. A very special man."

Annabelle paused and took another sip of wine. Lilly

wanted to respond, but she hadn't been able to swallow the lump in her throat.

"Anyway, we'd planned on seeing Leon while we were here. I knew he was ill; Jeremy told me. We'd had to cancel once, which I regret. Really regret. After he died, his son reached out to tell us about the service."

"Did you know Fred?"

"Jerry knows—knew—him. Leon reached out when Fred was in college, and asked about an internship. Jerry said he'd help out, for old time's sake, he told me. Turns out Fred was a great production assistant, so Jerry hired him the next summer and after college. Jerry and I weren't together by then, but I met him a couple of times. Oh no, Fred. I should call him—"

"I'll call him later," Lilly said. "Poor Fred; first his father, now Jerry."

"Both heart attacks—so scary. You just never know, do you?"

"No, you don't," Lilly said. *If they were both heart attacks*, she thought.

"When we saw Mitch at the memorial service, well, nostalgia started to flood in for all of us. That theater. Some of my best memories, the best times of my life were in that place." Annabelle started to cry, but didn't bother to wipe the tears at first. She stared over at the fire and then back at Lilly. "Nostalgia is a powerful drug, isn't it? We all decided to have Thanksgiving dinner together, and spent the entire dinner talking about the old days. I'm not even sure if Mitch suggested we be in the reading, or if Jerry inserted himself. I should have said something at that moment—told them both it was a terrible idea. But I didn't."

"Why was it a terrible idea?" Lilly asked.

"Because I knew once we all started working together, the bad memories would come back."

"Bad memories?"

"We were so young when we were all together at the Stanley. Stanley Sayers. Another lovely man," Annabelle said. "Did you see anything during Mel John's tenure? One of the summer shows?"

"I don't think I did," Lilly said. "I've been trying to remember. I feel like I might have seen one of the Oscar Wilde shows."

"That would have been done during the regular season. He did what was expected during the regular season. It was during the summer that Mel did what he wanted. Leon and Stanley were always so supportive of those summer productions. You wouldn't forget one of Mel's shows," Annabelle said. "It's not that they were all wonderful, because they weren't. But they were all done with artistry, passion, and panache. Nothing was out of bounds. Those first few years were some of the best years of my life. Certainly the best years of my artistic life."

"I've never worked in theater, but from the stories I've heard, passion runs high."

"It does. We were so young. You know how life is so black and white when you're young? The edges get blurry and life gets grayer as we get older. When Mitch and Jerry decided to work together, I think they were both hoping that time would soften those edges."

Lilly waited, but when Annabelle didn't say more, she asked her about those edges.

"Artistic temperaments, for sure. Disagreements. But toward the end of the Mel years, it had all become a soap opera. Mel was a few years older than we were. It wasn't that he was particularly handsome, because he wasn't. But my, he was brilliant. A bright, hot, brilliant flame of energy. We were all moths drawn to him."

"Anyone in particular?"

"We all loved Mel dearly, even though it cost us everything."

"What do you mean?"

"Have you ever had a passion so great that it consumed you? At the beginning, it's fine. You can keep everything balanced. But over time, the balance is lost?"

Lilly nodded, even though she didn't know that she'd ever lost balance in her life. She had felt passion, though. She allowed herself a moment to think of Alan, but then she concentrated on what Annabelle was saying.

"We all lost our balance. There were five years at that theater. The last two were a nightmare. Mel and Mitch had broken up. Mitch wasn't even there that last year. He may have been in rehab by then. I should have been, as well, but it took me a couple of more years to hit bottom. By then, Jerry and I were done. It took us a few more years to get divorced. That was ugly. Jerry and I didn't speak again until a couple of years ago. He got in touch after my second husband died."

"I'm so sorry," Lilly said. "You've had a difficult time of it."

"I can see you don't read the gossip sites, Lilly," Annabelle said. "My haunted past and lost career have been fodder for several stories these past couple of months. Yes, difficult times. Most of my own making, I'm afraid."

"I'm sure that's not true—"

"All that wasted time. Oh, Jerry. My dear Jerry. All that wasted time." Annabelle started to cry.

"But you were working together again?" Lilly said

quietly, wishing she'd read more about their movie project.

"We are. Were. He reached out a couple of years ago, after Blake died, and we started talking again. He encouraged me to focus on my career. These days, all I get are mother roles, but that's fine. Really, it is."

"You were wonderful in that movie that came out last year at the holidays."

"Thank you, that means a lot. That role was a gift. Even though it was small. Now, that's not fair. There are no small parts. It opened doors for me. But this role, the film we're working on? I'm so excited about it. Oh my, the movie. I wonder if, with Jerry gone. I hope they don't—"

"Annabelle, you've had a shock. Don't let your mind spiral out of control. One step at a time. You'll deal with the movie people tomorrow."

"You know, the movie wouldn't have happened if Jerry hadn't signed on as a producer. He only agreed to do this project because I was interested in the role. Oh, Jerry. I can't help but think this is all my fault."

CHAPTER 13

Lilly texted Bash close to midnight and asked if he was going to come over to the house that evening.

Rather than text back, he called. Lilly could hear a murmur of voices in the background, and she had to pay attention closely to what he was saying.

"Is Ms. Keys going to stay with you?" Bash said. "There will be questions, but there's a lot of work to do here first."

"She's going to stay here," Lilly said. "I just sent her up to settle in. She's had a bit to drink, and something to eat. She'd probably be happy to go to sleep."

"How is she?" Bash said. Lilly knew he wasn't asking about her health, physical or emotional. He was asking for Lilly's opinion.

"She loved him," Lilly said. "I think she's heart-broken, but she's still in the shocked phase."

"Do you think she could have killed him?" Bash asked.

"So, it's murder, is it?"

"They're treating it like murder. Did she still love him, do you think?" Bash asked. "Rumor has it that he had affairs over the years—"

"She said she had a happy marriage afterwards, and he's been a good friend since her husband died. I can't imagine her killing him."

"She's a good actress, though. She could be faking it," Bash said.

"Yes, there's that," Lilly said. "Have you told Trooper Harris about Leon?"

"I have, but her higher-up dismissed it for now. Captain Flavia. Looks and acts like the seasoned detective he is. Long on experience, short on charm. Anyway, Leon didn't die of cyanide poisoning."

"Cyanide? Poor Jerry."

"Yeah, that's the assumption right now. Not a good way to go. Painful."

"Not an easy poison to get, surely," Lilly said.

"You'd be surprised. Especially these days. Delia and Ernie are going to be staying for another hour or so. They've been helping with organizing who was where when."

"Is Roddy still there?"

"He is. Since he was with you in the upper gallery, he's not a suspect. He is a good observer, so he's been filling in gaps."

"Does being in the upper gallery remove him as a suspect because he was with me?"

"No, because you all stayed up there and didn't rush downstairs after the show. The food that killed him was delivered a couple of minutes before the show started. You were already upstairs."

"Was what killed him a—"

"Listen, Lil, I have to go. Could you get Annabelle to stay with you until we talk to her tomorrow?"

"Yes. If you're going to be here before nine o'clock, call me. Otherwise, the house will be moving then."

"I'm not in charge. Of anything. But I'll try and let people know about the timing."

"I'm sorry, Bash. You deserve to be in charge. I for one would feel better if you were. You take care, and come by for a chat if you have a chance."

"You can bet on that; thanks, Lil," he said, hanging up.

Lilly tried to stay up, but around one, she finally decided to go upstairs. Luna came up with her, and Lilly didn't have the heart to kick her out of the room, so she left her door cracked a bit. She'd started to read her book, and then the next thing she knew, she had a crick in her neck, and the lights were still on. She took off her glasses and rolled over, noting that the hall lights had been turned off, so everyone was home.

At eight o'clock the next morning, she came down and found Ernie bustling in the kitchen. When he saw Lilly, he stopped what he was doing and walked over to give her a hug.

"How are you, my friend?" Lilly asked him.

"I'm so tired that I feel as if I'm dreaming," he said. "I tried to sleep in, but I couldn't."

"You know that Annabelle's here?" Lilly said.

"Yes, and Mitch came back with us."

"Oh, did he," Lilly said.

"I put him in the room next to Annabelle's. I didn't think you'd mind." Ernie did his best not to look at Lilly. "The whole cast could have come over. Plenty of bedrooms, and each one with its own amazing assortment of bed linens, towels, soaps. You could turn this place into a bed-and-breakfast in a flash."

"Perish the thought," Lilly said. The idea of greeting strangers in the morning as a way to make a living made her shudder. "The bedrooms being prepared at all times is my mother's training; always be ready for guests. Most of the bed linens were Viola's. Buying new sheets was one of her indulgences. Keeping the old ones was one of her habits. When I married Alan, he'd have retreats here, so we got all of the bedrooms fixed up with new beds, and we added the extra bathrooms. I got used to having linens ready to go in each bedroom."

"Delia told me about a couple of those retreats. They sounded like camps for intellectuals. I can't believe you had them before the kitchen was redone. Your old kitchen was charming, but not very functional. That must have been tough."

"We ordered out a lot," Lilly said, laughing. "Though Alan did excel at large breakfast casseroles. Speaking of which, I put one together last night."

"You did what?" Ernie asked.

"It's no big deal," Lilly said, going over to the refrigerator and pulling out a large glass pan. "I took Delia's waffles and put some ham and cheese and a dash of mustard on them, then poured milk and eggs over the top. Let's put it in now, since it will take about an hour."

Lilly and Ernie futzed in the kitchen for a few more minutes, electing to make an urn of coffee for the rest of the guests. Ernie took out some of the roll dough that hadn't been used on Thanksgiving and cut it into pieces. After he'd rolled the pieces in melted butter and then cinnamon and sugar, he put the monkey bread in the second oven. They both went out to the back porch, bringing their coffee with them. Lilly rubbed her upper arms to warm up, and went to the blanket chest and took two out, handing one to Ernie. He turned on the remote for the fireplace, and then both wrapped themselves up and sat down.

"If it's too cold, we can go inside," Lilly said.

"The sun's out, and the fireplace helps. Let's see if we can take it," Ernie said. "I love this room more and more."

"So do I," Lilly said. She was thrilled that Meg Mancini was able to make strides in such a short time. The room was becoming more of a four-season porch now, but there was still work to be done.

"What time did you all come in?" she asked Ernie.

"Around two," he said, setting his phone on the side table to keep track of the baking with the alarms he'd set. "We were almost the last to leave."

"Are you off the suspect list?"

"Only because I didn't go near the food tables and I kept talking to people. I was heading to get a plate, but then Harry Lentz wanted to talk about the new seats for the theater, so I didn't get there."

"Harry's off the list as well?"

"Officially, no, he's still on there. He met me with a plate of food. Including cupcakes."

"I saw those. Where were they from?"

"The Cupcake Castle."

"I didn't know they made mini cupcakes."

"It was a special order."

"By?"

"Me," Ernie said miserably. "Mitch loves cupcakes, and when we needed to get more food, I talked to Kitty about making a huge batch of minis for the reception. She was game, but she didn't get them to the theater until the show was just going up."

"Where did she leave them?"

"She gave them to Bash, and he put them on the table. They stayed in the boxes until the end of the show."

"Do you know who took them out of the boxes?"

"Scooter oversaw the volunteers, and they did the food setup. They were actually quite lovely—the cupcakes. They were all in red cupcake papers with white frosting. Kitty molded theater masks in different colors of chocolate for the top. Each color was a different flavor. Scooter put some out for audience members, but saved the rest for the VIP reception."

Ernie picked up his phone and looked on Instagram for some photos. "Here you go. Scooter took a picture right before the audience came out. See the sort of rainbow way they set them up?"

Lilly took the phone. She jumped a bit when the alarm went off, but Ernie got up to check on the baking. She scrolled through his phone and noticed that pictures of Jeremy Nolan were all over the platform. She saw one that was taken just moments before he died. She clicked and made it larger.

Ernie came back onto the porch and put a cup of coffee down next to her. "They both need more time, but the coffee's done."

"Thank you. What color paper did you say the cupcakes were in?"

"Red. Why?"

"See this picture?"

Ernie took his phone and paled at the picture. "Dear God," he said.

"I'm so sorry. I should have warned you."

"It's all right. I've seen the pictures already. That's why I didn't sleep well. Look how happy he looked at that moment."

"He did, indeed. That's a blessing, don't you think? That he was happy?"

"It also makes the whole thing sadder. Enough about that. What did you want me to look at?"

"Look at the cupcake he's putting in his mouth."

"Right—"

"It's in a silver cupcake liner."

Lilly went into the kitchen to check on the casserole. It was done, but the beauty of the bake was that it would be fine to eat for hours as long as it was kept warm. Which her oven could do.

"Hungry, or should we wait?" she asked Ernie.

"I'm starving," he said. "I've been eating the monkey bread, but something with protein would be great."

Lilly took out a pile of plates and put them on the counter, so people could serve themselves. While Ernie gathered the napkins and silverware, Lilly put some casserole on two of the plates and carried them to the table. She was about to sit down when Delia came in. Before too long, Mitch and Annabelle came down, as well. After a flurry of coffee pouring, juice distribution, casserole cutting, and monkey bread explanation, everyone settled in at the kitchen table for the meal.

Whenever guests ate in the kitchen, Lilly could swear

she heard her mother admonishing her. While her parents were alive, the kitchen was only used for cooking. Breakfast was served in the breakfast room, and all other meals were eaten in the dining room. She and Alan had lived the same way, though they'd used the breakfast room for most meals. While Alan was sick, they'd begun planning the kitchen renovation, but the execution had been left to Lilly and Delia. Ernie had helped a great deal, which was how he and Lilly became the friends they were now. Between the renovation and the fact that Lilly had turned the breakfast room over to Delia for an office, most meals were in the kitchen or on the back porch, both lovely spaces. Still, Lilly knew her mother would have insisted that Annabelle and Mitch eat in the dining room.

There was a great deal of small talk, none of it having to do with what had happened the night before. During one particularly long pause, Delia jumped in with a new topic.

"Ernie, are you still planning on taking today off? I have a project I'd love your thoughts on."

"I am," he said. "What's the project? More work on the porch plans?"

The back porch had been enclosed years ago; winterizing it was turning out to be a feat of engineering, since insulation, windows, and heating ducts all had to be configured. Though Mary had been overseeing the project, Ernie had been working with Delia, helping her learn hands-on what it would take to convert the room. Lilly was grateful to everyone, since it was moving the project along at a fast clip.

"No, Mary's coming over to talk about the changes Lilly requested later this week. This is more of an historical project. I want to start opening up the dumbwaiters in the house, and I'd like your advice."

"The dumbwaiters?" Ernie said. "What dumbwaiters?"

"The original house had dumbwaiters that went from the third floor all the way to the basement. There were also dumbwaiters that went from the second to the third, and from the first to the second," Delia said. "It must have made sense at one point, probably because of servants and family members and who needed what where. Anyway, they were boarded up years ago. I found some plans for the house when the dumbwaiters were put in, and there were four. I've found two. I'd love to figure out where the other two are, and to try and bring them all back to life."

"It sounds complicated. How would you use them?" Annabelle asked, cutting a bit more of the casserole and putting it on her plate. Lilly was pleased that she was eating this morning. The dark circles under her eyes indicated a restless night. Lilly understood that well.

"I live up on the third floor, so I'd love to be able to use them to move books and my computer up and down stairs. I'd also like to see how they work in general. I suspect the basement to the third floor was for coal and wood back in the day. Nothing in this house is typical, so it's also going to be a discovery of how the captain thought."

"Who's the captain?" Mitch asked.

"Lilly's relative who built this beauty," Ernie said. "He was a sea captain, and quite the character. I actually admire his aesthetic. The house is laid out more for function than for show. Huge rooms down here, but all with a purpose. Upstairs are a rabbit warren of rooms, but that meant a lot of people could stay here at once. I love that he had sinks put in every room—obviously a bit of luxury that he admired."

"My father told me that he tended to invite some rather notorious people to stay, so the sinks and the extra bathrooms were to appease his wife," Lilly said. "She didn't like sharing a bathroom. You know, the house grew over time. It started as a modest house, but as his fortunes grew, the house grew as well. You can barely see the original house, but traces are still here if you know what you're looking for."

"I remember back when we spent summers here, we'd drive by and wonder who lived in this house. It's one of the few things that are actually more glorious now than I remember," Mitch said. "I'd love to get a tour and see the plans, if you don't mind—"

"I don't mind that at all," Lilly said. "Ernie and Delia can join us. Between the three of us, you'll get the whole picture. Ernie waxes on and on about the post and beam structure."

"It's built like a ship—"

"And Delia can give you historical background on the history of Goosebush and how the house fits in," Lilly continued.

"Don't take this the wrong way, Lilly, but I'm glad that your family didn't have enough money to renovate it during the last century," Delia said. "They would have mucked it up. There's so much history that's been saved over the years. When renovations were done, they were in the vein of putting wallboard up instead of tearing it down and starting again. That was less expensive for your relatives, but it also ensured that the layers of wall-paper and paint choices could all be found."

"Like the fireplace in your library," Ernie said. "The room was probably servants' quarters at some point, and then it was turned into a mud room, and then—"

Mitch took out his phone and began tapping.

"What are you doing?" Lilly asked.

"Taking notes. There's something about this house, and hearing the stories. I'm not sure how to ask this, but do you think there are ghosts here?"

"I'm sure there are," Lilly said matter-of-factly. "Why is everyone looking at me like that? The house has been in the family forever; it's seen its share of life and death. I'm sure there are spirits around."

"I think that spaces absorb the energy of those who have passed away there," Annabelle said quietly. "As terrible as all of this is, there's a part of me that's glad that if we had to lose Jerry, it would be at the Stanley after a performance. Just like Mel."

Mitch reached over and took Annabelle's hand. They both looked down at the table.

"I didn't realize that Mel John died at the theater," Lilly said quietly.

"Neither did I," Delia said, looking annoyed. "Of course, finding out anything about that time in the theater has been challenging. How—"

"Delia's been working on a history of both the theater and the Goosebush Players," Lilly said. "They are inter-twined in challenging ways."

"And some things are made up. A lot of things are made up," Delia said.

"History is written by the winners," Mitch said. "Mel

ran the Goosebush Players for those five years, but he
hated it. He felt that the work the Players did was pedestrian at best. I think he was being harsh, but that was Mel.
He lived for the summers, when he could do the work he
wanted to do. He was meant to do."

"He died way too soon," Annabelle said. "I always
thought he was so old, but now I realize that I'm older
than he was when he died."

"Much older."

"Hey, now—" she said, taking her hand and hitting
Mitch on the shoulder.

"I just mean, he was only forty-five years old. In a
more just world, he'd still be working."

"Would you both mind if I ask you some questions
about those summers?" Delia said. She glanced over at
Lilly and, for once, read her expression correctly. "Not
now, of course. When you're up to it."

"I'd be delighted," Annabelle said. "Seeing those pictures that Portia showed us brought it all back."

"Oh, darn it!" Delia said, jumping up from the table
and running out of the room.

"Was it something I said?" Annabelle asked.

"Delia's mind works in mysterious ways," Ernie said.
"She'd likely forgotten something and needs to take care
of it. Who wants more coffee?"

Ernie had just filled up the cups when Delia came running back downstairs. She was winded, with good reasons. Three flights up and down in five minutes was quite
a feat.

She plopped down in her seat, holding two packages
close to her chest. She waited for a minute until she could
catch her breath.

"I meant—these were for last night—thanks to Lilly and Roddy, I have some gifts for you to thank you for being part of the reading this weekend." She handed Mitch and Annabelle each a package with a card.

"The cards are from the company," Ernie said. "You may want to read them later."

Mitch nodded and set his card aside. Annabelle opened hers, but then stopped reading and wiped a tear from her eye. They both opened the packages. The small bound book included all of the photos that Delia had asked to be scanned. Lilly had spent a small fortune having them made into booklets overnight, and she'd been pleased at how they came out.

She wasn't the only one who was pleased. Mitch and Annabelle both looked through them quickly, and then pointed out pictures to each other.

"This is lovely; thank you so much," Annabelle said. "I hadn't seen any of these pictures before. What wonderful memories—"

"And great stories," Mitch said. "All of which I'll tell you at some point, Delia. Most of which aren't fit to print."

"I believe that everything is fit to print," Delia said. "Honestly."

"This is one of Delia's missions in life. Getting people to separate facts from truth by providing all points of view of their story," Ernie said.

"I don't like the idea that history is written by the winners," Delia said. "I like the idea that everyone's story matters. And that facts and the truth aren't always the same thing."

"What do you mean—" Mitch started to ask, but he

was interrupted by the gate buzzer. Ernie got up and buzzed the intercom to find out who was there, but all he heard were garbled voices.

"Lilly, we need to get the buzzer fixed. I'm going to make that my mission," Ernie said. He walked over to the kitchen door and picked up the mini-binoculars that were left there. He stepped out on the kitchen stoop and came back in quickly.

"Trooper Harris is here," he said, putting the binoculars down and buzzing open the gate. He left the kitchen door open. The chatting in the room had stopped, and any joy on Annabelle and Mitch's faces was gone.

CHAPTER 14

Lilly stood on the landing outside her kitchen door and watched Trooper Harris get out of the back seat of the dark sedan that had pulled into her driveway. She'd been tempted to wait and see if they walked all the way around the front of the house, but she'd decided that wasting time didn't serve the moment.

She stepped inside the kitchen and moved into the room until all three officers were in and the door was closed.

"Ms. Jayne, this is Captain Flavia. Captain, this is Lilly Jayne."

Lilly and the older officer nodded at each other.

"We'll need a place to set up that has some privacy," he said to Lilly. "Seems these VIPs are to be given special treatment. Not the way I like to run investigations, but then again, I don't like much about these types of investigations."

"I see," Lilly said. "Why don't we set you up in the dining room." She took them through the kitchen and into the hallway. She pointed out the restrooms on the first floor and then went into the dining room.

"Let me just put the table topper on," Lilly said. She walked to the side and lifted up the heavy leather table covering. Trooper Harris put down her things and helped Lilly lay it out.

"Afraid we'll ruin it?" Captain Flavia asked.

"More concerned that you won't be able to settle in because you'd be afraid you would," Lilly said. "The table isn't precious, but it is treasured."

"I hear you're off the suspect list," Captain Flavia said. "I've still got questions."

"Of course," Lilly said. "Let me get my notes." She went to her library and picked up the sheets of paper that she'd printed out. When she went back into the dining room, the three officers were sitting at one end of the table. Lilly sat at the other end.

"I'm sorry that we're so late," Trooper Harris said. "But our interview with Ms. McGee took longer than expected. Is Ms. Keys still here?"

"She is," Lilly said. "She and Mr. Layton are in the living room with coffee. Speaking of which—"

"They should have gotten your statement last night," Captain Flavia barked. "You've probably forgotten a million details by now."

Lilly paused, and then she handed him the statement she'd worked on last night. She handed Trooper Harris the other copy she'd brought in. She'd edited it, of course, and typed it before she came downstairs. Trooper Harris looked it over and then passed it to the third officer, who was there to take notes, as had been explained. Lilly had forgotten her name.

"That seems very detailed. Anything else to add?" Trooper Harris gave Lilly a smile, and opened her notebook.

"I'm sure you've already looked into the silver foil."

"The silver foil."

"I was looking at some of the pictures on social media this morning. Ernie mentioned that he'd placed the cupcake order from the Cupcake Castle at the last minute." Both officers nodded, and Lilly went on. "I was surprised that they came from the Cupcake Castle, because Kitty usually only bakes large cupcakes. Quite delicious, really. Anyway, Ernie told me about the special order, and the red paper linings with white frosting, and different-colored masks to denote flavor. I saw a picture of Jerry—"

"Jerry? You knew the victim?" Captain Flavia asked, making a note.

"They'd used my house for rehearsal, and I had a couple of meals with them. He asked me to call him Jerry, which I did. I hadn't met him before this weekend, though I knew who he was, of course."

"A fan of his movies, huh? I wouldn't have figured you for the action movie type," Captain Flavia said.

Lilly forced her face to remain neutral. She wasn't sure if Captain Flavia was baiting her, dismissing her, or just being a jerk. She regretted mentioning the silver paper. She should have waited to tell Bash.

"What about the silver paper?" Trooper Harris asked.

"I saw a picture of Jerry right before he, just as he was

about to eat. I noticed that the cupcake in his hand seemed to have a silver cupcake liner. I'm assuming that's the one he ate."

Captain Flavia turned and stared at Trooper Harris, who was going backwards in her notebook.

"I just thought I'd share what I'd noticed. That's the only thing that I would have added to my statement," Lilly said. That was true, of course. That said, she'd left out several other observations that she didn't want to pass on without knowing if they were important. Given the way this was going, she was grateful to have held back.

"Anything come up at breakfast this morning? It looked like you were mid-meal. Sorry to interrupt. Looked pretty cozy when we walked in," Captain Flavia said.

Lilly tilted her head and gave him her best icy stare. She still had it; he seemed a bit flustered and looked away.

"Captain, when I have guests, I give them food," she said. "And we don't discuss murder over breakfast. At least not at my house. Chief Haywood had indicated that you'd let me know when you were on your way. We didn't have time to clean up." After breakfast, she had planned to bring up the murder, but Captain Flavia didn't need to know that.

"Chief Haywood has nothing to do with this case," Captain Flavia said. He looked over her statement and then read it again. He made a couple of notes and then looked up at her. "Seems thorough. I guess we're done here. If anything else comes up, we'll talk to you—"

"Good enough. I was planning on taking a walk. Would that be all right?"

"The theater is a crime scene," Captain Flavia said.

"And it's too far to walk to, at least for me. No, I was thinking about getting some air."

"Fine—"

"And my other question is whether you'd all like some coffee."

"Thank you, Ms. Jayne," Trooper Harris said. "That would be great."

Captain Flavia shot her a look, but nodded. "Send in Ms. Greenway, will you?" he said.

"Certainly," Lilly said, smiling and leaving immediately.

She went into the kitchen to oversee the coffee service, which Delia and Ernie had already put together.

"Delia, you're next," she said. "Captain Flavia is a delight, so be prepared." Delia left to go to her office, and Lilly opened the door to the dining room.

"Sorry to startle you, Captain," she said, not at all sorry. She put the tray down on the sideboard and walked out without serving it. The youngest officer stood up, and Delia came in the other door carrying her stage manager's prompt book, computer, and notebook. Lilly went back into the kitchen and closed the door.

"What a jerk," Lilly whispered to Ernie.

"Captain Flavia? Yeah, he showed up last night. I overheard him talking to someone, complaining really, that these high-profile cases were career enders."

"Only if the case isn't solved," Lilly said. "Though the silver paper discovery makes that unlikely, don't you think? I mean, those cupcakes could have been brought in any time."

Ernie took out his phone and scrolled to a picture that the Cupcake Castle had posted. It showed the boxes of cupcakes being sent to the party. One of the trays had cupcakes with both red and silver paper.

"Then they were part of the order. Which means that anyone could have eaten it," Lilly said quietly.

"I know. Though it did appear on his food plate near his champagne glass." They both stopped talking when Annabelle came into the kitchen.

"How did it go?" she asked Lilly.

"He's a delight," Lilly said. "Though he may be nicer to you. Delia's in there now."

"He'll probably have me go last," Annabelle said. "I hope you don't mind us hanging around here for a bit longer."

"You're welcome to stay for as long as you'd like, Annabelle," Lilly said. "Honestly. As you can see, it's a large house, plenty of room."

"You're very kind, but I'm going to go and stay with Mitch for a couple of days."

"Take care of yourself," Lilly said. "Spending time with a friend is very comforting. Tell you what, why don't you settle into the library while you wait."

"No, that's your room. I can sit in the living room—"

"Where the curtains are drawn. You need some daylight. I'm going to take a walk, and then I'll be in the greenhouse."

"You have a greenhouse?"

"Does she have a greenhouse," Ernie said. "You might have seen it when you were outside. Big glass and wrought iron structure. Looks like something out of a movie? I'll show you around if you'd like. I give a much better tour of the place. Lilly is far too modest to sing her own praises. That okay with you, Lilly?"

"That's fine," Lilly said, laughing. She waited until

Annabelle was out of the room with another cup of coffee before turning to Ernie.

"Are you kicking me out for some reason?" she asked him.

"I am," Ernie said. "First of all, Roddy is next door and wants to catch you up on last night."

"Okay—"

"And also, Delores said she was going to the Star for lunch. I thought that maybe you'd be interested in that."

"How was Delores last night?" Lilly asked. They were both huddled by the coffee urn, whispering while looking at each door.

"She made a bit of a scene, but was actually fairly well behaved, for her. She was on Roddy's list."

"Roddy's list?"

"Roddy, Delia, and I made a quick list of people to track, and she's on his list—"

"Ernie, you're next," Delia said, poking her head into the kitchen. "They'd like you in ten minutes or so. Lilly, I'm going into the breakfast room to keep Luna company. Do you need me?"

Lilly looked at her young friend and gave her a smile. Poor Delia; she looked exhausted. "Delia, I'm fine. Go and take care of Luna. I'm going to go over and see Roddy," Lilly said.

"Yes, he should be all set up by now," Ernie said, leaving the kitchen.

Lilly went up to her room and put some leggings on under her dress. She grabbed her phone, a pen, and a notebook and put them in her pocket. She headed back downstairs and took her boots out of the hall closet. She was sitting on the stairs pulling them on when the hall restroom door opened and Trooper Harris stepped out.

"Sorry, didn't mean to startle you," she said to Lilly. Lilly finished zipping her boots and looked up. The officer held her hand out, and Lilly accepted the help up.

"No worries," Lilly said. "I hope you have everything you need. Let Ernie know if you'd like more coffee or something to eat."

"You're very kind," the younger woman said. "I wanted to say that I was, am sorry if the captain was—"

"Trooper Harris—"

"Liz, please."

"Liz, you are both doing your job. I understand completely. This crime needs to be solved quickly, I'd imagine. There must be a lot of pressure. Otherwise, you might be leading the investigation."

Liz looked over her shoulder and then back at Lilly. "I'm up for a promotion, so I might have been, but still. As you said, this needs to be solved well, and quickly. He's abrupt, but he's a great detective. I'll learn a lot working on this case. From lots of people."

"I'm sure you will," Lilly said. "I know you need to get back in there, but please feel free to ask for whatever you need."

"Thank you so much. I *will* talk to you later."

Lilly smiled. "I'll look forward to that."

Lilly peeked out of the side windows of her front door. She didn't see anyone out there at first, but then she noticed the vans across the street in the boatyard parking lot. She sighed and walked through the house to the kitchen and grabbed the key. She let herself out the back and through the gate. She didn't look to her left, but she suspected that there were prying eyes watching her. She relocked the gate and made her way over toward Roddy's back door, moving quickly behind the garage so that she was blocked from the street as much as possible. The French doors in his kitchen were slightly ajar, and he poked his head out and gestured to her. She walked over, and he let her in, then closed the blinds over the door.

"This is so annoying," he said.

"What is?"

"The press people who've decided to park outside and knock on my front door every five minutes."

"They've figured out that Annabelle is at my house." Lilly sighed. Roddy took her coat, and she put on her glasses and pulled out her phone. She texted Delia and Ernie to let them know what was going on, and that they should warn Annabelle. "The poor thing."

"Do you think it's affected her?" Roddy said.

Lilly looked up and cocked her head at him. "What does that mean?" she asked. She realized she'd become very protective of Annabelle.

"Sorry, I'm short-tempered. Let me start again. Good morning, Lilly. How are you?"

"I'm fine, thank you, Roddy. How are you? I hear you had a late night."

"I was afraid it was going to be later for a while, but when Captain—"

"Flavia. The charmer."

"Exactly. When he showed up, he started to move things along. I tried to listen in to what he was saying. Apparently, after he looked over the notes that Trooper

Harris had made, he decided that they could limit the numbers of people with access and then run them against motives. Something like that."

"Really? Seems a bit cut and dry, doesn't it? Shouldn't motive come first?"

"I agree that his methods seem geared toward a quick result. Here, come see what I've been working on."

Lilly walked into the living room. Roddy's house had been undergoing renovations since he moved in, but this part was done. The house was smaller than Lilly's, but it still had a Victorian flair, with high ceilings, plaster adornments, ornate fireplaces. Roddy had taken great pains to restore, but his furnishings were all mid-century, done with minimalistic accents. Somehow it worked. Lilly found his home very relaxing by its lack of fuss.

She looked at the large piece of paper he'd pinned to the drapes. He gestured to have her sit down, and after he was assured that she didn't want anything to drink, he handed her a file folder.

"What's this?" she asked.

"Notes from Delia and me. Ernie said that you had some notes as well?"

"I did. I do. Believe it or not, I may even be able to send it to you. Hold on." Lilly fussed with her phone, using the app as Delia had taught her. She found the document and sent it to Roddy via email. She looked up proudly, and he expectantly held on to his phone and smiled when it pinged.

"Brilliant! I'll be right back."

While he was gone, Lilly opened the file folder. She read over the notes and then looked up at what Roddy had been working on. It seemed like a timeline of sorts, with a list of names at the bottom.

Delia's report focused on the facts she knew, nothing else. They included who was backstage and when, the time the show started, the time it ended, and what happened afterwards from her point of view. Since she hadn't made it to the front of the house, she didn't have a lot of detail about that time. One thing she made clear was that she didn't believe any of the technical staff could have gone out to the lobby and come back without her noticing.

Roddy's commentary was very similar to Lilly's before the show. He said that most of the tickets had been picked up before he left the table. Warwick had left and Nicole stayed. Lilly wondered about the latecomers and who they might have been.

Roddy came downstairs. He handed her a copy of her notes. She saw that he'd already marked his up.

"Not a lot to work with, is there? We were both upstairs well before the show started."

"To be fair, it was a helluva climb," Roddy said. "Tamara came up around the same time we did."

"I thought it was interesting, seeing a part of the theater that the audience doesn't get to see," Lilly said. "We missed the delivery of the cupcakes, and didn't get downstairs until people had started to eat. Not very helpful. Warwick said that Scooter stayed in the lobby. Maybe she saw something? Does Ernie have anything to share?"

"He was in the men's dressing room. Annabelle and Jerry each had their own, though Jerry hung out in the men's dressing room."

"We should ask Portia if Annabelle came into their dressing—"

"I called her this morning to check in," Roddy said. "She said that Annabelle didn't come into their dressing room. She saw Mitch walk back towards hers about twenty minutes before the show started, but other than that, she didn't see anyone go past the door. Portia did say that Annabelle was late lining up to go onstage, and seemed out of breath, but Portia chalked that up to nerves."

"Where was Portia's dressing room?"

"Closer to the stage. Annabelle's was closer to the back door." Roddy paused. "You know, I've been doing some research on Annabelle. Her divorce from Jerry seemed quite traumatic for her career. She didn't make another film for eight years, and by then, she was past the romantic lead stage, and had moved into character roles."

"Which she's very good at," Lilly said.

"True. But have you seen her when she was young? She was stunning. One of the articles I read wondered if he'd blackballed her in the business."

"They're working together now, or they were," Lilly said.

"Apparently she had a very, very hard time after her second husband died," Roddy said. "A nervous break-down, one article said. Another one said she tried to do herself in. Jerry had to guarantee the film and agree to play a small role in order to hire her."

"Wow," Lilly said.

"Wow? Is that it?"

"Roddy, I've spent some time with her. Granted, she's an actor, but I really think her grief was real. *Is* real. None of this jibes with the woman I've been talking to."

"To quote Delia, facts and truth."

"I know."

"One fact. She could have run out of the side door around to the front and done something to the cupcake."

"How could she have been sure Jerry would eat it?"

"There was a plate of food set aside for each of them. She could have even poisoned her own, and then given it to him."

"The silver foil—"

"What silver foil?"

Lilly explained, and found the picture on her phone to show him. "Of course, the silver foil cups might not mean anything. Captain Flavia wasn't impressed with the idea. Seemed to dismiss me."

"What did Bash think?" Roddy asked.

"I haven't told him."

"Well, then I know where we're going next," Roddy said. "Let's head into town and talk to Bash. I'll buy you lunch while we're out."

"Sounds good. How will we get past the reporters, though?"

"My dear lady, have you forgotten that I own a car with a very, very fast engine?"

CHAPTER 15

Lilly thought Roddy was joking about a fast car being the plan for getting out of the driveway, but he wasn't. His garage was next to his house, an addition from the 1930s. The upstairs of the garage was an in-law apartment, or used to be. Like the rest of the house, it had fallen into disrepair. Lilly hadn't been in the garage itself and was impressed by how much work Roddy had done—pouring a new floor, adding what looked to her like mechanic's tools along the side. In addition to Roddy's red Jaguar, he had an Aston Martin up on blocks and a Jeep in the third bay.

"Are you restoring that?" Lilly asked him while he held her door open, waiting until she was settled before closing it. Getting in and out of his car was a challenge for Lilly, but not for Roddy, who slid in and rubbed his hands together.

"I am," he said. "It's in terrible shape, but I'm in no rush. I enjoy restoring older cars. The puzzle of getting it going again calms my mind."

"I see a Jeep joined the Jag," Lilly said.

"I took your advice about winter driving to heart. The Jeep will be much more practical."

Roddy turned the engine over and gave it a minute to warm up. "I will admit, this garage is ending up to be a wonderful asset that I didn't expect. At first I was troubled, because it sits in the middle of the drive and was so large. As it turns out, it's fairly good for privacy, and I'm able to indulge in projects like the Aston. The second floor is wonderful for storage."

"You know, you could put up a trellis with a swinging gate between the garage and the wall to my house to really block off the backyard. People were peering in as I came through the door."

"If we avoid having celebrities hiding out because another movie star was killed, that may help with privacy. But yes, let's plan on that. It's shady there, so I was planning on putting a gravel area, perhaps with a tool shed of sorts, in that area. I'll add it to my project list. All right, the car should be warm. Ready?"

Lilly nodded. Roddy hit the remote to open the garage door and eased his car out. He waited until he had just cleared the door and hit the remote again. People started to gather at the end of his driveway. He revved his engine and started to move at what Lilly thought was an alarming speed. A couple of people stepped forward on the street, but he didn't slow down. Camera lights went on, but still he kept his speed up. One person jumped back, and then everyone seemed to understand that he wasn't stopping, so they made quick exits by running up on the embankments on either side of the driveway.

At the end, he paused for a moment, but when he saw that no cars were coming, he took a quick turn to the right.

"Are you all right?" Roddy asked.

"I'm fine," Lilly said, lying a bit. "You could have hit someone."

"This car can stop on a dime," Roddy said. "If we'd paused, they would have surrounded us. We do have an intrepid someone following us, though."

"Take the first right off the rotary, and we'll get rid of them," Lilly said. Roddy loved learning back roads from Lilly. The town was so old that most roads had been cow paths that fed into rotaries. Most but not all of them connected to other roads. It took a while, but Roddy finally got the follower lost in a maze. He extricated himself, and they headed to the police department.

When they arrived and asked to see Bash, they were ushered right back to his office. He started to stand up, but Lilly waved her hands to have him sit back down.

"You escaped?" he asked Lilly.

"I did. Met with the charming Captain Flavia already. He's talking to the rest of the household now."

"He talked to Scooter McGee this morning," Bash said. "He used our interrogation room. He also had Virginia Blossom come in to give her statement."

"Do you think either of them are suspects?"

Bash shrugged. "He talked to Scooter for quite a while. But he's not sharing anything with me. Annabelle Keys stayed with you last night, Lilly? Is she still there?"

"Yes, and Mitch is there, as well."

"What's it like having a movie star in your house?"

"Everyone keeps talking about movie stars like they're a different species. She's lovely. Come by, and I'll introduce you."

"No can do, Lilly. Captain Flavia made it very clear that I'm off the investigation."

"What do you mean?" Roddy asked. "You're the chief of police."

"State took over. This high-profile a case, I'm not that surprised, actually. Normally they'd keep me in the loop, but Captain Flavia has a 'my way or the highway' reputation. So here I sit."

"Surely you're still gathering information," Lilly said.

"I'm doing some background research and paying attention to visitors," Bash said. "I tried to talk to Flavia about Leon, but he didn't want to hear it. He said, and I quote, that 'thinking like that just complicates what is probably a simple case of revenge or jealousy.'"

Lilly nodded. "Trooper Harris seems like she's a bit more open-minded."

"She is, but he's her boss."

"Unfortunately. Well, you don't mind an old friend coming in for a chat, do you? Perhaps making a few observations during the conversation?"

"I always love talking to you, Lilly. You know that."

"Did you hear about the silver cupcake liners?"

"Like the one around the cupcake that Jeremy Nolan ate?" Bash said, smiling.

"Yes, that one," Lilly said.

"I've got some of the details. There was a special order of cupcakes done online, for Delores. Her favorite, red velvet with cream cheese icing. Kitty used the silver paper linings to keep them separate."

"Jerry was eating a cupcake meant for Delores?" Roddy said. "That confuses things."

"It gets more confusing," Bash said. "Guess who ordered the cupcakes?"

"Ernie?" Lilly asked, though he would have told her.

"Jeremy Nolan."

Roddy whistled, and Lilly moved forward in her chair. "Jeremy Nolan ordered the cupcakes that killed him?"

"Looks like."

"Does Captain Flavia know that?"

"I just told him. And, of course, I never mentioned it to you."

"Of course not—"

"It's just that you're good at putting pieces that don't look like they belong to the same puzzle together."

"Were all the cupcakes poisoned?" Roddy asked.

"Not all; not sure how many yet. They're still figuring out how the poison was introduced, but it looks like cyanide. That's all Liz could share so far."

"It's amazing that more people didn't die," Lilly said.

"It is. Especially since a little goes a long way with these types of poison," Bash said. "They're testing all of the cupcakes now. If more of them have cyanide, it could be that Jeremy Nolan wasn't the intended victim. If his is the only one, then that's a different focus."

"Interesting. You know, there's something else I've been thinking about," Lilly asked. "Virginia cornered me last night. She says that she and Leon had been talking about doing business together. I can't help but think the theater is a part of a lot of stories these days."

"I'm going to call—" Bash stopped talking when he heard a skirmish outside his door. He opened it just as Delores Stevens was trying to let herself in. She tumbled forward, but Bash caught her by the arm.

"Someone is trying to kill me," she said, righting herself and recovering her composure quickly. She thrust a piece of paper towards Bash, but it fell on the floor. Roddy picked it up, stood, and handed it to Bash.

"We should be going," Roddy said.

"Thank you for being willing to serve as one of the wreath judges, Bash. I know how busy you are—" Lilly said.

"Busy? I should say he's busy. Or at least he should be. One person dead, another one threatened . . ."

"Have a seat, Delores, and tell me what this is all about."

Delores glared at Lilly, who jumped up and stepped aside so that Delores could sit.

"Lilly, I'll call you later to get the details."

"Thank you, Bash. Delores, take good care, won't you?" Lilly said, letting herself out of the office, Roddy close behind.

"Should we go and have lunch?" Roddy asked.

"How about a walk first?" Lilly said. "Alden Park?"

"My car is in a four-hour spot, so lead on."

Roddy had won the contest to design Alden Park, and Lilly knew he liked to visit it often at various times of day and in different light. She didn't mind. Renovating the park had been a dream of hers for years, and she was thrilled that it was going to be done next spring. Of course, she wasn't going to really celebrate until they cut the ribbon at the opening ceremony. The project had already had several false starts.

Lilly had an ulterior motive for going to visit the park. She had to picture what the layout for the garden sculpture event was going to look like. If she was going to enter a piece—and she really didn't see how she couldn't—she needed to understand what the parameters were and how the event was going to be set up. Although it wasn't for another two weeks, Lilly saw that there were signs up around the park, and areas were already being cordoned off. The plan seemed to be to use the entire park, and Lilly was startled by the number of entries they seemed to expect. She looked around and then saw someone scurrying over to her.

"Lilly, hello," Scooter said.

"Hello. Scooter, do you know Roddy?" Lilly asked.

"I met Scooter last night while we were fighting the sea of unhappy patrons," Roddy said. "I must say, I was very impressed that you kept such a cool head."

Scooter smiled, though not for long. "I wish I'd never volunteered to be there," she said.

"It was a terrible night," Lilly said quietly.

"He didn't even know me," Scooter said.

"Who?" Roddy asked.

"Jerry. I knew him, back all those years ago. He didn't recognize me at first. I get that. It's been a long time. But even when I told him I knew who he was, he didn't know me. How's that possible? Am I that forgettable?"

"Take a deep breath," Lilly said. "Scooter, you look exhausted. You're not making much sense. Jerry didn't know you. And that upset you?"

"Of course it did," Scooter said. "We had a deep and

profound relationship. I loved him. He changed my life. How could he act as if it didn't matter? How dare he?" Scooter threw her clipboard and watched as papers flew off it. Roddy went to retrieve it and the papers.

"Scooter, did you talk to Captain Flavia this morning?"

"Yes, at the police station. What a terrible man. Men are terrible, aren't they, Lilly?"

"Did you have a lawyer with you?" Lilly asked gently. She stepped closer to Scooter and put her hands on her upper arms to hold her steady.

"No, why should I?"

"That depends. Did you tell Captain Flavia what you just told me?"

"I may have mentioned it. He had me all confused. He kept asking me about setting up the cupcakes, and asking who had access. At one point, he did ask if I knew him— Jerry, I mean—before last night. At first, I wasn't going to tell him. It's so embarrassing. To be forgotten like that."

Lilly took a deep breath and gently squeezed Scooter's arms. "Scooter, next time they want to talk to you, I want you to bring a lawyer with you. Promise me you'll do that."

"I won't need a lawyer, Lilly. Don't be silly. He died of a heart attack, right? He sort of deserved it, don't you think? Not that he had a heart to begin with. He just used people and broke theirs, that's what he did."

"Whoa, calm down. Hush, you're exhausted. You didn't mean that."

Roddy walked back over towards them, having retrieved all of the papers. He stood back a bit.

"I didn't get much sleep last night," she said. "But I

promised Ernie I'd work on the grid for the event," she said.

"I can help with that," Roddy said quietly.

Scooter looked at Lilly and then at Roddy. "I am very tired. Bucky's going to come and pick me up in a little while. What time is it? Oh, dear. Five minutes ago. He hates it when I'm late."

"Scooter, promise me you'll tell Bucky what happened this morning. Tell him I suggested you bring a lawyer with you next time. Is that him? Double parked?" Lilly took Scooter by the elbow and led her out to the car. She opened the passenger door and helped Scooter in.

"Lilly, good to see you—" the man in the car said.

"You too, Bucky. Listen, Scooter's had a rough time of it. Take care of her, all right?" Lilly reached into her pocket and pulled out a card. "Give me a call this afternoon so we can catch up."

Bucky looked over at his sister with concern, and Lilly closed the door carefully. She turned around and went back into Alden Park.

"What was that about?" Roddy said. "You don't think she—"

"No, of course not. Scooter's harmless," Lilly said. "But if I was Captain Flavia, I'd probably think she was guilty. He doesn't strike me as a person of great imagination. He does want to close this case. That's what worries me. Now, what was it she was supposed to be doing?"

"Marking off a grid, from what the notes said. I will say it's probably for the best that I'm taking over. She'd started off the grid with the wrong scaling, so it wouldn't have worked."

"If anyone can figure it out, you can. Do you need to look around?"

"For a few minutes, if you don't mind," Roddy said. They walked around Alden Park, looking at the notes that Ernie had left for Scooter. Earlier in the month, the entire park had finally been tilled, and hay had been put down as a mud shield for the winter. It was a clean slate, but it looked barren and uninviting. Lilly had to wonder how they were going to pull the Garden Sculpture and Lights event off so that it would be festive and not depressing.

"I can do this grid work for Ernie," Roddy said. "I have the drawings on my computer. I'll check with him to see exactly what he needs. Lilly, are you listening? Are you still worried about Scooter?"

"I am, but I texted Bash and told him not to let her talk to anyone without a lawyer. He's going to call Bucky and make that suggestion. I also gave Bucky my card so he could call me."

"Isn't that out of Bash's purview?" Roddy asked.

"This isn't his case," Lilly said. "Besides, he's known Scooter forever. She used to babysit for him."

"You really believe she's innocent?"

"In more ways than one," Lilly said. She slipped a bit in the mud and grabbed Roddy's arm.

"How will this place be festive for this garden sculpture event? Maybe they should—"

"Maybe *you* should relax and let someone else be in charge," Roddy said, offering his arm, which she took. "The Beautification Committee has a subgroup that is working on it. You specifically said you didn't want to be involved."

"No, I specifically did not want to be *in charge*," Lilly said. "But I never said I wouldn't help—"

"Mary Mancini has taken it on," he said. "She knows that if she needs our help, she has but to ask. So far, she hasn't. The event is almost two weeks away. Plenty of time. Speaking of which. We should work on our submission."

Lilly looked at Roddy and shrugged. "As long as I'm not doing it alone. I'm still not sure I understand what the goal is."

"Festive pieces with lights, so that they'll be fun to walk around and look at. I don't quite understand it myself, but there is a website with more information. What say we involve Delia and Ernie in the planning? And perhaps Warwick and Tamara? That will guarantee something will be created, even if it is desperately off. I believe the goal of the event is to have fun."

"I've never been very good at fun. Sounds like I have a lot of opportunities to let go of my control issues," Lilly said.

"Or focus your control on having a good time with friends."

"I could do that," Lilly said, pulling his arm tighter.

"Lilly, you mentioned Leon when we were in Bash's office. What about him were you and Bash talking about?"

"He's running some tests to double-check Leon's cause of death."

Roddy stopped walking and turned to look at Lilly. "For any reason? He was quite ill, wasn't he?"

"Yes, he was. He was on borrowed time. But he also had a healthy heart, and so dying of a heart attack was unexpected. Bash is making sure he's crossed his t's and dotted his i's. Leon deserved that."

Roddy nodded, and they started walking again. "He did, indeed. Good for Bash for being concerned. You and Leon were good friends, weren't you?"

"I've known him for years. Knew him. Still hard to believe he's gone. Anyway, my mother did amateur theatrics in college and was a big supporter of the Goosebush Players in different ways. We'd host fundraisers every summer, that sort of thing, so I got to know him through those events, though not well. When his wife Betsy died, rather than retreat, he became more social and started to volunteer more, host parties, come to events. Warwick and he were good friends."

"I only went to that one cocktail party at his house as your guest, but it was a lot of fun. The canapés were delightful."

"He loved to cook, and watched those baking competitions like it was his job. I benefited from his experimentation more than once. When Alan got sick, he'd come to the house once a week, make a fabulous meal, and share it with us. He'd tell us stories about rehearsals and productions. He was a wonderful storyteller and made us laugh until our sides hurt. Then he and Alan would sing Gilbert and Sullivan or other songs. Leon was a good, good friend. I really expected we'd have more time. I think Leon was counting on that to get his life in order." Lilly's phone rang, and she fished it out of her pocket, slid the green button on the screen, and turned on the speaker. "Ernie, how are you?"

"How am I? Well, Captain Charming and Trooper Sunshine just left, but not before they made Annabelle cry and Mitch lose his temper. The press is outside, and the only reason they aren't storming the front doors is because they left some troopers stationed out front."

"That sounds awful."

"The movie company is sending some PR people

down here to help," Ernie said. "They'll be here in a couple of hours. In the meantime, I'd stay away. I'll call you when the coast is clear." Ernie hung up the phone, and Lilly turned to Roddy.

"Poor Ernie," she said.

"It sounds terrible," Roddy said. "We could sneak you in the back gate—"

"Your house is probably under siege, as well, after our exit. Let's go and see if Tamara is in," Lilly said.

"Then we'll go to lunch," Roddy said.

Lilly hated that the door buzzed whenever someone walked into the real estate office Tamara owned. She knew it was to alert people of customers coming in, but still. Whatever happened to a small silver bell on the front desk? She was going to get Tamara one as a Christmas gift.

Pete Frank stuck his head out of his cubicle and stood up. Lilly still wasn't used to running into her first husband during the normal course of a day. They'd been divorced for almost forty years—how was that possible, Lilly wondered—and they had nothing in common, and less to say to one another.

"Lilly, how are you?" he asked. "Terrible news about last night. Heard that you're in the middle of it, again."

"What do you mean 'again'?" Lilly said.

"Come on, Lil, you've got to admit—"

"You've got to admit that she's fixed a lot of wrong in the past few months," Tamara said, coming out of her office. "Including some wrong that was coming your way, Pete. Saved your butt, as I recall. Lilly, Roddy, what a nice surprise. Come into my office."

Tamara turned around and went back into her office. Lilly and Roddy followed her, and Roddy closed the door.

"I still can't believe you married him," Tamara said.

"Hey, I was young and stupid," Lilly said.

"Glad you got it right the second time."

"Amen to that."

"I've got to admit, though, Pete's been doing good work lately. Sold a couple of houses this month. I think Rhonda's been lighting a fire under him."

"Bless her heart, she's been trying to do that for years," Lilly said. The conversation paused, mostly because talking about Lilly's first husband and the woman he left her for was not a favorite topic for long conversations.

"To what do I owe the pleasure of this visit?" Tamara asked.

"We've just been over to Alden Park," Roddy said. "Lilly's worried that it won't come together for the event."

"I'm not worried about that," Lilly said. "Well, a little worried about that. I'm also worried about Scooter." Lilly told Tamara about how Scooter was behaving in the park.

"Did you tell Bucky to watch out for her?" Tamara said.

"I told him to call me later."

"I'll give him a call. He'll take care of her. Again. She's always being taken care of," Tamara said. "That's part of the problem. She doesn't have a lot of survival skills. What was she doing in Alden Park?"

"Taking measurements for Ernie," Roddy said. "Working on a grid for the sculpture event. I offered to do it for her. I was afraid that Lilly would if I didn't."

"Lilly, you have nothing to do with this event. We both agreed that we needed to step back," Tamara said.

"I know, but it's a muddy hayfield right now. Hardly festive," Lilly said.

"Mary Mancini's on top of it. The Christmas trees are being delivered on Thursday, so that will help. And the first couple of installations are going up this weekend."

"And you know this how, Miss 'we need to step back'?"

"I may or may not have checked in with Mary this morning. Just making sure we're on track. And I wanted to talk about the 'made in Goosebush' hashtag idea. Thanks for sending that email, by the way. I'm glad Portia's on board."

"What did she think?" Lilly asked.

"She loved it. In fact, look at this." Tamara held out her phone, and Lilly and Roddy watched the video that was playing. Portia Asher was talking about how she'd like to see the floral displays all made in Goosebush, because that mattered. Lilly swallowed the lump in her throat.

"That's lovely," Lilly said.

"Oh, that's only the beginning. There are a dozen posts by other people already. Mary is going to start doing daily videos in the store, demonstrating how to create certain effects with things they have on hand. So that's what I've been up to this morning." Tamara looked at her phone, clicked through her texts, and then she looked over at Lilly. "Did I hear that Annabelle Keys stayed with you last night?"

Lilly and Roddy quickly filled Tamara in on the morning activities. At the end, the three sat in the office in silence.

"Well, maybe it's best to let the police handle this one," Tamara said.

"Agreed," Lilly replied, sighing. If only she had confidence that Captain Flavia was interesting in solving the entire puzzle.

"I wonder what the note Delores found said?" Tamara asked.

"'Next time it will be you,'" Roddy said. He looked at Lilly and shrugged. "I read it before I gave it to Bash."

"That's fairly dire. Where does Delores getting threatened leave everything?" Lilly asked. "We don't even know if Jeremy was the intended victim, or if it was Delores."

"The police will figure that out," Tamara said.

"Tell you both what, let's discuss it over lunch at the Star. My treat," Roddy said.

CHAPTER 16

The Star restaurant was busy, very busy for a Monday. Lilly suspected it was a combination of extended holiday visitors and people being sick of leftovers. Stan offered to have the three of them sit at the bar, but Lilly wasn't sure. She never liked having her back to a room, and the three of them needed to see faces in order to understand conversations.

"I would have saved you a table if I'd known," Stan said.

"I know you would have," Lilly said. "We're all a little discombobulated. We'll figure something out." Lilly smiled at Stan and turned to leave.

"Lilly, do you have a minute?" Stan asked.

"Of course," she said.

"Let me go see if I can snag a table in the café," Tamara said.

"I'll go with you," Roddy said.

"Lilly, Virginia Blossom is going to send me a business proposal this week. I know that you're in the middle of what happened last night—"

"I'm not in the middle of anything," Lilly said.

"I heard that you've taken Annabelle Keys in."

"Well, yes, there's that. But I'm not too busy to talk to you, Stan. Send me the proposal when you receive it if you'd like. Planning first would have been better, but we can catch up."

Lilly walked out to the front of the store and saw Tamara waving at her and pointing down at a table. Lilly was pleased. She loved sitting near the bookstore. She walked up to Roddy, who was waiting in line.

"Is this all right with you?" he asked.

"More than all right. I love the café food. What are you ordering?" she asked.

"I thought I'd get the roasted beet and feta salad."

"Oh, healthy—"

"And a kitchen sink cookie for dessert," he said. "With a cup of tea."

"I still think it's healthy," Lilly said. "There are nuts and oatmeal in the kitchen sink cookies. That's how I justify my obsession with them."

"What are you going to get?" Roddy asked.

"What's Tamara getting?"

"The California cobb salad," he said.

"Ah, well. I'll get a chicken Caesar salad. And a cookie. Tea sounds good."

"Sit down," Roddy said. "I'll be able to carry all three lunches back."

Lilly smiled and went to sit down. She wove her way

through the crowd. Tamara was seated in the very back, close to the wall and right next to the bookshelves that delineated that edge of the store. Because Stan liked to play with space, the bookshelves were on wheels so the seating capacity of the café could be expanded. Today everything was at capacity.

"Busy today," Lilly said to Tamara as she finally made her way to the table. Tamara put her fingers to her lips in order to silence Lilly. She tilted her head to the bookshelves.

Stepping back, Lilly looked between the shelves to see who was standing in the bookstore. She saw the fiery red mane of Virginia Blossom, but she couldn't see who she was talking to.

Lilly sat down next to Tamara.

"They had me come in again to answer questions," Virginia was saying.

"That must have been terrible," the other voice said.

"Who is that?" Lilly whispered.

"Not sure," Tamara said. "They just started talking about the murder."

"Like I would have killed such a handsome man," Virginia said.

"I saw you talking to him right before."

"That's why they called me in. I was the last person to talk to him. Except his ex-wife."

"She didn't look happy."

"No, she didn't, did she? I read that they were getting back together, but let me tell you, that wasn't the vibe I was getting. It's such a shame," Virginia said.

"He was so talented."

"I've never had an affair with a movie star," Virginia

said. "Actors, sure. But never a movie star. That would have been fun."

"I guess so," the other voice said.

"I mean, if someone was going to die, it's a shame it wasn't that odious Stevens woman. That would have made my life easier, frankly."

"Ginny—"

"Don't 'Ginny' me. You know I always get what I want, no matter what's in my way. Let's get out of here. They don't have any good magazines. Like that's any big surprise in this backwater town."

Lilly and Tamara watched the front of the store. Virginia and another woman walked by the café. Roddy had just turned with his tray of food and narrowly missed crashing into the two women. In the brief second that it took for Virginia to recognize him and look around, Lilly had the satisfaction of seeing her face when she saw her and Tamara.

"She really does need to learn to pay attention to who she's talking to, even indirectly," Lilly said.

"She was a little—"

"Callous? Self-involved?" Lilly asked. Roddy arrived at the table, and she reached up and took the beverages off Roddy's tray and then the salads. He picked up the bag of cookies and then leaned the tray up against the bookshelf.

"What did I miss?" Roddy asked.

"A terrible human being having too loud a conversation in a restaurant," Lilly said.

* * *

Roddy parked at the back of the library, but they walked around to the front to go in. It wasn't a direct route; they could have gone through the lower entrance and down the hall, since Lilly had an access card that let her in. But entering through the main hall always replenished Lilly, and today she needed that.

The Goosebush Library, this version of it, was a repurposed elementary school. The old library, a somewhat tragically designed building with no personality, was razed for a new school building. For a brief moment, the town considered the same fate for the elementary school, but cooler, more thoughtful heads prevailed. The school had been built in the late 1800s, and served many grades for a long time. Marble floors and a soaring entranceway led to good-sized classrooms with wooden floors. The building was solid, a brick structure with concrete decorations. Lilly was on the committee that pushed for the building to be given to the library rather than a developer, and the thrill she felt every time she walked in reinforced her decision.

The large foyer had a circular desk as its centerpiece. The walls were covered in art, much of which was available for lending through a new program that had just been launched. There were also re-creations of old maps and paintings of Goosebush throughout the years. Tours were given of the library on Saturdays so that people could appreciate the building more fully.

Whenever he entered the library, Roddy always paused and took a moment to look around. Lilly liked that about him—his attention to the details, all of them.

"What's that?" Roddy asked, walking over to the left.

A large wreath adorned the wall, taking the place of the hand-drawn map that was usually there.

"That's the library wreath," Lilly said with some pride. "My mother made it twenty years ago when the library was first opened. See the paper flowers? They're all made of books and magazines. The ribbon is made from a sail. There are bits of sea glass and shells inside. She called it 'Goosebush Holidays.' It took her months and months to make it."

"The colors on the flowers—from a distance, they look red and green and blue, but up close, you can see the printing."

"Those took forever. She'd rip out pages of magazines, and then she'd sort them into colors. Alan would bring her all sorts of journals and travel magazines."

"It's really lovely," Roddy said, taking out his phone and snapping a few pictures. He looked down and started tapping on the screen. "An original made-in-Goosebush piece."

"Indeed. In fact, that's how the wreath competition started. The next year, my mother held a flower-making class in the summer and then a wreath-making class in the fall. Both were held here in the library. She charged a small amount to raise funds for the library. The wreaths were displayed, and a couple of people donated them to a fundraiser. Then the wreath making became its own fundraiser."

"With a literary theme."

"That's new," Lilly said. "But I like it. Beauty and craftsmanship are so hard to judge, so we started adding creativity categories. The event is a lot of fun."

"And a lot of work, but thanks to the committee who runs the event, I don't have to do much of the work," a younger woman said, walking up to the two of them. She was wearing a beige pantsuit and polka dot shirt and wore large red hoop earrings.

"Dot, how are you? I didn't see you there."

"The front desk let me know that you were here, so I thought I'd come by and say hello. How are you doing, Lilly? A terrible thing to happen last night. It made me just as glad that we couldn't get tickets."

"The performance was wonderful, but yes, overtaken by a terrible loss of a lovely man." Lilly shook her head and set her face with pursed lips and a clenched jaw. She had no intention of talking about the murder with anyone. Well, anyone outside the Garden Squad. "Tell me, how is the wreath competition going?"

"Slowly," Dot said.

"Really? Why?"

"I hate to admit it, but you were right. Great literary titles aren't inspiring people to enter a wreath. Especially since we're having them come down here to draw a title."

"Plus the entrance fee that you added to the mix."

"Looks like you were right about that, as well. I didn't think there would be resistance to a twenty-dollar fee."

"Who's signed up so far?" The three of them walked over to the circulation desk, and Dot walked behind it to get the list, which she handed to Lilly.

"All members of the committee," Lilly said. "People who well understand the challenges the library is facing with funding right now. Tell you what; let's do a few things to shake it up. First, let's tell people that the next ten people to enter will have their entry fees waived.

Then waive them all, and I'll write a check to cover the loss."

"Lilly, you don't have to—"

"Nonsense. The wreath auction is a major part of the fundraiser we're doing in December. The second thing you'll need to do is expand your list of what are great books. Add some romances. Some science fiction. When all people see is *The Mill on the Floss*, it doesn't inspire creativity."

"There's a lot you could do with *The Mill on the Floss*," Dot said.

"Unless the thought of rereading that book gives you ugly flashbacks to high school English, which it does me. That brings me to the next thing. *You* make a wreath based on *The Mill on the Floss*."

"Me? I have no talent—"

"Which is why you'll social-media yourself going to the Triple B and getting materials from Mary Mancini. And you'll use the 'made in Goosebush' hashtag along with the wreath event hashtag. I have no idea what I just said, but you'll figure it out."

"Perhaps I'll have Minh take one on—"

"In addition to you. Come on, Dot, you know people give money to people. They want to get to know you better. You've only been here a couple of years, and it takes New Englanders time to warm up."

Dot sighed and shrugged. "All right. My wife will help."

"Good. Now, Roddy, I didn't see your name on this list," Lilly said.

"An oversight," Roddy said. "Let me rectify that." He signed his name and gave Dot twenty dollars. She pulled the fishbowl out, and he drew a name, immediately making a face.

"What did you get?" Lilly asked.

"*Moby-Dick*," Roddy said. He grimaced. "I am having first-year English memories of not excelling at my essay on symbolism."

"You can draw another one," Dot said.

"Oh no, I'll enjoy the challenge," Roddy said. "Though I'm not sure how to incorporate a harpoon and whale blubber in a festive holiday wreath."

"Please, don't even try," Lilly said, giving him a smile. "Make it symbolic."

Roddy and Lilly went down to the Historical Society. Lilly took out her key to let them both in and was amazed at the transformation. Sure, all flat surfaces were covered in piles. But the piles seemed to have some order amongst the chaos. Especially if the determined look on Minh's face as she was reading one of the documents was any indication.

"Minh, sorry if we startled you. I didn't think you were coming in today," Roddy said.

"I was working upstairs until one o'clock and then I thought I'd come down and tackle some more of the theater paperwork. Delia texted this morning and asked me to look through another box that she'd put in the back."

"Delia texted you?" Lilly asked.

"Yes, Roddy connected us so that we could confer on the project a bit before I dove in. I didn't want to step on her toes, so I adapted her system to my own." Minh made a gesturing sweep of her arm to the piles at hand.

"This looks very impressive," Lilly said. "And you

said this is the theater archives. Could you walk me through your process?"

"Of course," Minh said. "Delia sent me the documents she was working on, which were so helpful. She asked me to make notes on documents if they had to do with the Stanley Theater, which used to be the Goosebush Theater, and the Goosebush Players. This is why some context matters. I never would have understood that they were so separate otherwise. Honestly, it's still sort of confusing. Anyway, I've been going through the boxes of materials and adding colored tabs to them along with some Post-it notes to clarify dates and any other large-scale tags I'd add once they're in the system."

"Tags?" Lilly asked.

"Ways to tell the computer how to categorize the items. You know, like I'd tag the directors, or the play-wright, or the actors, designers, that sort of thing. You never know what's important to whom, so my process is to start with some global categories, and then add tags so that people can narrow the search. We'll scan all of the documents at some point. But for the short term, for the show programs, I'll just scan the cover, the title page, and the cast and crew lists for now, and then we'll make a note of where they are in the archives."

"You're going to do all of that?"

"Yes, it's easy peasy to get that done," Minh said. "Delia had a lot of this organized from the outset, but I've added some tweaks. I want to run them by her before I start, though. Seems only right, since she's in charge here."

"In charge by default," Roddy said. "She'll likely be thrilled by the work you've been doing."

"She seems pleased, but we haven't had a chance to meet yet. She was going to come by today, but she got tied up. Understandable, given that she was working on the show last night. Poor Jeremy Nolan. He was one of my son's favorite actors, let me tell you. I feel as if I know him, seeing all these pictures of him from the archives over the past couple of days."

"There were a lot of pictures?" Lilly asked.

"Lots. One of the boxes that Delia had pulled but hadn't gone through was a donation from the Stanley Theater for the archives. It looked like James Jentry donated them back in 1992, but they hadn't been cataloged properly."

"Who was James Jentry?" Roddy asked.

"He was an artistic director of the Goosebush Players. And he ran the theater," Minh said.

"His nickname was JJ," Lilly said.

"Ah, I wondered—" Minh said, making a note.

"He took over after Stanley Sayers died," Lilly said. "He ran the theater for years. Minh, you said the donation was made by him?"

"That's what the paperwork indicated," Minh said. "It's a good thing she found them. None of the pictures were in sheets; they were just tossed into file folders. Some of the eight-by-tens stuck together, but the photographs from rehearsals had been printed on that matte stock, the kind that looked like linen if you saw it up close, remember that? Those pictures stood up to being tossed in a box, but just barely. Do you know if there's a budget for getting archival boxes and appropriate storage materials? I'd be happy to get these taken care of—"

"We'll find a budget," Lilly said. She was realizing that unless she jumped in, Minh would keep talking, and

Lilly would lose her train of thought. "We'll find a budget for your time, as well."

"I understand that this is a volunteer-run organization, and I'm happy to do my part," Minh said. "It's helping me learn a bit more about Goosebush in the meantime, and I'm grateful for that. Very grateful. What an interesting town—"

"Minh, we've needed to hire someone to get this place organized for quite a while," Lilly said. "We had a part-time person working here for years, but that didn't work out, for a number of reasons. Before I can make a formal offer, I'll need to have Delia speak with you, but in the meantime, we can afford to have you help us get organized. You mentioned JJ donating the box. Which years did it cover? All of the previous years?"

"No, that's what's odd. It only covered the years from 1983 to 1989."

"Not so odd," Lilly said. "Those are the Mel John years."

"Mel John. Yes, he's a category. Let me double-check . . . yes, he's the purple flag. See all of the purple flags in these stacks? That means he's mentioned in some way."

Lilly walked over to the large table that dominated the front third of the Historical Society. A countertop separated the back two-thirds. When someone came in, they could request documents from the volunteer on duty, or they could look at the books that were available for everyone to read. The table was covered with several piles, the tops of which each had years written on them. Lilly wandered, looked around, and finally found the 1980s in two piles on the countertop.

"Where are the James Jentry materials?"

"Back here," Minh said.

"May I see them?"

"Of course," Minh said. "Let me see, why don't we move this here, and that there. Yes, here you go." A space was now cleared on the countertop. "You can look at the box here; that way it won't get mingled with anything else. I haven't categorized the box materials yet."

"I understand," Lilly said. "I won't take anything, though I may ask to make copies of things."

"I'll get the scanner and computers warmed up," Roddy said.

"Anything in particular you're looking for?" Minh asked.

"Mel John interests me," Lilly said. "I've heard about him a few times this weekend. I wish I'd seen some of his work, particularly; from what I understand, his summer work."

"Yes, that confused me," Minh said. "He worked for the Goosebush Players during the year, but the summer seemed to be different. 'John's Players' were how they were referenced. It's going to take a while to figure this all out. Maybe we can go through the box together, and you can hand me things? I'll start to sort them that way? But whoa, I'll need to make more space if I'm going to pull that off. My system takes space, at least at first."

"Here, I'll help you," Lilly said. She walked through the opening in the countertop and around to face the same way as Minh. Roddy was sitting at the desk in the back, turning on computers and scanners. That area was where Lilly saw the most progress. There was actually a good deal of floor space for people to work, and a couple of extra six-foot tables had been set up. Lilly picked up stacks of papers and handed them to Minh, who put them on one of the tables in some sort of order that meant something to her. Lilly had to pause once in a while to let Minh fidget with the piles. She started to look through them while she was waiting. One pile was smaller and seemed to have nothing to do with the theater.

"What's this?" Lilly asked.

"Oh, that's my pile. Sorry about that. I should have asked permission—"

"No worries," Lilly said. "Are you doing some research?"

"On the Preston family. I noticed that Albert Preston died a few years ago, and his family was from Goosebush."

"Yes, on both counts," Lilly said.

"He didn't have any children?" Minh asked.

"No, no children. He married his wife, Gladys, later in life. He was devoted to her, bless him. She died last summer."

"I read about that," Minh said. "Did you know Albert? Let me rephrase that. I know you did; I saw a couple of pictures of you with him during some garden tour?"

"He was a wonderful gardener. So was Gladys, though she was a little less traditional than he was. Their house was on Shipyard Lane. All three houses had wonderful gardens, and they held an annual garden party that was the height of the season while Albert's parents were alive. Albert kept it up after they died, but Gladys and he weren't as social."

"Was he . . . what was he like?" Minh asked quietly.

"He was a very nice and gentle man," Lilly said. She looked at Minh and paused. Far be it for Lilly to pry, but there was obviously something Minh was processing. "You know, Ernie Johnson bought the Preston house. He's been working on clearing it out all fall. There's lots of Preston family materials, from what I understand. If you're looking for something in particular, he could keep an eye out."

"Oh, that would be great. How can I get hold of him? I don't think I've met him yet. Of course, I haven't met many people. I just got here."

"Ernie runs Bits, Bolts and Bulbs," Roddy said from the desk. "Remember, I told you about his store. A wonderful place to get the things you mentioned needing for your apartment."

"Right, you did tell me about that. I need to go there, don't I? I sure do. But today I'd like to keep going on this project. Is that all right with the both of you?"

"I could use your help," Roddy said, flashing a smile at Minh, who blushed in return. "You will need to go to the Triple B later this week for your wreath materials, though."

"Triple B? Bits, Bolts and—oh, I get it. See, those are the sort of things I need to learn. Places have names, but then they have what people call them. Like that 'John's Players' business. Were they really called the John's Players, or was that a nickname? I'm still figuring that out. Wait, what wreath?"

"You're going to make one for the auction. Just don't let Dot pawn off *The Mill on the Floss*," Roddy said. "I've been drafted, as well. Perhaps you should also enter a garden sculpture? There will be an event a week from Saturday in Alden Park."

"I live in a one-bedroom apartment, for now," Minh said. "I'll need a bigger place next summer when the kids come home from school, but right now I don't have the room to do a sculpture. I was tempted, though, let me tell you. I love that sort of thing, I really do. Gets my creative juices flowing. Creativity is so important. Anyway, my kids will be here next week for their winter break, so we'll be at Alden Park for the big lighting up, for sure.

"Okay, now the countertop is clear. Let me get my toolbox. Ms. Jayne, why don't we look through the box?" Minh opened what looked like a fishing tackle box, but was full of pens, tabs, index cards, highlighters, and more. She was ready to go to work, and Lilly was happy to assist.

CHAPTER 17

"I hope I didn't interrupt anything," Tamara said a little while later, after Lilly had gotten into the car and buckled her seat belt.

"Well, yes and no. Minh was sorting through a box she'd found that James Jentry had donated—"

"Hold up. Minh?"

"Minh Vann. New to town. Works part-time at the library—"

"Right, I met her—"

"And as of this afternoon, part-time at the Historical Society, pending Delia's approval. She thinks like Delia, but in overdrive."

"That's a little scary, don't you think?" Tamara said.

"As long as they use their power for good, it's very helpful. She has a process when she is going through things that is very, very methodical. I would have dumped the box out and just started to sort willy-nilly, but she has a process. I tried to hurry it along, but Roddy sided with her."

"The box was from James Jentry? JJ, who used to run the theater?"

"The same. Interestingly, in the box were the records from Mel John's years. Delia had found them when she was looking for materials, but hadn't opened the box yet."

"That must be interesting."

"It may be, but we won't know for hours at the rate they're going. She'd taken the top two folders out, and they were jammed with pictures, so she's being very careful about what else is in the box that could give context. Roddy is helping her by taking notes in the database and then doing scans. I was getting impatient."

"I wonder what's in there?" Tamara asked. "Do you think it has anything to do with the murder? They're saying it may have been a crazed fan, by the way. The person who killed Jeremy."

Lilly rolled her eyes. Obviously, the press hadn't heard the Delores angle, if that's what it was.

"I think it's odd, is all. First Leon dies, then Jeremy Nolan shows up at his funeral, then *he* dies. Maybe Jerry's death has nothing to do with current events. Maybe it's all about what happened thirty-odd years ago."

"You're reaching," Tamara said. "But I'm not going to stop you. You may not have a method like Minh's, but you have a mind that sorts through unrelated facts and comes up with a truth."

"Hopefully the right truth," Lilly said. She'd become more aware of the impact her forays into investigation had on other people, and treaded lightly these days. That said, she also could not bear for injustices to stand.

"In Lilly, I trust," Tamara said, reaching over and patting Lilly's knee. "Thanks for taking time out and coming to this open house with me."

"My pleasure," Lilly said. "I'm fascinated by the opportunities that the church offers."

A new, larger Catholic church had been built in Goosebush, and the old Goosebush church had been deconsecrated and was being sold with some restrictions about its future use. Because it had been built on an odd V-shaped plot of land, and height restrictions were firmly in place in that part of Goosebush, most people thought that the building, the small meeting house, and the rectory would be kept intact and that some sort of business enterprise would take over the space. Lilly was curious about what the approval process was going to be like. As with many things, her goal was to stand back but also make sure that the decisions were made well.

"This realtor open house was very last-minute," Tamara said. "I don't think the interest is as high as they thought it would be, especially with the zoning restrictions."

"How much are they asking?" Lilly asked. Tamara told her a number, and Lilly's jaw dropped.

"Mind you, it isn't the church who's inflated the price. The original developer wants to make a profit."

"The original developer is an idiot," Lilly said. The man had purchased it from the diocese and agreed to use the space within two years or sell it. Over the past twenty-two months, he'd put four plans in front of the board of selectmen, and two of them had gone before a town meeting. Each was more ludicrous than the next, at least in the eyes of the zoning commission. Six-story buildings with tennis courts. A nightclub complex. A shopping mall. The closest was a restaurant, but the neighborhood wasn't thrilled about the idea of a restaurant that could seat one hundred and fifty people. He might have gotten that one passed if he hadn't alienated everyone in town with his social media screeds and public relations assault.

"He is. Rumor has it that he expected people to jump at the opportunity, but the realtor open house tells me that he doesn't have a lot of interest, and he's scrambling. Pete visited when it first opened and suggested that I go by. He's going to make a list of people who may be interested."

They parked in the church parking lot, another asset for the space. Tamara signed in, and she and Lilly walked in what used to be the back door of the church. Tamara immediately saw some people she knew and went over to talk to them. Lilly got them both a cup of tea and brought Tamara hers. She could have stayed and talked real estate, but instead she wandered around, looking at the building as well as the people investigating the opportunity. Virginia Blossom walked in and started surveying, careful to avoid any conversation. She moved along the outer perimeter of the room, in the opposite direction of Lilly.

Lilly had been to the church many times for various life events of friends, but she'd never seen it empty before. Not really empty. The pews were still there but pushed to the side. The building had started its life as a Congregational church, so it had those lines as its base. Stained-glass windows had been added, and the altar had been expanded. Looking around, Lilly saw a beautiful space with a lot of potential. She stepped into the middle of the room to look up at the choir loft.

"This place is meant to be a theater," a voice said. Lilly turned around. Delores had arrived. She was wearing black from head to toe, with dark glasses and a slash of red lipstick. Even by Delores standards, she looked dramatic, and that was saying something.

Lilly looked around, but it didn't appear that anyone was with her. And no one was getting close, so Lilly finally took a deep breath and channeled her mother. Manners mattered. She walked over to Delores.

"I agree," Lilly said in a much quieter tone. "Or it certainly deserves to have sort of a grand future."

"The other buildings will house actors and provide shop support," Delores continued, ignoring Lilly. "The Stevens Center. This will be Tompkin Theater. It's perfect."

"Tompkin Theater? After Leon?" Lilly asked. "That's very nice."

"Well, after all, it's dear Leon who is making this possible," Delores said. "His will is quite generous."

"Is it?" Lilly said carefully. The reading of the will hadn't happened yet, but her conversations with Fred had her thinking that Leon's will was no such thing, at least as far as Delores was concerned.

"We had a wonderful dinner just a few nights before, before dear Leon passed away. He surprised me with a codicil that made his intentions clear. Dear Leon. Such a good, good friend. Yes, yes. This is perfect," Delores said. "And without the ghosts of our current artistic home. Honestly, I don't think I could bear to walk in that building again."

"Ghosts?" Lilly asked.

"Both real and imagined," Delores said. "No one should suffer as I've had to." She turned and walked toward one of the side doors. Lilly watched as she stopped and said something to Virginia Blossom. The younger woman replied, and Delores turned and quickly walked out the door.

Tamara walked over to Lilly and handed her the specs of the property. "Interesting information in here," Tamara said. "Since I'm on the board of selectmen, I can't show too much interest. That said, and much as I hate to agree with Delores, this would be a great space for the performing arts."

"Or a gallery and small music-performance space," Lilly said. "By the way, I won't tell anyone you agree with Delores."

"Thank you," Tamara said. "Want to go out and look at the other buildings?"

"Sure," Lilly said. They went out the side door, and took a few steps over to the rectory. Lilly had always loved that old house, but she'd never been in it. Renovations had turned the first floor into multiple conference rooms, in addition to a kitchen and dining room. Upstairs there were several small bedrooms and three sitting rooms.

"Nice retreat potential," Tamara said.

"Or a crystal shop like the one we visited in the Berkshires last fall. I hope some of those renovations can be undone on the first floor. That particle board is awful."

"A crystal shop would be fun," Tamara said. "I loved that place. Incense, candles, tarot readings. That would be great in there. The old Sunday school building would be fabulous for educational programs. Dance lessons, theater camps."

"It's a shame the developer didn't talk to us," Lilly said.

"It's a shame he didn't embrace what was here instead of presenting plans that tore everything down," Tamara said. "He should have driven around the neighborhood a bit and seen what would fit in."

"It's an odd lot of land, so imagination is required. But the potential is great. This old rectory is a beautiful building that likely has some history to it."

"You know, there are times when the slow pace of Goosebush is challenging," Tamara said. "But then I look at projects like this, and how something being thrown up would have been a disaster."

Lilly waited until they were in the car to tell her about Delores's mentions of Leon.

"Well, if Leon left her a pile of money, that could make her a target for someone," Tamara said. "Do you think it's true?"

"I hadn't heard anything," Lilly said. "I wonder if Fred has heard anything about it?"

"You should update him."

"I'm planning on calling him later this week. I should go by Leon's house first, so I have a sense of what we're dealing with in order to get it on the market. I haven't been up to it yet. Will you come with me?"

"What, now?"

"He gave me a set of keys."

"I can't believe Fred and his wife are serious about selling. Are they not coming back to help clear things out?"

"Not that I know of. I'd imagine they took what they wanted with them, and may have marked other things for shipping. Honestly, I haven't dealt with it at all."

"It's been just over a week since his funeral, Lilly. Give yourself a break. Sure, we'll go over on our way back to your place and look around. Maybe Fred missed some paperwork about the theater that would be helpful. Do you have the keys with you?"

Lilly picked up her bag and smiled. "I'm always prepared."

It took Lilly a moment to locate Leon's keys in her purse. The tag on the keychain that Fred had given her had numbers on it, which she assumed was the code to the alarm system. Both worked, and she let herself in. The house smelled of a ripe cat litter box, and Tamara waved her hand in front of her face.

"Whoa. They didn't clean up after Max before they took him on a plane, did they?"

"Apparently not. The refrigerator is probably a nightmare, as well. I hope they brought the garbage out."

"I have people who can help us clean up," Tamara said.

"That's good," Lilly said. "It's cold in here. Let me turn the heat up a bit." Lilly looked to her left, and the usually pristine living room was a jumble. The shelves were mostly empty, there were shadows on the wall where pictures once hung, and the furniture had been sorted into two groups that were on each side of the room.

"We'll deal with that later. Let's look for any paperwork Fred might have missed, and we'll work on a strategy for tackling the house. Now, Leon's office is over here, right?" Tamara asked.

They opened the door and walked into a cyclone of

paperwork. Lilly didn't know where to start. She turned on her phone and texted Fred.

I'm at your father's house. His office is a mess. Is that your doing? Or might someone else have been here?

She put the phone back in her pocket and looked around. Tamara was looking at a wall of photos, and Lilly walked over to join her.

"I can't believe Fred wouldn't want these," Tamara said. "Look at that picture. When the girls were little, they'd invite us over for pool parties. Fred was in between Rose and Ty, but that didn't matter. We all had wonderful times here."

Lilly looked around. "Leon didn't edit the pictures on this wall, did he?" she asked. "There's a picture of Pete and me the summer we got married. And then that's one of Alan and me when we moved back to Goosebush."

"None of these pictures are formal, or even that good. They must be memories that made him happy. You know, Leon was always a bit scattered," Tamara said. "He'd start talking to me about three different ideas at once, and it never made sense right away. But eventually it all came together."

"I wonder what idea he was cooking up with all of this." Lilly turned around and gestured at the piles of paper on every surface, the double-shelved books and the plastic storage containers strewn about. "Who knows what's where? I wonder if Fred went through things carefully. I don't want some stranger looking through Leon's papers and finding a personal letter he got from his wife, or some diary that had family secrets."

"With this much paper, that could happen," Tamara said.

"This is a much bigger job than I supposed."

"But one that Leon's friends can help with. Warwick will pitch in," Tamara said. "I agree, we need to take care of Leon's legacy first and foremost, so it's important we all look through this stuff."

Lilly sighed and looked over at Tamara. "I suppose the best way to start is to sort things into piles after we get a better sense of what's here."

Lilly went over to Leon's desk and stacked all the papers into one pile. She quickly sorted through them but didn't see a will or letter that might be helpful. The chair was piled high, as well, so she did the same thing. Again, no will. But lots and lots of papers that included bills, notes, charts, and printed emails.

Tamara brought an armful of papers that she'd taken from on top of the credenza and put them on the desk. "There's nothing here."

"Nothing here either," Lilly said.

"The file cabinets are locked. Did Fred give you those keys?" Lilly nodded and handed her the key ring.

Lilly felt her phone buzz in her pocket and looked down at the screen. "Fred apologizes. He said that they were in a rush to get out and didn't leave instructions. He'll call me later." Another text came in, and Lilly read it out loud. "'Sorry I didn't call you back last night. I'd heard about Jerry, and it knocked me for a loop.'"

"Poor Fred," Tamara said. "I know this looks bad, but we can get it straightened out. Here's another pile, under 'William Shakespeare.'"

"What do you mean—oh, the bust of William Shakespeare. Leon did like busts, didn't he? An interesting assortment of characters."

"Having all these faces staring at me would creep me out. Here's what Will was holding down. Looks like cast lists, articles, some notes."

Lilly looked around. "Maybe that's how Leon organized? 'Thomas Jefferson' is sitting on top of this file cabinet, and it's full of legal documents. Is that shelf full of theater files?"

"Sarah Bernhardt is on top of Playbills. Here's a *Complete Works of William Shakespeare* that's holding down another pile of papers. Hello, what's this?" Tamara pulled a piece of paper out of the book carefully and unfolded it. "Welp, this is interesting." She handed the paper to Lilly.

"This is what Delores was talking about," Lilly said. "Unsigned, but still. She wasn't lying."

Tamara found the right key on the key ring and unlocked the top file cabinet drawer. It was completely full. "That's a lot of paper."

"Who knows what's what?" Lilly said. "I'm sorry, Tamara, I had no idea this was such a huge project."

"Tell you what, my house is five minutes from here. I'll run down there and get some boxes so we can get the paperwork out of here. This looks like older stuff, but who knows." She opened up the lower drawer, which was also full. "I'll get a lot of boxes."

Lilly opened the file drawer in the desk. It was empty. She texted Fred, and he told her that he'd taken those files with him.

"While you're gone, I'll organize a bit. Looks like Leon had pulled out Christmas decorations. Fred may want some of the ornaments in these plastic bins."

"He may have meant to take them," Tamara said. "But the stuff on top is mail from weeks ago. Presumably Leon put it there."

"I wonder why Leon had them in here so early? He hadn't started decorating. For now, let's move this box over here to clear a path." Lilly bent over to pick it up; then she put it right back down. "Oof. What's in here?"

Lilly opened the box of ornaments and found the expected items in the first layer of cardboard sections. The ornaments looked old and well used. She lifted the layer out carefully and looked underneath. The three iron file boxes covered with a Christmas tablecloth explained the weight. She looked up at Tamara.

"Those look promising," Tamara said. "And well hidden."

Lilly lifted one of the strongboxes out and looked at it. "They're all sealed. See. He put stickers over the locks and signed them. Let's take them with us."

"I'm heading out to get those boxes," Tamara said. "If Warwick's home, I'll have him come and help. We'll do a quick walk-through and get anything of value out of here this afternoon." Tamara looked at her watch. "How is it only four-thirty?"

"It's been a long day," Lilly said. "But I'll feel better if we get Leon's personal business out of here. You know, I can't help but wonder if someone's looking for these boxes."

CHAPTER 18

Lilly was sorting through the papers on the desk once more. She noticed a bill from a storage unit and wondered if Fred planned on cleaning it out or if she'd need to add this to her list. Honestly, she didn't mind helping with these sorts of things. But it did strike her that Fred was either being obtuse about the amount of work that needed to be done, or for whatever reason, he didn't care.

When Leon told her he was sick, he indicated that he had a few projects he wanted to get done. "I hope I can count on your help when I'm ready. You've got such an orderly mind," he'd said.

"I'm happy to help," Lilly had said. And she'd meant it. Leon had been a bit absentminded, but she had no doubt that his intentions were to leave a clear plan. She looked around at the papers and shook her head. He'd just run out of time.

Crash. Lilly heard a noise from the other end of the house. She called out but didn't hear a reply. She walked into the kitchen and turned on the hall lights for the bedroom wing of the house. "Hello?" Her heart was pounding, so she took a deep breath. She heard another sound, and then a cry from down the hallway.

She walked down the hallway and called out again. Another cry, coming from the door on her right. She opened it, and a gray ball of fur flew towards her.

"Max? Oh Max, why aren't you in California?" She knelt down and picked up the big Russian blue cat. Leon had adopted Max three years ago. Or, as he'd put it, Max had adopted him. The big gray cat melted into her arms and began to purr. She carried him back into the room and noted that he had plenty of food and water.

Lilly walked back toward the office and sat down in the desk chair, still holding Max. She had begun to shake; she was so angry. She fished her phone out of her pocket and dialed Fred's number. He didn't pick up, so she left him a message. She didn't mince words. How dare he leave his father's cat alone? Did he just assume she'd come sooner? What would have happened if she waited until after the holidays? What would his father say?

"Lilly?"

"Warwick, I'm in the office," Lilly said.

"What do you have there?" Warwick came into the room carrying several flat boxes and some packing tape.

"Max. Leon's cat. He was in the guest room."

"In the what?" Tamara said, coming in with more boxes. She put them down and came around to the other side of the desk. Lilly relaxed her hold, and Max let Tamara pick him up. "Poor baby boy."

Warwick went down the hallway to explore and came

back carrying a note. "I don't think he was suffering," he said. "There was an automatic feeder, and one of those water fountains. The TV was on, and there are lights. Fred left a note and a copy of his medical records, so he obviously expected someone to come and get him."

"He's okay, Lilly. Such a cuddle bug, this cat. He must miss Leon, though," Tamara said.

Lilly put her arms up, and Tamara handed her back the cat. Lilly nuzzled his neck again, and he licked the side of her face. She looked at the note, which was generic instructions about taking care of Max. "He'll come home with me," she said.

"You sure? We could take him," Tamara said. Warwick gave her a look, but he didn't say anything. He was planning on getting a dog in the spring, but if they had to make it work, they would.

"I'm sure. Luna's still little, but she'll probably like having a furry friend. And Max will have people home all the time, so he won't feel alone."

Tamara bent down and gave her best friend a quick hug.

"Listen, my friend, this all sucks. I hate to use that sort of harsh language, but it's a fact. Leon isn't here. Poor cat, being here, without Leon, not knowing what was going on. This mess. Let's pack some stuff up and get out of here. We'll come back and look around more in a couple of days. We can come up with a plan and let Fred know what it is. Fred. I thought he had more sense than to just up and leave the house like this."

Lilly nodded and looked up at Tamara. "I think we should get the house rekeyed. And reset the alarm. I'll call Mary at the Triple B so we can make that happen tonight."

"Why the urgency?" Warwick asked.

"If someone was supposed to come and get Max, someone has a key. Who knows how many keys are out there? Also, look at this place. Leon was scattered, but he wasn't a slob. Maybe someone's been looking for something."

Tamara nodded, and Lilly picked up Leon's desk phone and gave Mary a call.

"You're keeping me busy! I'll be over within the hour."

"Is there someone else I should call?" Lilly asked. "I'm afraid I've gotten into the habit of thinking the Triple B can solve all my issues."

"I wish more people thought like you did," Mary said. "I used to change locks all the time in rentals. Do you have an idea of the types of locks there are?"

"No idea, but I'll bet Tamara does." Lilly handed her phone to Tamara. Tamara did a walk through the house, discussing the security system and sending Mary pictures of the locks on the doors.

Lilly stood up and gently put Max on the chair. The cat stood for a moment and then circled around and laid down.

"Do you need help?" she asked Warwick.

"Nah. I'm packing the files into boxes; that's it for tonight, right?"

"Right," Lilly said. "I'm going to go pack Max's things."

Lilly walked toward the bedroom. She always liked Leon's house, mostly because it was so very different than her own. A true mid-century ranch, it was built with a combination of wood and polished concrete with stainless steel. It hadn't been updated but felt strangely mod-

ern. For a moment, just a moment, Lilly envied whoever
was going to live in the house. One side had views of the
water, and the other side had a private backyard, complete with a pool. The gardens were in terrible shape, but
that could be fixed. Lilly shook her head. She could never
live here; who was she kidding? She loved Windward and
could never leave. That didn't mean she wouldn't do
what she could to get this house in shape. It was too late
in the year to do much to the gardens, but she'd come
back and make some notes for the new owner.

The kitchen was open to the hallway with windows
that overlooked the pool in the backyard. Lilly walked
over to the sink and looked out. Turning on the outside
lights showed the outline of the pool and the walkways.
How many wonderful cocktail parties had she enjoyed
out on that patio? How many times had she walked the
paths to help Leon order the plants he'd need for the season? She blinked back tears and turned the lights back
off.

After finding gloves, trash bags, and liquid soap under
the sink, Lilly headed to the back bedroom. She held her
breath while she emptied the litter box. She took it into
the guest room bathroom and rinsed it out, putting it into
another trash bag and sealing it up. She turned over the
automatic feeder and put the entire contraption in a bag.
Ernie could figure it out. She emptied the fountain in the
sink. She was concerned about how Luna would react to
the gurgling water, but nevertheless, she put it in another
bag.

Lilly piled all of Max's things near the door. The cat
carrier was large and made of hard plastic. She looked inside and saw a pile of blankets that was obviously Max's
bed. There was a fine layer of gray fur on the blankets,

but Lilly would sort that later. She took them all out to re-fold them. She was shaking out one particularly nasty old blanket that might, at one point, have been a crocheted shawl but was now a bundle of yarn held together by knots and cat hair. On the second shake, she realized something was stuck to it. Maybe newspaper that Leon had lined the carrier with? No, it was large and white. A piece of tape adhered it to the fabric, so she separated it carefully and patted the furry strips onto the envelope rather than ripping them off. Turning it over, she saw Leon's handwriting. She flipped it around to read what he'd written. "In the event of my death" was what he'd scrawled along the flap, along with his signature.

She sat down on the bed and stared at the envelope. "Oh, Leon, my dear friend," she whispered. "What was going on with you?"

After a few seconds of staring, and trying to decide what to do, Lilly called Bash. She told him about the un-signed document they'd found in Shakespeare, the mess in the house, and about the white envelope she found taped to what must have been Max's favorite blanket.

"Did you open it?" he asked.

"No, of course not," she said. What she didn't say was that she'd thought about it for a good minute. Had the seal not been signed, she would have taken it home and steamed it open. Probably.

"Are you still at Leon's?" Bash asked.

"I am, but heading home soon." She was telling him about Max when her phone vibrated, which meant a text was coming in. She put Bash on speakerphone and put her glasses on with her other hand. Then she read the text.

"Well, this is interesting. It's a text from Fred. Delores was supposed to take Max, so he texted her. She was worried that Sir Ralph wouldn't like it. Sir Ralph is, apparently, a pet squirrel. She said she was trying to find Max a home. At least that's what she told Fred."

"Leave it to Delores to have a pet squirrel. Listen, hang tight. I was heading home, so I'll be at Leon's house in a couple of minutes. I'll pick up the letter and the envelope."

"Delores probably has a key if she was the person who was supposed to get Max. Other people may have keys, as well. Mary's coming over to change the locks."

"You're that worried?" Bash asked.

"Cautious. The house was a real mess when we came in. Given everything, that may be how Fred left it on Thursday when he flew back to California. Or maybe people have been in here. I was going to take his files and personal papers with me. Or do you want us to leave everything here?"

"No, it's as safe at your house as anywhere. Mark the boxes, and keep things together. As far as anyone is concerned, Leon had a heart attack. Nothing's come back to indicate that isn't true so far. The medical examiner is leaning towards a finding of inconclusive, which means we can keep looking into it. Sort of."

"Are you going to tell Captain Flavia? About Leon and the note?"

"He thinks he has his case closed," Bash said. "Didn't you hear?"

"Hear what?"

"He arrested Scooter McGee this afternoon. About a half hour ago. Ernie said that her brother was hiring her a lawyer."

"Why does he think Scooter killed Jerry?" Lilly asked.

"I guess this will all come out now. Apparently, she had an affair with him years ago. She was young, and took it very seriously. When it was over, she had a breakdown. She's been a bit obsessed with him ever since."

"Obsessed? Is that what Captain Flavia said?"

"No, that's what Scooter said. And what an audit of her social media profiles shows. Liz, Trooper Harris, said that they found a detailed scrapbook of his career at her house."

"That's not a reason to kill him."

"There's more. Twenty-five years ago, she was taking one of those Hollywood tours and saw him. She lunged for him, and his security held her back. She was out of control and was detained. She said she wasn't trying to hurt him, but there's an arrest report. That was right before she went into rehab."

Lilly nodded, vaguely remembering her mother mentioning Scooter's troubles. Troubles were how her mother's generation described anything from an ulcer to an arrest. "So that's it? No more investigation into Jerry's death?"

"That's it for them. For me? I'm going to get that envelope to Leon's lawyer. And I'm going to keep asking questions."

CHAPTER 19

Max wailed the entire car ride, making Lilly doubt her decision to bring him home. What would happen if that was his normal state? Constant cat wailing was not something she either wanted or needed in her life.

"How was the ride over?" Tamara asked, walking towards Lilly's car. Warwick and Tamara followed her back to her house. They'd all left once Mary showed up, followed by Bash a few minutes later. He'd promised to get a set of keys and the new code to Lilly.

"Loud and miserable. I hope to heaven that he calms down. Poor cat; he doesn't know what end's up."

Tamara carried some of Max's things into the kitchen, and Lilly followed with the carrier. Delia and Ernie were sitting at the kitchen table, drinking tea and eating cookies, when they walked in.

"What do you have there?" Ernie asked, standing up.

"Max. Leon's cat. He needs a home," Lilly said. Her voice broke on the word home, and Ernie rushed over to her, leading her to a chair. Once she'd sat down, he took the cat carrier from her and put the entire thing on the table.

"Hello, Max. If you need a home, you picked a good one, buddy. Let's get you set up. First, we'll get the rest of your stuff out of the car, if there's more?" Ernie asked.

"Oh, there's more," Warwick said, walking in carrying two boxes. "Lilly, where do you think these should go?"

"Delia's office for now," Lilly said. "She may be called on to help us go through them. Here, let me help you."

"No, you and Tamara stay here. We'll get the boxes," Delia said. Lilly smiled at her young friend and watched her follow Warwick outside, with Ernie following behind them.

"Luna, stop," Lilly said, and Ernie turned quickly and picked up the kitten. He handed her to Tamara, who held her close.

"I really hope she stops trying to make a run for it all the time," Lilly said. Max had stopped wailing, and she put her fingers through the grate of the carrier. He rubbed his head against them and started to purr.

"Having Max will be good for Luna," Tamara said. "My family always had two cats. They keep each other company."

"I hope so, because I don't need any more drama."

"I heard you talking to Bash. Do you really think something happened to Leon?" Tamara said.

"Honestly, probably not. Being sick combined with trying to figure out how he wanted to leave things must have been stressful, and that probably took a toll. But I do feel obligated to make sure Leon's wishes are carried out. Looks like he may have been worried about that, what with codicils being written and packages being left in cat carriers."

"Plus the boxes hidden with the ornaments."

"I forgot about those. I should tell Bash—"

"Later. Will Bash let you know what's in the packet?"

"I think so," Lilly said. "He was the first one who wanted to make sure Leon died of natural causes. Of course, I think that may have been a knee-jerk reaction given what's happened here in the past six months, but still. I'm impressed by his inquiry."

"I can't believe he got shut out of the investigation into Jerry's death. If I was him, I'd be royally ticked off." Tamara held Luna on her shoulder, and the kitten was falling asleep.

"That farce of an investigation?" Ernie said, carrying two boxes and heading across the hall to Delia's office. He came back in a few moments, fuming. "Did you hear what happened?"

"I did—" Then she stopped. Lilly knew that Ernie needed to tell the story, which he did for the next ten minutes.

Delia and Warwick each brought in more boxes while Ernie talked. He'd just finished when they brought in the final boxes and brought them to Delia's office. Ernie went and shut the kitchen door, checking to make sure it was locked.

"Scooter McGee? Can you even imagine? That woman couldn't hurt a fly," Ernie said.

Delia came into the kitchen and looked through the Max's bags Lilly and Tamara had brought in. She took them with her to her office. Warwick went down the hall to wash up, but Lilly and Tamara stayed at the kitchen table with their coats on.

"Did Scooter get out on bail?" Lilly asked. She was petting Max through the grate of his carrier, waiting for Delia to get him set up.

"She did," Delia said, coming back into the kitchen. "I checked in with Portia, who's been in touch with Bucky." She picked up the rest of Max's things and carried them into her office.

"What made Captain Flavia focus on her?" Warwick asked when he came back into the kitchen. He put his hands on Lilly's shoulders. "I'll take your coat, Lil. Yours too, sweetheart."

"A long-ago love affair she obsessed over for thirty-plus years," Ernie said. "Plus, the cupcakes."

"The cupcakes?" Tamara asked. She put Luna on the table and stood up so that Warwick could take her coat. Once her arms were out of her sleeves, she scooped the kitten back up and sat down.

"Scooter says that Jerry called and asked her to order the cupcakes," Ernie said. "This is according to Portia. Anyway, the receipt of the online order was on the box office computer. She had his credit card number because he'd donated to the Players. Problem is, there's no record of him calling the box office."

"That's odd," Lilly said. "Maybe Delores was—"

"Sorry to interrupt, but how about if we introduce Max to his new home?" Delia said, coming back into the kitchen. "Lilly, he seems to like you, so why don't you take him out of his carrier?"

Lilly opened the door, but Max didn't move. She reached in and picked him up. "All right, sweetheart, let's see what Delia has set up for you." She walked across the hall, Tamara and Luna following them. "See? Here's her office. Your litter box is right here." Lilly put him down in the small bathroom, and he sniffed his litter box but then ran back to her. She picked him back up.

"Here's your food, Max," Delia said. "I know you had that automatic feeder, but I'm putting that away. It wouldn't be good for Luna to eat your food, and it's not good for you to graze all the time. No offense, Max, but you look a little heavy. Stairs and watching your food intake will help with that." Max watched Delia, and looked back at Lilly.

"She's in charge," Lilly said, kissing him on top of his head.

"I put your toys over here, but they're going to get mixed up with Luna's. I really hope the two of you get along. If you don't, we'll figure that out. I'll leave your carrier right over here, with the blankets from home, in case you want to sleep in there tonight, but I'll also put one of your blankets over here." Delia took out the least furry blanket and moved it onto the couch.

"You know he doesn't understand you, right?" Tamara said.

"Oh, he understands," Delia said. "Try putting him down, Lilly, and see what happens."

Lilly put Max down gently, and Tamara put Luna down at the same time. The two cats faced off, and then Max turned and went to his food dish. Luna followed, but Max hissed, so she went over to her own dish.

The three women stood and watched them for a few minutes, and then Delia turned to Lilly.

"How are you doing, Lilly?" she asked.

"I'm tired," Lilly said. "You must be tired, too."

"I took a nap this afternoon," Delia said. "Ernie and I

put some lasagna in the oven a while ago. We're sick of Thanksgiving food, so he's going to make soup tomorrow. Why don't you both clean up, and we'll eat in a bit."

"Ernie was telling me about what happened to Scooter," Lilly said.

"We'll talk about it over dinner," Delia said. "Hopefully Roddy will make it in time. Go upstairs. You too, Tamara."

Lilly nodded, and went up the stairs to her room. When she was younger, she lived on the third floor, but she'd moved to the second floor when she and Alan moved in. After he died, she moved into her parents' old room, which also had a sitting room and bathroom. She could see the water from her bedroom window, and that always calmed her. She was going to shut her door, but a gray head nudged its way in.

"Max! Well, that's fine, I guess. This is my room, and my sitting room. I'm going to take a quick shower, but I'll leave the door open for you. Yes, the bed is very comfortable. Make yourself at home."

The shower soothed Lilly, and she got dressed in comfortable clothes. She was leaving her room as Tamara was coming out of the guest room she considered hers. She was wearing yoga pants and one of Warwick's coaching fleeces.

"It's amazing what closing my eyes for ten minutes does," she said.

"I was afraid that if I laid down, I'd sleep through," Lilly said.

"Hey, I found a makeup case in the guest room. Annabelle must have left it."

"Bring it downstairs. I'll have Delia let her know. Hard to believe Annabelle was here just this morning."

"That's the only sign she was in the room. Ernie must have stripped the bed. It looked too inviting, I needed to stretch out. The last twenty-four hours are catching up to me." Tamara smiled at her friend, and Lilly nodded. "You know, you don't have to fix this for Scooter. She'll hire a wonderful lawyer and probably get off."

"And whomever did this will get away with it."

"Lilly, you're not responsible for the whole world."

"No, but we're all responsible for our corners of it. I know you agree with me, Tamara. Scooter can't go through life with everyone thinking she's a murderer who got off."

"You're right, you're right. I know you're right," Tamara said.

When they got to the first floor, they both looked in the living room, but it was dark. Tamara put the makeup bag on the hall table. They walked toward the kitchen and heard voices coming from the back porch, so they went out there.

"Sorry, we started without you," Ernie said, jumping up and holding a chair for Lilly. "Let me get you a drink. Wine? Lemonade? Something else?"

"Red wine sounds wonderful," Lilly said.

"For me as well, but make mine a half a glass. I have to drive home," Tamara said, sitting down on the chair that Warwick pulled out for her.

"No, you don't," Warwick said. "I was just about to ask Lilly if we could stay tonight. We have a situation at the house. When I got home, the hot water was out. I went downstairs—"

"No. Do not tell me," Tamara said.

"I'd called the plumber, and she went by while I was

with you. We just had a talk about it. We need to replace the tank."

Tamara closed her eyes and shook her head. "That was supposed to last until next summer," she said.

"I told the hot water heater that when I went downstairs and the floor was flooded. The tank didn't listen," Warwick said. When Tamara didn't smile, he went on. "The plumber's going to install that tankless system we looked at. She can do it tomorrow, Wednesday at the latest. Sorry to presume, Lilly, but Delia and Ernie offered the guest room."

"You're always welcome," Lilly said. "I like having the Garden Squad around."

"Speaking of which," Ernie said, hopping up to let Roddy in the porch door. He was carrying an archival box and had a roll of paper under his arm. Unlike everyone else, he looked full of energy.

"Hello all! Just back from the library. Minh is still there, finishing up some scanning."

"That's a long day for both of you," Lilly said.

"The hours flew by. It was fascinating. I learned a lot about some ideas she has for archiving and digital storage. Delia, you're going to enjoy talking to her. You both speak the same language."

"Her credentials are very impressive," Delia said. "I look forward to learning from her."

"I floated the idea of working part-time for the Historical Society by her," Lilly said. "Pending your approval, of course. One warning, though. She likes to talk. A lot."

"She's lonely," Roddy said quietly. "She's uprooted her life and moved across the country without knowing a person here, all based on a possible family tie."

"Why would she do that?" Delia asked.

"Her story to tell. I only know bits and pieces, but I'm filling some of it in. Suffice it to say, she enjoys her work but is also looking for ways to fill her days. The theater project is helping do that."

Lilly smiled and put her hand on top of Roddy's. "You're right; I was being unkind. Though she does talk a lot. We'll have her to dinner soon. Maybe this weekend? We'll all do a better job of making her feel welcome. I'll go first."

Roddy turned his hand over and gave hers a squeeze. "Thank you, Lilly. She'll appreciate that."

"Okay, I can't stand it anymore," Ernie said. "What's in the boxes, Roddy?"

Roddy smiled at Ernie and then turned to Delia. He loved telling stories on his own timeline. "Delia, one of the boxes you found was a donation by James Jentry," Roddy said.

"I think I remember that one. I didn't look in it yet—"

"We did. He donated all of Mel John's files. *All* of his files. He must have just emptied drawers, because it was a jumble. Minh is still sorting things. In the meanwhile, I've got some of the records she'd already scanned, plus some articles that pertained to the question Lilly texted this afternoon." Roddy accepted the plate of lasagna that Ernie offered him and lifted his glass of wine to the group in a silent toast.

"What was the question?" Warwick asked.

"How many people have died in the theater," Lilly said. "I was curious, so I texted Roddy on my way over to Leon's house. I saw Delores this afternoon, and she mentioned ghosts. I thought I'd ask." She went back to nibbling at her lasagna.

"That's a little dark, don't you think?" Ernie asked.

"Given the last two weeks, do you honestly blame me for having dark thoughts?" Lilly asked.

"Lilly always asks questions that have the most interesting answers," Roddy said, pouring himself some water from the pitcher. "As it turns out, six people have died in the theater. Including Jeremy Nolan."

"Six people? In the theater, or are these associated with the Goosebush Players?" Lilly asked.

"The theater. In the past forty years, since the building became a theater, six people have died. Stanley Sayers died there, but you must have known that already," Roddy said.

"Wait, what?" Delia said, coming into the room with a new loaf of garlic bread. "I didn't know that. How could I not have known that?"

"Thanks, Delia. I love this bread. Stanley didn't officially die *in* the theater. He died out in back of the theater," Tamara said.

"What happened?" Delia asked.

"He had a cigarette and keeled over," Lilly said. She and Tamara both looked at each other and then looked down at their plates.

"Not exactly," Roddy said, looking at both women. "Minh found a couple of articles that indicated that he may have committed suicide."

Tamara and Lilly looked at each other. Tamara shrugged. "Delia, the story that we all agreed to believe is that he died after smoking a cigarette. Stanley killing himself was an idea no one could deal with, especially his daughter. I think my father was the first one to say 'he died smoking a cigarette' when someone asked, so that's what we all said."

"Not to give us an out, but the facts weren't clear," Lilly said. "There wasn't a note. There was just Stanley and a gunshot wound at the side of his head."

"Wow, from gunshot to smoking a cigarette. That's some impressive cover-up," Ernie said. "Really. I'd never heard that story in all these years."

"We all agreed to believe our false truths," Lilly said. "Stanley was such a lovely and generous man. Everyone felt guilty about not knowing his level of despair, so we implicitly agreed to lie."

"My world is rocked. No really, it is," Delia said. "It's going to take a while to process this. While I was doing my research, Stanley always came off as such a bon vivant."

"People are complicated," Warwick said.

"They are indeed. In the meantime, let me tell you about what other entries I found in the potential ghost category. James Jentry died in the theater," Roddy said.

"During rehearsal of *A Midsummer Night's Dream*," Tamara said. "Or was it *Twelfth Night*?"

"Very good, Tamara. *Twelfth Night*. He died during tech, according to an article. I believe the quote was that he died in the saddle, an unfortunate turn of phrase."

"JJ was a good guy," Tamara said. "My father was on the advisory board of the theater, which meant that he gave them money. JJ came over to dinner once a month or so. He and Dad would tell these terrible jokes and kill themselves laughing."

"Tamara, I may ask you for more JJ stories for the project," Delia said.

"There was also a set designer who died in 1992," Roddy said, determined to finish his story. "He had some sort of accident in the shop. Then there was a rather large donor to the theater, who had a heart attack during a show in 2009."

"I remember that one," Warwick said. "He was the father of one of my students. He was a generous donor to the school programs, but he wanted everyone to know about it. He had a real 'my way or no way' attitude. After he died, a lot of dirt came out about his affairs."

"Business or personal?" Ernie asked.

"Both," Warwick said.

"Ouch."

"Yeah, it was pretty tough for his family."

"What happened to his kid? Do you remember?" Ernie asked.

"Of course he remembers," Tamara said. "He remembers every student who needed extra help."

"She's fine," Warwick said, smiling at his wife. "She's living in Boston, finishing up medical school. Her mother still lives in town."

"Who is it?" Delia asked.

"Molly St. John," Roddy replied. He shrugged and looked around the table. "She would have found out easily enough."

"So, Jerry, JJ, Stanley, the rich guy, the set designer. Who's the sixth person?"

"I know this one. Mel John," Delia said. "They found him in the lobby after a show one night. A drug overdose."

"Do you know who found him?" Roddy asked.

"No, who?" she asked.

"Jerry Nolan and Annabelle Keys."

* * *

"Here's where you are," Roddy said, closing the door to the greenhouse behind him. "I was wondering where you'd gotten to."

"It's been a long day," Lilly said. "I needed to spend some time with plants."

"Would you like me to leave?" he asked.

"No, you're welcome to stay."

Roddy wandered over to her but stopped a few feet away. She continued to mist her plants for a few moments before speaking again.

"It's all so dark, isn't it? Suicide, drugs, death."

"It is. But there's an opportunity to find some answers that may help—"

"Help who? Leon's son? Scooter? Annabelle? How will us learning about what happened almost forty years ago help any of those people? I'm so tired of darkness."

"I understand," Roddy said. "I really do. Lilly, please take care of yourself tonight. Feed your plants. Think of an idea for me and my bloody wreath. Better yet, make my wreath."

Lilly stopped misting and smiled. "I can help you make your wreath, if you'd like. I have frames, and can show you how to wire things on it. The process is actually very meditative. I will, however, leave the decoration up to you."

"You can't blame a man for trying," Roddy said, flashing a smile that she returned. "Bloody *Moby-Dick*. What book did you get?"

"*Murder on the Orient Express*."

"What? How did you get that title?"

"I suggested it, and then I drew it out of the bowl."

"Quite a coincidence."

"Isn't it?" Lilly said, and then she laughed. "I think

that Dot was just as happy I picked it. She really thought that her high literary taste books would be a major hit."

"Sometimes people have to learn on their own," Roddy said. "Then you can help them make sense of what they've learned so they can do better the next time."

"Maybe so," Lilly said. "I don't feel as though I'm good for much else right now."

"Ah, Lilly, my dear friend, don't you know what a gift that is, your clarity of vision, for us all?"

Lilly blushed a bit and put the mister away. "Here's where I'm working on my wreath. As you can see, we have a lot of materials you can use. These are the frames," she said, gesturing to a pile of wire frames on a high shelf. "You'll need to decide on the size, and what materials you want to cover it with. If you want another shape, we can cut up frames and solder them together."

"Interesting. I suppose seaweed wouldn't be a good base for the wreath?"

"The smell wouldn't be very festive. You may be able to replicate the look with something else. I love my plants, but I'm not above spray-painting branches and using faux materials if they work. Maybe you could use raffia, or ribbon—who's banging at the door?"

Lilly stepped over and saw Max looking through the lower panes of glass, crying for her, pressing his shoulder against the door.

"You have a new friend," Roddy said. "Tamara told me what happened. Dreadful woman, that Delores Stevens. You know, looking for motives, it seems as if quite a few people would have them against her. Sorry, off topic for this evening. Are you going to let Max in?"

"No, too many poisonous plants in here," Lilly said. "I'd already anticipated having to cat-proof my holiday decorations because of Luna, but Max can get in a lot more trouble."

"Are many of your plants poisonous?"

"Yes, especially for cats. Humans require a much higher dose, but a lot of these plants have medicinal properties that can be harmful if enough is ingested."

"I've been reading up on medicinal plants this fall," Roddy said, picking up one of the wreath forms. "After learning about the nefarious plants Miranda Dane planted in her garden, I was fascinated. Some of the poisonous plants are actually lovely, but not really in keeping with *Moby-Dick*." Roddy started wandering around the greenhouse, looking at the shelves of the potting benches. He picked up a pinecone from a pile and tossed it up in the air. "I hadn't noticed how many craft materials you have in here. It's all rather inspiring." He put the pinecone back down.

"That's one word for it," Lilly said. "While you're being inspired, how about coming up with our garden design project? I have no good ideas."

"I've got one. Do you mind if I borrow a wreath form? I need to understand logistics of *how* before I fall in love with my idea of *what*."

"Take this one," Lilly said. "It was one my mother started but never finished. You can see how she wired things on. Don't worry about being careful—she stopped working on it because she decided it was ugly. She was right."

Lilly handed Roddy a half-finished wreath made of all sorts of ribbons and ornaments. He smiled and took it from her, ideas already percolating.

CHAPTER 20

L illy went to bed early and slept in. It didn't make a world of difference, but it did help. When she woke up, Max was sleeping on the other side of her bed, and he started purring when she reached out and petted him. That helped more.

Lilly dressed, intentionally picking a bright-colored dress rather than the black she had been wearing. She'd been thinking about Leon, about his friendship, about his zest for life. No matter what, she knew the best way to honor his memory was to find moments to enjoy today.

When she walked into the kitchen, she was greeted by Ernie's "She wakes!" as he jumped up and poured her a cup of coffee.

"I am, finally," Lilly said. "What have I missed?"

"Nothing. Mary called and told me to take the morning off. Some reporters have been coming by, and she hopes they lose interest by the afternoon. I've been catching up with the reading Roddy brought over."

"Has that been helpful?" Lilly said.

"Interesting. It's actually helping me appreciate the Stanley a bit more. I'm enjoying seeing what Stanley Sayers envisioned for the place. Listen, I love being part of the Goosebush Players, but the quality has been going down for the last few years. Maybe getting some more programming into the Stanley, some more challenging work for people, would be good. I know that Leon was thinking about that."

"If Delores buys the church, you'll have that opportunity."

"What do you mean, 'if Delores buys the church'?"

"Didn't I tell you about that part of the open house? She says that Leon was planning on leaving her a small fortune, and that she was going to use it to open another theater."

"I just got an email from his lawyer about the theater being named in his will, details to follow, so I'm not sure that's true."

"Why did you get the email?" Lilly asked.

"Apparently he'd named me vice-president of the board on the documentation."

"Ah, that's good. Was that recent?"

"Must have been. He hadn't actually talked to me about it, but it shouldn't be a problem. The board is mostly advisory. Or was."

"I really hope that Leon was very, very clear in his intentions," Lilly said. "No one wants this to be a long, drawn-out affair."

"You said that right. Hey, listen, I forgot to mention

this. Minh Vann is coming by this morning. She finished scanning documents, and is going to meet with Delia."

"Where is Delia?"

"In her office, teaching one of her online classes. She also has office hours, so she's going to be in there for a while longer."

"I'm glad you'll meet Minh," Lilly said. "You know, she was asking questions about the Preston family."

"I'll be happy to—" The doorbell rang, and Ernie stood up to go to the door. "Where should we meet with her?"

"The living room," Lilly said. "She's a guest; may as well treat her as such. I'll be right there." Lilly went into her office and grabbed a notebook. She looked at herself in the mirror and put on some lipstick.

As she got closer to the living room, she heard laughter coming down the hall. It was Ernie's. She walked in, and the conversation stopped.

"Nice to see you, Minh," Lilly said.

"I'm really happy to be here. I'd driven past the house many times, of course, but I didn't realize it was yours until today. It's so lovely, and there's so much to look at."

"Minh was just telling me a story about learning the history of Goosebush, and how much Delia's work on the Alden Park bodies helped her decide to move here."

"I heard laughter," Lilly said. "Delia's work is many, many things. Funny has never been one of the words I'd use to describe it."

"No, I was talking about the time I went on an archae-ological dig with my son. It was supposed to just be a fun exercise to help him get a badge, but then it ended up being one of those parents-can-be-nightmares events. I got a reputation as the cool mom to a lot of kids that weekend."

"It was a great story," Ernie said. "Minh, would you like coffee or tea? Lilly and I were just going to have a mid-morning snack, and we'd love for you to join us."

"Coffee would be great, thank you," Minh said.

"I'll be right back," Ernie said.

"Thank you for doing all that scanning," Lilly said, gesturing to the pile of documents on the coffee table. "That's a lot of information."

"It is, and I'm sorry about that. I know how over-whelming it can be when you ask people like me one question, and I give you a dozen answers."

"I'm used to that, actually," Lilly said. "Delia is the same way. She believes in looking at every angle before answering a question."

"I've put some Post-its on the items I think you may find the most useful," Minh said. "I also wrote up a sum-mary page of what I included. I don't want to overstep, but I thought it may be helpful."

"Oh, Minh, thank you so much. That's exactly what I need. I feel a bit overwhelmed these days. And since I have no idea what I'm looking for, guidance will help."

"I'm glad. I've been grateful for the project. I'm not sure how much Roddy has told you about why I'm here—"

"He hasn't said anything, actually. He's only men-tioned that he's enjoyed talking to you. I'm glad you came by today. I was wondering if you'd like to come to dinner on Saturday. Unless you have other plans?"

"No. No plans, I mean. Yes to dinner. That would be so nice. It's hard to move . . . I've had a tough year. So much happened. First, I had a really terrible divorce."

"A new environment can be very helpful after a breakup," Lilly said. "After my first marriage broke up, I moved to London. It did me a world of good."

"I, for one, am glad you moved back; otherwise, we never would have met," Ernie said as he came in carrying a full tray of coffee, scones, and cookies. "I know you loved living over there."

"What's not to love? I went to the London School of Economics," Lilly said. "And then I stayed for a few more years. It's a wonderful city."

"I've never been," Minh said. "I was actually going to do some traveling, but then my mother died in April."

"I'm so sorry," Lilly said, putting down her coffee cup.

"That's what brought me to Goosebush, actually. See, right before she died, she told me a secret, one that I was the last to know. My father wasn't my biological father. She'd been pregnant when she married him. He must have figured it out when I was born full-sized, three months early. They never had a good marriage, and he always favored my younger brother and sister, but I never put it all together."

"Did she tell you who your father was?"

"No, she didn't. She wouldn't. She wasn't an easy woman. That's probably why I go overboard with my kids. Anyway, after she died, I looked through her things, but I didn't find any records except that she'd been in the Army for three years. That's where she met my father, the father who raised me. She always regretted leaving the Army. I did a DNA test, and that's when the Preston family came up."

"Interesting," Ernie said. "You know, I bought the Preston house last month—"

"I want to be honest about why I'm in Goosebush," Minh said, looking at Ernie. "I want to meet people, and to make a home here. But I'm also trying to figure out my family history."

"Albert Preston was in the Army for a few years," Ernie said.

"I know. But from what everyone says, and what I've been able to find out, he didn't seem like the kind of person who'd leave my mother. But maybe he was. Or maybe it's another Preston. The person with the DNA connection was a second cousin, or something like that."

"I knew Albert," Lilly said. "It's hard to tell about a person, isn't it? But my sense of him was always that he wasn't the type of man to walk away from a responsibility."

"It may be a wild goose chase," Minh said.

"I've been going through the house, slowly," Ernie said. "Gladys was a collector, and she never threw anything away. When I bought the house, I thought it was all junk, but it's not. There are a lot of treasures in there, more in the keepsake sense. Why don't we figure out a time for you to come by?"

"I'd love that—"

"I've found some of Albert's things, and there may be his DNA on something. An old hairbrush or something?"

"That would be wonderful," Minh said. "I don't want to cause any trouble, trust me. It's just that—I always thought I knew who I was, you know? I was married, a daughter, a mother. Then this year, my youngest decided to study abroad, my marriage fell apart, and then my mother passed. So, who am I? I'm fifty-five, and I have no idea."

"I don't know you well, Minh, but you do strike me as someone who will figure it out," Lilly said.

Delia stepped into the living room, and everyone turned to look at her. "Sorry, I didn't mean to interrupt. Hello—Minh? I'm Delia Greenway. Why don't you come back to my office, and we can talk there. Bring your coffee with you. I hope you're not allergic to cats?"

"No, I love cats," Minh said.

"Minh, come see me before you leave," Ernie said. "I'll give you my contact information, and we can set up a time for you to come to the house."

"Thank you both so much," Minh said.

"Oh, and Lilly? I put those metal boxes in the dining room. That may be an interesting diversion this morning," Delia said.

Lilly went into the dining room to look at the three metal boxes. All were locked. Under normal circumstances, given what was going on, that wouldn't have stopped Lilly. But Leon had gone a step further. He'd put large labels across them that said STANLEY HISTORY and signed each. "Only to be made public with the permission of Fred Tompkin, or on the occasion of the 50th anniversary of the theater" was written in block letters. She took a picture of the boxes with her phone, and a close-up of one of the seals.

This entire situation didn't feel right to her. Who knew what was in these boxes? If she called Bash, they'd be part of the public record. She thought about Stanley Sayers. Forty-year-old secrets being made public without an understanding of whether they were going to be useful to the current situation or not? And what was that current situation? Jerry Nolan had been killed. He lived a public life. Anyone could have killed him. She didn't know enough about him to draw up a list, but she hadn't tried beyond what she knew.

Lilly couldn't imagine the case against Scooter would stand up in court, would it? She ordered cupcakes for Delores that Jerry asked her to order, but that were used to kill him. Was that how she got revenge from all those years ago? Lilly thought about the woman she knew now, and she couldn't imagine Scooter having that depth of passion. Anyway, Scooter would probably go free. Why wasn't that enough for Lilly?

Wandering into the kitchen, Lilly got a scone from the cooling rack. Bless Ernie and his stress baking. She poured herself some more coffee, and grabbed a second scone. She went out to the back porch. The fireplace was on, but the room was still chilly. After renovations, the room would be warmer, but now the windows were leaky, and Mary had been talking about ways to add extra insulation to the walls. As much as Lilly loved the rustic feel of the porch, she loved the idea of being able to sit out there in the winter better. She texted Mary to tell her she was reconsidering the new wallboards on the porch. That change would make the winterizing much easier. Lilly looked out to her gardens and smiled. She was too addicted to this view to worry about the porch looking too polished. She needed to trust Mary. She got a text back from Mary with a smiley face emoji, and message that she'd send design options as soon as she was at her desk.

Delia had suggested that they always leave the remote to the fireplace on the mantle so they could find it. It made sense, but it also meant that she needed to get up again. She walked over to take the remote and looked to the side of the fireplace. She saw Max curled up in Luna's cat bed, with Luna spooning against his belly. Max opened one eye, flicked his tail, and went back to sleep. Lilly turned the fireplace up and went back to her seat.

She texted Fred and asked for the name of Leon's lawyer. She texted the pictures of the boxes and said that she wanted both of their advice on how to move forward.

Will get back to you, Fred texted.

Is Max okay? was his next text.

Lilly stood back up and took a picture of the sleeping cats and sent it to him. He sent back a heart emoji in reply. She had no idea how to send emojis, but obviously needed to learn.

She'd taken a sip of coffee and started on one of the scones when another text came through, also from Fred.

Do you think Scooter killed Jerry? he asked.

No, she replied. *But I think they've stopped looking for who did.*

He didn't text back. Lilly started to make some notes. She could faintly hear Delia and Minh talking. It was a constant hum.

"Did you look at Minh's notes?" Ernie said, coming into the porch and sitting down. The cats both stirred and gave Ernie a glare before settling back down. "Whoops, sorry. It's great that they're becoming friends, isn't it?"

"One of the nicer things to happen in the last few days. Though I could still throttle Delores for not taking him in."

"I hear you," Ernie said. "But he seems to have recouped. Fred didn't leave until Thursday, so he wasn't alone for too long."

"Still. She's an idiot," Lilly said.

"She is. Maybe an idiot someone is trying to kill, or have you given up that thought?"

"No, I'm still confused about what's been going on. More now than ever. Seems like the more we know, the more confused I'm getting," she said. "And no, I haven't read Minh's documents yet."

"She made three copies of the summary, color coded."

"I left my copy in the living room."

"Sit down, Lilly. I brought you one. The summary references the articles in the packet," Ernie said.

"She's very thorough."

"Yeah, I'm impressed. Are she and Delia still talking?"

"They are," Lilly said. "I can't imagine what about."

"She's very open with her life story, isn't she?" Ernie asked.

Lilly laughed. "We're a couple of cranky Yankees, you and I. We'd be hard-pressed to tell someone our favorite color until we'd gotten to know them for a few weeks."

"Never mind our search for a long-lost father."

"I don't begrudge her the search," Lilly said. "What a shock that must have been. But I can't imagine Albert, the Albert I knew, turning his back on a child."

"I never knew him, but feel like I did him from the stuff at the house," Ernie said. "Are you okay with me helping her?"

"Of course. As we've learned, nothing good comes from hiding the truth. It's not like there's any money left, not that that's why she's looking."

"There's the house—"

"That was mortgaged to the hilt. If you hadn't bought it, all of the Preston family history would have been in a dumpster by now. I say let her do her research, as long as you're up to it."

"I'm more than happy to help her. I was worried about sullying Albert's good name."

"I really don't think he'd mind." Lilly looked down at the scanned documents and flipped through them. Ernie was right. Minh had distilled the information and put it in chronological order. She was impressed by the thoroughness of the connections she'd included. Minh would be an excellent addition to the Historical Society and the archiving project.

She looked up at Ernie and sighed. "Very interesting. But I'm not getting a sense of the time, you know? If Jerry's murder had motives that started back then, I'd love to understand what. I miss Leon. I'll bet he had stories. And not the rose-colored-glasses stories of people like Mitch and Annabelle, who were in Mel John's direct orbit. They had a cultlike love of the man. I wish I'd seen one of those shows that he directed. I have no sense of the brilliance everyone is talking about."

"Why don't you talk to Portia?" Ernie asked. "I bet she could give you some insights. When they were all talking about those days during rehearsal breaks, she had lots to offer to the conversation."

"Portia! That's an excellent idea. Do you want to come with me?"

"I'd love to, but I'm heading into the store. Why don't you bring Roddy with you?"

"Perfect," Lilly said. She picked up her phone and dialed. "Hello, Portia? I was wondering if you'd be up for a visit later? How about lunch? I could pick something up at the Star and bring it over. How does that sound? No, it's no bother. Yes, I'm sick of turkey, too. I'll see you in a bit."

CHAPTER 21

L illy parked out in the back of the Star and walked around the building. Stan had offered to deliver her order, but she'd insisted on picking it up. She realized she hadn't thanked him for doing the room exchange on Sunday. Only two days ago—how was that possible? No wonder she felt so exhausted.

As Lilly walked by the Cupcake Castle, she noticed no one was in there. Not only that, but there were empty display cases. Though she wasn't overly fond of Kitty Bouchard, she didn't think the younger woman deserved having her business suffer because someone poisoned one of her cupcakes. She made a note to herself to ask Bash if she'd been cleared completely.

Lilly walked into the Star and was surprised at how busy it was. She walked back to the restaurant area and walked over to the bar.

"Lilly, good to see you," Stan said.

"Good to see you, as well," Lilly said. "Why are we whispering?"

"There are still a lot of reporters here," Stan said. "I figured you'd rather not be pointed out in case someone wanted to talk to you."

"Thanks, Stan. Why are there still reporters here?"

"Death of a movie star," Stan said.

"There's been an arrest."

"A judge told the prosecution that the evidence was slim, and that they needed to come back this afternoon with more," Stan said. "Haven't you been watching the news?"

"Avoiding it, actually," Lilly said.

"Yeah, well, there are a lot of armchair detectives looking for other reasons Scooter may have killed Jeremy Nolan. We all know that Scooter didn't do this, but a long-ago love affair is fueling the tabloids. Then there's the Delores angle. She gave an interview this morning indicating that she may have been the intended victim."

"Do people believe that?" Lilly asked.

"Only the people who know her," Stan said. "No, seriously, that interview added a lot more fuel to the fire of interest. I hate to say it, but it's been good for my business, since they all like to eat and use my wi-fi."

"I went by Kitty's store. It's closed."

"Yeah, I called her this morning to order some cupcakes. She was going to stay closed for a couple of more days, but I told her to open up. She's been a person of interest, as well, at least for the media. The Delores angle may shine more light on her. It's a mess."

"It is that," Lilly said. "And it keeps getting messier.

Thanks for getting lunch together for me. How much do I owe you?"

Stan slid a paper folder across the bar, and then he went back to the kitchen to get her order. She looked at the bill and knew that he undercharged. She took out her cash and estimated what it should have cost and added a large tip. She folded the paper back up and put it under a bottle of ketchup.

"This is a wonderful feast; thank you, Lilly," Portia said, spooning some more coleslaw onto her plate.

"Yes, thank you, Ms. Jayne," Portia's grandson Chase said. "We were getting a little sick of turkey at every meal. Sorry I have to eat and run, but I have to go to work."

"Where are you working, Chase?" Roddy asked, taking another bite of potato salad.

"At the Triple B," Chase said. "Today's my first day. I'm going to help them stock shelves and do social media. At least that's what Mary said."

"That's great," Lilly said. "I didn't realize they were hiring."

"Apparently, the 'made in Goosebush' movement is taking off," Portia said. "I went down to the Triple B yesterday, and Mary said that things were flying off the shelves. I'm so glad. She said she needed some help, and I volunteered Chase."

"I'm glad to do it," Chase said. "Plus, the store discount I'll get will help our renovation budget go a little further."

"You're renovating?" Lilly asked. Portia's house was a rambling cottage that had been winterized long ago. She hadn't been able to afford to do much maintenance over the past few years, and the house showed the neglect.

"My son helped me get an equity line so I could take care of things," Portia said. "And Chase is helping my dollars go as far as they can. We've had a plumber come in to redo some of the pipes, but Chase is changing out the sinks and toilets. He's also putting bars and rails in my bathroom, like I'm some old lady who needs the help."

"Gram, I'm only doing it now so that it's there when you need it. Dad did the same thing when he renovated his own bathroom. Okay, I'm off. See you tonight." He bent down and gave his grandmother a kiss on the cheek. "Thanks again for lunch, Ms. Jayne. Good to see you, Mr. Lyden. I'd love to come by and see your Aston. I've always wanted to check out one of those engines."

"Any time," Roddy said.

The three of them watched Chase go. Lilly turned to Portia and smiled. "He's a delightful young man. You must love having him live with you."

"I do," Portia said. "I think he likes it here. I'm easier on him than his folks, so that helps. My daughter-in-law is very tough on him, but I try not to interfere."

"It's nice that he's around to do some of the renovation work," Lilly said. "Another set of hands makes a huge difference."

"I try not to ask him to do too much. I want him to have his own life, you know? But he says he enjoys helping out."

"That's wonderful," Roddy said.

"Enough about me. What's going on with Jerry's murder? Have you solved it?" Portia said. "There's no way Scooter killed anyone, at least not on purpose."

Lilly smiled at her directness. "Delores may have been the intended victim," she said.

"That would make more sense," Portia said. "It certainly widens the pool. Don't look like that, Lilly. You know it's true. She's one of the most unpleasant people I've ever met. What are you doing about Scooter?"

"Nothing," Lilly said.

"Nothing?"

"I don't want to stir things up," Lilly said. "The police are looking into it."

"Then why are you here?" Portia said. "I assumed you wanted my help."

"Questions about the past. What was Mel John like?" Lilly asked.

"Mel? Do you think all of this has something to do with Mel?"

Lilly paused and took a sip of her iced tea. "Portia, I'm not really sure. What I do know, or suspect, is that the police are going to be looking for current-day motives. Arresting Scooter showed that they are considering the past, but focused on now. Thirty-some-odd years ago may not have anything to do with Jerry's death, whether he was the intended victim or not. But I'd like to know about those times. I suppose it's because I'm thinking about Leon these days. The theater and the Goosebush Players, they both meant so much to him. I can read articles, but I'd love some context."

"Leon was a very good man," Portia said. "A better-than-average actor. A wonderful singer. A lousy dancer, but you can't win them all. But in context of the theater and the Goosebush Players? You have to understand Stanley. Did you know Stanley, Lilly?"

"Not well. My parents did, though."

"He was a huge personality. Lit up a room just by showing up. Stanley and Leon were as close as father and son. They shared their love of theater, but it was different for Stanley. Stanley wasn't a performer. He was an engaged audience member with a big wallet and great taste. He truly loved the art of theater."

"He was the person who had the idea to convert a failed home improvement store into a theater?" Roddy asked. "I've always wondered about taking that leap."

"Goosebush has had its up and downs economically, as have most towns. We've always been blessed because we're so close to the water and to Boston, but still. Opening up a larger store was a huge leap for our town, one that a lot of people didn't want to make. When it failed, Stanley bought the property and proposed opening a theater, all at his expense. He made a deal the town couldn't refuse. Most people expected him to give the space to the Goosebush Players and call it a day, but he had other ideas. He rented it to them, but then he worked on producing more adventuresome work on his own. Most of it was awful. Then he met Mel John."

"How did they meet?" Lilly asked.

"Stanley used to go to Boston, New York, Providence, all over, to see work. He saw three or four shows directed by Mel, and made it a point to meet him. By then, Mel had burned folks out, so when Stanley offered him a chance to come to Goosebush, Mel took it."

"What do you mean he'd burned people out?" Roddy asked.

"I don't use the word 'genius' lightly, but I'd use it for Mel. He was almost childlike in his enthusiasm for the work. His joy was contagious, and people followed along. The thing was, it wasn't everyone's cup of tea. And he never stayed on budget. He burned bridges with a couple of theater companies and hadn't worked in a year when Stanley met him. He came down that summer, and Stanley gave him free reign and a healthy budget. The work was great, so Mel stayed on. The Goosebush Players needed a new artistic director, so Mel took that on as well, with the understanding that he'd do more traditional fare with them, and then he could do whatever he wanted in the summer."

"Did he stick to that agreement?" Lilly asked.

"Yes and no. He did traditional fare, but his take on it. Cross-casting, rewriting endings, darker tones. Lots of new plays. Business was good, though. Especially while Stanley was writing the checks. No expense was spared, and they were lavish productions. People flocked to them."

"Did Jerry and Annabelle do work all year, or only in the summer?"

"Mostly the summer, but they'd come in for special projects."

"How about Mitch?" Roddy asked.

"He and Mel were a couple for two or three years," Portia said. "They broke up right before that last summer. I remember Mel was pretty broken up about it."

"Did they break up because Mel started seeing someone?" Lilly asked.

"Mel loved Mitch. He also loved Jerry, but that was different. Jerry was Mel's favorite actor to work with. Mel called him his muse. No, they broke up because Mel was a selfish jackass. So was Jerry. I do remember that Annabelle was a wreck that last summer, but I wasn't around much. My kids were all getting older, so we took a cross-country trip."

"Did Jerry and Annabelle break up that summer?" Lilly asked.

"Not that I remember, but like I said, I wasn't around. Listen, you have to understand something about both of those men. They were extraordinarily talented. Incredibly charming. Tons of fun. But they were very selfish and devoted to themselves and their own pleasures, both artistic and carnal. Jerry used to flirt with me, and I was in my forties and married. He was devoted to himself. For what it's worth, I know he loved Annabelle. Poor thing, she had her own demons."

"What sort of demons?" Roddy asked.

"She drank. Did drugs. Was quite the party girl. Now you've got to remember, it was the eighties. But still, the booze and drugs got in her way. She might have been partying to spite Jerry, or because of him. But she was a wreck by the end. She could barely function."

"She and Jerry found Mel when he died, according to one of the articles I read," Lilly said.

"Yeah. That was always odd. If you'd told me that Mel John was going to die of a drug overdose, I would never have believed it. The man didn't drink; he didn't do drugs. It only takes once, I'll grant you. But still, Mel was high enough on life. He didn't use any other substances. Such a tragedy. An incredible loss for us all. Stanley was brokenhearted."

"And then James Jentry took over," Lilly said.

"JJ. He didn't take over right away. Stanley didn't like him. He thought he was pedestrian. That's a quote. But then Stanley died—"

"Killed himself," Lilly said gently.

"Talk about a shock. I never would have believed it. But you never know what someone's going through, do you? Stanley was such a great guy. I always felt badly that I didn't tell him that. I hope he knew."

"I'm sure he did," Lilly said gently. "What happened after he died?"

"Stanley left the theater to Leon. Leon, not being a man of artistic vision, hired JJ. JJ melded the theater and the Players together. Like I said, he was a good guy, but not nearly as talented as Mel. He hired Delores. He ran things for a few years, and then he died, and Delores took over."

"His death was unexpected?" Roddy asked.

"He died during tech, a heart attack," Portia said. "Delores was sitting next to him. Must have been awful for her. She and JJ were close, if you know what I mean. Still, Leon was pretty quick to hand over the reins to her."

"Why do you think Leon did that?" Lilly asked. "He always seemed quite devoted to Delores."

"I've never liked to think too much about it," Portia said, pausing dramatically. "There were rumors that Leon and Delores were an item at one point, but I hope that's not true. I think he was bamboozled by her, like so many others."

"But not you?" Lilly said.

"Oh, I've been bamboozled by Delores over the years," Portia said. "She has a way of getting what she wants. But not anymore. There were a lot of us who were sick of how she was running things, and we were working on making changes. Leon was listening, bless his soul. Now we'll have to figure out another way. If she's got people believing that someone wants to kill her, she may get a sympathy vote from the board, but not from me."

* * *

"Well, that was bracing," Lilly said, getting back into the car. She turned up the heat in the car and rubbed her hands together. "This time of year is so beautiful at the beach, don't you think?"

"Stunning. The clarity of the cold air and the light is simply stunning. What a wonderful idea, taking a walk on the beach. Thank you," Roddy said, turning his collar back down and smiling at Lilly.

"I imagined it may help your creative flow with your *Moby-Dick* wreath."

"Is that why you suggested we carry bags with us?"

"Between trash and trinkets, I knew we'd pick things up. And we got both. It used to be, before plastic bottles and recycling, a walk like today would have garnered us a lot of sea glass. But alas, or probably happily for the sake of the oceans, broken bottles aren't as prevalent. And people are pretty good at recycling, so there's not much trash. But still, I like to do my part."

"Sea glass would have been lovely. But I appreciate the driftwood I found, and the shells."

"We do have several jars of beach glass at the house if you need some."

"Thank you; I might. I do wish that the seaweed was feasible, but I trust you on the smell. I took some pictures. Maybe we can find something that looks the same."

"Do you remember the grasses I have in the front of my house? One of the last things I do every fall is cut them back. We could do that today, and you could dry it."

"Excellent." Roddy sat back and closed his eyes for a moment. "It was nice to clear my head for a bit."

"Agreed. One of the reasons I own this car is that it can drive on the beach. I make the trek regularly in the winter. Shorter walks, but just as edifying. The sea air isn't helping me make heads or tails of what's happened over the past couple of weeks, though."

"Portia added to the complexity of the stories," Roddy said. "It made me think of Delia, and her facts versus truth. There are a lot of truths out there. You know, I did some research of my own last night. I realized I'd seen a couple of shows Mel John directed when I was going through the files with Minh. I'd forgotten, but then I looked at his biography and made the connection. I found some photos online, and the memories came flooding back."

"You remember them all these years later."

"They would be hard to forget. I remember certain moments, so affecting. Mel working in a more intimate space? That would have been extraordinary to see. People like Portia were fortunate."

"If nothing else, these conversations are helping me remember part of Leon's true legacy," Lilly said. "His love and support of the theater all these years."

"You know, we're looking at this from two different angles. If Leon's death is connected to Jerry's, it seems as though these stories are important. But if Leon died of natural causes, the story is different."

"Agreed," Lilly said. "Maybe we should just look at Jerry's death—"

"Or Delores's attempted murder—"

"Right, that. We look at that as the puzzle that needs solving. Leon's death is only about context."

"That sounds like a good plan moving forward," Roddy said. "Still, I can't help but wonder if—"

Lilly's phone rang, which startled her. The display said it was Delia. With Roddy's help, Lilly used her steering wheel controls to answer it.

"Delia, I'm in the car—"

"Delores is on Facebook going live now. Pull over and watch."

"Won't it be available to watch later? We're almost home."

"She'd done three lives today and she's erased them all. Just watch it." Delia hung up. Lilly was five minutes from home, but she did what she was told and pulled over. She took her phone out of her purse and hit the Facebook app and found the Goosebush Players page. Sure enough, Delores was rambling about the sacrifices she'd made for her art over the years. She was showing pictures of a young girl as an example of someone whose life had been forever changed by the art. She pronounced it *ahhrrt*. Lilly winced. Roddy had taken out his phone and was recording it. Delores went on and on for several minutes before finally signing off, daring someone to try and kill her again.

Lilly looked over at Roddy and shook her head. "Do you think she's drunk?"

"Perhaps," Roddy said. "She certainly doesn't appear to be in her right mind."

"Does she ever?" Lilly pulled up her contacts and called Bash.

"Hey Lilly, how are you doing today?"

"Hanging in there," she replied. "Any news from Leon's lawyer?"

"Nothing definitive. It's difficult for me to push too hard. I don't want to raise any flags about Leon's death since I have no proof, and the ME has signed off on the death certificate. I hear you have a call in to him, as well. Something about boxes?"

"He and Fred are conferring about steps on that front. I found them last night, but I hadn't looked at them until today. Sorry, I should have called you first."

"No, it's fine. The lawyer told me about them, and said that since you were helping with probate, they would consult with you. Having two fronts on this is probably better. One of us will get answers. Still nothing on the tox screens they're running on Leon's death."

"I thought you said the ME signed off—"

"To get probate started. The tests are as a favor."

"Listen, Bash, this probably has nothing to do with anything, but are there police reports on Mel John's death? Would it be possible for me to look at them?" Lilly asked.

"Funny, Liz—er, Trooper Harris—asked the same thing. I'm pulling them for her. As far as I'm concerned, they're public record. I'll send you a copy."

Roddy made a face, and Lilly muted the phone. "JJ and Stanley," he said.

Lilly unmuted the phone. "Could you send me a copy of James Jentry's death, and Stanley's, as well?"

"Liz asked for those, and for two other people. Both of them died at the theater. Want me to send those along too?"

"As long as you're not breaking any rules," Lilly said.

"We're all breaking rules. Liz is on her own mission; Captain Flavia will have her badge if he finds out. I'm locked out of one case, and trying to make a case where there probably isn't one. Sending you information to feed into that brain of yours? A rule I'm happy to break. Listen, how about if I drop them off at your house?"

"Perfect. You're welcome to come to dinner—"

"I'm actually meeting Liz for dinner. I hope to have all the files out of the archives by then, but it may take until tomorrow." Bash hung up the phone.

"If nothing else, we'll have more facts to deal with," Lilly said to Roddy.

"I can't help but feel that I should feel more satisfied by the news than I am," Roddy said.

CHAPTER 22

L illy and Roddy pulled up to Lilly's gate. While they were waiting for it to open, someone jumped out of a black town car that had been idling across the street.

"I'll deal with this," Roddy said, getting out of the car. He conferred with the person, and then they both walked back to the car.

"Hello, Lilly," Annabelle Keys said, getting in the back seat. "I'm sorry to be so dramatic, but I came by to pick up my things I left. Delia said she left them in the front hall, but no one was home. I'm an idiot; I should have called."

"Annabelle, it's good to see you. Is your driver going to wait?"

"He is," she said. "I have a rehearsal tonight."

"The movie is going forward?" Lilly asked, pulling up and making sure the gate closed behind them.

"I know it may seem heartless, but yes," Annabelle said. "Jerry's role was small enough that they can recast. He was also one of the producers, but they're figuring that out. Canceling it would have cost a lot of people their jobs."

"Understandable," Lilly said. "By the way, this is Roddy Lyden. Roddy, Annabelle Keys."

"A pleasure," Annabelle said. "Tell me, why does it smell like the ocean in here?"

They walked onto the back porch and then opened the door to the house. Two balls of fur ran out to greet them.

"Who's this lovely gray man?" Annabelle asked, leaning down and petting Max's head.

"He was Leon's cat," Lilly said. "He needed a new home. His first placement didn't work out. You sure I can't offer you a cup of tea?"

Annabelle looked at her wrist and smiled. She took her phone out of her pocket and dialed. "Louis? I'm going to be a while longer. Do you want to go and gas up the car? Great. Text me when you're back." She hung up and turned to Lilly. "I'd love a cup of tea."

"I'll make it. Do you both want to go sit on the porch? Or in the living room?" Roddy said.

"Living room," Lilly said. "It's cold out here. Thank you, Roddy."

"I'll go get the bags out of the car, as well," Roddy said.

"Leave them out by the patio. We can rinse them off there."

Lilly showed Annabelle into the living room and went to check the front hall. Nothing was there, so she went and looked in Delia's office. The makeup bag and a pair of gloves were on Delia's desk. She walked back into the living room and noted that both cats had joined Annabelle on the couch.

"Your friend—Roddy? He's very handsome," Annabelle said. "A special friend?"

Lilly smiled and blushed. "My next-door neighbor. He's only been here a few months, but a good friend."

"Handsome men are a tonic, aren't they?" Annabelle said. She moved forward on the couch and looked at some of the printouts of pictures that were lying on the coffee table. "Speaking of which. These pictures. Look at how young we all were. Youth is so beautiful, isn't it?"

"I've been doing some research on Mel John," Lilly said. "Part of the theater project that Leon started. His tenure at the theater wasn't well known to me, so I've been trying to understand what brought you all together."

"We were so young," she said. She was wearing her reading glasses on a chain, and she put them on to look at the pictures more closely. "Those were a remarkable five years. The most remarkable of my life."

"I read that you were the person to find Mel John," Lilly said.

"Jerry and I. By then, our marriage was over. I was taking so many drugs. Jerry was having another affair, but that was nothing new. We were arguing one night after a show, and we found Mel. I don't remember much after that."

"Mel died of an overdose?" Lilly asked gently.

"There was a needle in his arm," Annabelle said. "I had no idea. He was so judgmental of drugs. Hated that I took them. Kept telling me it would kill my talent. Which it did, for a while."

Roddy came into the room and put the tea tray on a table. He looked at Lilly, who nodded.

"I'll be back in a tick," he said.

"I'm so sorry to bring it up," Lilly said. She handed Annabelle a cup of milk tea and watched her take a sip.

"You know, for years and years, we ignored those days," Annabelle said. "Mitch, Jerry, and I never talked about them when we saw each other, which wasn't often after Mel died. I went into rehab, Jerry and I got divorced, Mitch went his own way. We never talked about Mel, or what happened to him. Until last week. Last weekend, on the way back from rehearsal on Saturday night, Jerry said that being back in Goosebush, he was starting to remember things. He wanted to check something out when we were at the theater. He didn't say what. I can't believe that was only three days ago."

"How's Mitch holding up?" Lilly said.

"He's all right. Staying with me. We both feel so badly about old Scooter. I remember how crushed she was when Jerry ended his affair with her. But still, to hold that much resentment for all these years?"

"You knew about his affair?"

"Affairs. He had several while we were married. He flirted with everyone all the time, so it was hard to keep track. I didn't know about all of his affairs, because most of them barely lasted a night. His affair with Scooter ended earlier that last summer. For what it's worth, I do think he cared about her. He just cared about me more."

"He sounds like a very difficult man to be married to," Lilly said. She smiled at Roddy when he came back into the room, and handed him a cup of tea.

"He was. He was also the love of my life," Annabelle

said. "Do you know what no one mentions when they talk about that sort of passion?"

"What's that?" Lilly asked.

"That it can kill you," Annabelle said.

"Or get you killed," Roddy said quietly. Annabelle looked at him and then looked down at the pictures again.

"I should get going," Annabelle said, putting them down. "Are you sure this is all I left? I've misplaced another small bag. Maybe it's in the car?"

"I just cleaned out the car," Roddy said. "I didn't find anything else there, though you're welcome to look through the bags. They are in the back of the house."

"If you don't mind," Annabelle said. "It's a small bag of vitamins and medications. I can replace them, of course, but that's so difficult."

The three of them walked through the house into the patio area. Annabelle looked through the bags that had been in the back of Lilly's car.

"I'll keep an eye out in case it got mislaid somewhere else in the house," Lilly said as they let themselves back into the house and walked toward the living room.

"Thank you so much," Annabelle said. "Sometimes I'm afraid I'd forget my head if it weren't attached." She pulled her phone out of her pocket. "Sorry, I have a call. Oh, it's my driver. I should run. Thank you so much for the tea and the conversation."

"My best to Mitch," Lilly said.

"What's going on?" Ernie said as he walked into the dining room. Roddy put his finger to his lips, and Ernie covered his mouth.

"Thank you for clarifying his intentions. Yes, that's

fine," Lilly said. "I have a couple of witnesses here. Of course. You're going on speakerphone now."

"Who's in the room?" a voice said.

"Roderick Lyden," Roddy said, spelling his name.

"Ernst Johnson," Ernie said.

"Ernst?" Roddy mouthed, and Ernie swatted at him. Lilly gave them both a look, and they settled down.

"Gentlemen, I'm Walter Peabody, Leon Tompkin's lawyer. Ms. Jayne has three boxes that are sealed. Do you see them?"

"Yes."

"And do you both swear that they are sealed?"

"Yes," they both replied.

"All right. According to what I believe is the most recent will of Mr. Tompkin, Lilly Jayne and Fred Tompkin are to work together as co-executors of the will."

"Sorry, Lilly, I didn't know he'd made that change," Fred said. "I would have let you know."

"He indicated that it was because of Ms. Jayne living in Goosebush, which is the heart of much of what he bequeathed. Mind you, he had changed his mind on several issues a great deal, but Ms. Jayne's involvement was in place for several weeks. I would have thought he might have mentioned it."

"He didn't, but he had less time than he thought," Lilly said.

"To clarify for the witnesses in the room, there had been some discrepancy about his exact desires. He had a number of different wills, some of which weren't witnessed but may still be binding. I've just told Ms. Jayne what I think his intentions were. His son receives half of his estate in every scenario, which makes him a fairly neutral party to the rest of the will."

"Though not a disinterested party," Fred said. "Lilly, Walter and I talked it over. You have my permission to open those boxes."

"As long as she keeps an inventory of what she finds, which is witnessed," Walter said.

"I get it, Walter. She'll do the inventory," Fred said. "I trust her. Obviously, my dad trusted her. There's just one thing, Lilly. Could you go through the contents yourself? Use your editorial eye. If there's—if I wouldn't want to know about something, don't tell me. Okay?"

"Okay, Fred, I won't. But remember, your father was a very good man. I'm sure that these are only family records he wanted kept safe."

After everyone hung up, Ernie sat down at the table. "What are you going to do if there's something untoward?"

"I'm going to keep it to myself, for now," Lilly said. "He'll be more open to hearing it in the future. Now, do you have any idea how to unlock these boxes?"

"A screwdriver?" Ernie said.

Roddy pulled one of the boxes towards him and looked at the lock. "A paper clip should do it. Let's get ready to do an inventory."

"I'm going to need to bow out," Ernie said, looking at his watch. "Lilly, I hate to tell you this, but I may need to have a meeting here tonight. Delia suggested it. We're bringing together the theater board."

"You're welcome to have your meeting here," Lilly said. "What's it about?"

"Have you seen Delores today? She's losing it. Spreading rumors about the theater. Making herself out to be a victim, working on getting sympathy. Well, remember the ticket list she gave Warwick the other night? I'm so glad you took a picture of that list. I called the people I knew, and she'd charged them for tickets. Five hundred dollars apiece. She told then it would go toward 'theater rental income,' but I don't think the Goosebush Players are going to see any of that money."

"Did Scooter have anything to do with those tickets?" Lilly asked.

"No, I asked about that. They all dealt with Delores directly. She's running a shoddy business, and I'm done. I don't care what she's going through, and I know that sounds terrible. The theater needs to give her thirty days' notice, and that's this weekend. I'm calling for a vote that we do just that."

"Is Delores coming?" Lilly asked.

"She may," Ernie said.

"Can I change my mind about using the house?"

"Lilly—"

"Just kidding. Godspeed, my friend. Roddy and I will go through the boxes and catch you up later."

CHAPTER 23

"This is what Leon thought was precious," Lilly said. "Pictures and diaries." They'd been looking through the boxes for hours, taking time to inventory each box carefully.

"The pictures seem to all be Stanley's," Roddy said. "He wrote on the backs of all of them. That alone is a gift, because they are candid shots of the entire company, not just the actors. We can see what pictures are from what year."

"And what production," Lilly said. "He put notes in each of these playbills. Listen to this: 'I've seen a dozen *Macbeth*s in my life, but never one that helped me understand the turmoil Macbeth felt in quite the same way. Jerry was sublime.' He goes on and on about why. He was a very thoughtful critic. Not all of his notes are praise."

"Lilly, look at these," Roddy said, handing her a stack of photos.

Lilly looked at the top one. It was a picture of Jerry hugging a young woman, but it looked like a rehearsal rather than a show. She was having trouble identifying the woman, so she flipped it over. Scooter was the woman in the photo. Lilly looked at the rest of the pile. They were all photos of Jerry and Scooter, but from different productions over three years. Each of the photos showed them touching or embracing in some fashion.

"These were all together?" Lilly asked. Roddy nodded. She looked through them again, and then she looked over at Roddy.

"The affair lasted three years?" Lilly said.

"Apparently. There are dozens of other photographs, but these had been separated," Roddy said.

"Why, do you think?"

"There are two options that leap to mind," Roddy said. "The first, that Leon wanted to blackmail either Jerry or Scooter."

"Impossible. At least I hope so. That would add an entire layer of sludge to this story, and make me think less of Leon," Lilly said.

"More likely, he took them out so that people wouldn't see them when they were sorting through candids."

"So he wouldn't embarrass Jerry or Scooter."

"Or Annabelle."

Lilly handed him back the photos, and Roddy put them back in the envelope and on the pile where he'd found them.

Roddy continued to look through the items from the box. "He really loved Mel John's theater. Look at this agenda item. 'Meeting with J. Jentry. Dreck. Search continues.' That supports what Portia said about him not being a fan."

"What is the date of entry?" Lilly asked.

"March 23."

Lilly took out her notebook to find something. "He died on March 28," she said.

"That would make James Jentry a suspect if we were solving Stanley's murder," Lilly said.

"If it was a murder," he replied. "Let's not get ahead of ourselves. Looking through this quickly, it seems that Leon was concerned about clearing up the history of the theater. Perhaps he wanted to protect Stanley's legacy, and make sure future generations knew more about the beginnings."

"By hiring Jentry, he was going against Stanley's wishes. Maybe he wanted to put it right after he died?" Lilly said.

The shouting from down the hall was getting louder and louder. Lilly had just thanked her lucky stars that she wasn't in the meeting when Delia came into the room. "Lilly, Ernie wants to know if you'd come and talk to us."

Lilly looked over at Roddy, and he laughed. "Have fun," he said. "And hurry back. We need some dinner. Perhaps I should order a pizza."

"Sounds good to me," she said. "Lock the dining room door behind me, Roddy. I wouldn't want anyone to wander in."

She turned to Delia.

"Lead on, Macduff."

"Lilly, we're hoping that you can share something, anything, about Leon's will," Ernie said.

Lilly looked at Ernie, and then she looked around the room. Delores was holding court in one of the club chairs. The other ten people were sitting in a semicircle on the other side of the room. Ernie sat on a folding chair that he'd offered to Lilly, but she'd refused. She stood by the fireplace and addressed the room.

"Leon's lawyer just emailed me with some more information," Lilly said. "He seemed to have left the bulk of his estate to the theater with some caveats about its use. He wanted the space to be renovated, and he also left an endowment to pay for staffing a new producing structure."

"But he left me, I have a letter—" Delores sputtered. "Are you going to let them win? Those that seek to vanquish me?"

"We found the codicil," Lilly said. "But it wasn't signed. Did you have a copy of the signed one?"

"No, Leon took it and told me he'd take care of it." Delores started to weep, but no one made a move toward her.

"I don't know what to say," Lilly said. "He may have sent it, and they haven't received it yet. Or maybe he filed it at home. We're going through his paperwork—"

"And I should trust you why?" Delores said, turning towards Lilly.

"Leon trusted me to do what he wanted. Right now, that looks like he wanted the theater to be shut down for a few months for renovations and open again next season, which I assume means next fall."

"That would be my understanding, as well," Ernie said. "That's what he talked about at our last board meeting."

"He changed his mind," Delores said. "I have proof—"

"All right, Delores. Here's what's going to happen. You're going to give us your proof at a board meeting on Thursday. We'll delay the vote on whether or not to renew your lease until then," Ernie said.

Delores stormed out of the room. No one tried to stop her.

"I hate feeling like the bad guy," Ernie said a little later as they were finally eating the pizza Roddy had ordered.

"You're only doing what's best for the theater," Delia said. "It's not your fault that it's coinciding with someone trying to kill Delores, and her being cut out of Leon's will."

"Delia, I'm surprised at you," Lilly said.

"What do you mean?"

"Facts. We don't know that anyone's trying to kill Delores," Lilly said.

"The challenge is that we don't know the motive of the murder," Roddy said, ignoring Lilly. "The cupcake was on the plate set out for Jerry. But the cupcakes were sent to Delores from Jerry. Was this a premeditated murder? Or was it a spur-of-the-minute crime of opportunity?"

"Poison feels premeditated," Ernie said.

"Agreed," Roddy said. "But honestly, without motivation, the entire situation is a muddle."

"You know, perhaps solving the puzzle of who killed Jerry will need more information in order to be solved," Lilly said. "I'll admit, I've come to be far more interested in Mel John, and his influence on all of this."

"What do you mean?" Roddy asked. He poured her some more wine before finishing the bottle in his glass.

"All three boxes that Leon sealed up had to do with the Mel John years at the theater. They included his father-in-law's agendas, which were more like daily diaries with his thoughts. Stanley's notes were also included. His passion for Mel's work was palatable. Jerry mentioned that Leon had reached out to talk about those days. One could surmise that Leon had intended to invite Annabelle and Jerry to the reading of Mitch's play."

"I know he did," Ernie said. "He was pretty excited about surprising Mitch."

"You know, Annabelle said that she and Jerry blamed each other for Mel's death before they talked it out. What if someone else blamed Jerry?"

"So, you think this could be revenge for a drug overdose from thirty years ago?" Delia said. "That feels like a stretch."

"Leon changed his will for some reason," Lilly said. "He talked about starting a new theater company, but with no names mentioned. Maybe he was trying to make amends for the past in some way."

"You don't honestly think that Leon had anything to do with Mel John's death?" Ernie put down his glass and stared at Lilly.

"I don't," Lilly said. "But maybe he was the person who talked Stanley into moving on quickly, then he reconsidered. Perhaps revisiting the work Mel did reminded Leon of the loss, and of how Stanley wanted the work to move forward."

"Do you think that emotions from that long ago would cause someone to lash out now?" Delia asked.

"They might," Lilly said.

"So maybe it could have been Mitch, or Annabelle? Especially if they blamed Jerry in any way," Roddy said.

"I can't believe for one second that Mitch could have done anything of the kind," Ernie said.

"It's very hard to believe," Lilly said. "But not impossible. I wonder how Mitch felt about those Mel John days?"

Ernie sighed. "You'll have a chance to ask him tomorrow. He's coming by to take Delia and me to breakfast so we can talk about the play."

Lilly nodded. "Why don't you plan on having breakfast here instead?"

Ernie looked miserable but nodded in agreement.

"I'll cook," Roddy said, and Lilly smiled at him.

CHAPTER 24

"Are you sure this isn't an imposition?" Mitch asked. He'd parked his car across the street and come in the front door.

"Roddy wanted to try out a new frittata recipe. And besides, it's easier to talk here," Ernie said, taking his coat. "Unless you'd rather go out?"

"No, honestly, the idea of a home-cooked meal and not having to deal with people staring at me makes me very happy."

"Do you mind if Lilly and Roddy join us?" Delia asked as she came down the stairs.

Mitch looked over at Lilly and smiled. "No, I'd love to hear what they thought of the play."

* * *

Breakfast discussion was spirited. Ernie and Delia both shared their thoughts on the reading, and Lilly and Roddy answered questions from the audience point of view. Mitch took copious notes, nodded a lot, and said things like "I thought so" and "excellent, excellent."

Lilly refilled everyone's coffee cups, and then she went back into the kitchen to bring out her contribution to the meal. Her mother called it "Breakfast Joy." It was a pastry made out of baking mix, butter, and cream cheese rolled out. The edges were cut, a large serving of whatever jam or jelly was handy was put down the middle, and then the edges were braided over it. After it was baked, it was glazed with confectioners' sugar and milk. It was Lilly's kind of recipe: simple to make, but with a big impact.

After everyone insisted they were too full before trying just one bite, the pastry went around the table twice.

"Mitch, it really was a wonderful evening of theater," Lilly said. "I'm sorry that it turned out so, well, so badly."

"Yeah, well, that was my own fault."

Lilly and Roddy looked at each other. "In what way?" Roddy asked.

"I never should have offered Scrooge to Jerry. I should have known he'd chew the scenery instead of giving it the nuanced reading I'd hoped for. I was standing at the back of the theater, and I could see his mugging from there."

"Well, I suppose—"

"I mean, the goal was to break out of the Scrooge stereotypes. Make people understand that they had Scrooge inside of them. But years of film work, they'd taken that nuance out of Jerry's realm."

"Hadn't he been onstage since his time with John's Players?" Lilly asked.

"No, he hadn't. Which is a shame, because once upon a time, he was a truly great actor."

"I've been helping Delia with some of the research into that period of time," Roddy said. "It helped me recall that I'd seen some of Mel John's shows in Cambridge and New York. Extraordinary work."

"He was a genius," Mitch said. "I was so young that I thought I'd have a similar experience again in my lifetime. I was wrong."

"Annabelle said that you and Mel were very close," Delia said.

"That's one way to put it. He was the first great love of my life. I worshiped him. We were together for four years. But he was a lot to handle, and I was young. I didn't know who I was yet, so Mel's personality was the focus for both of us. He was constantly bouncing ideas around, diving into research with great enthusiasm. He was like a black hole—he sucked everything into his orbit. I lasted four years, but then I had to leave him. I've always regretted that. Maybe if I'd been around that last summer . . ." Mitch leaned back in his chair and rubbed the bridge of his nose.

"Annabelle mentioned that last summer was very difficult."

"Poor Annabelle, watching Jerry have affair after affair," Mitch said. "Jerry had the morality of a cat in heat."

"Including an affair with Scooter?" Lilly asked.

"I wouldn't classify Scooter as an affair," Mitch said. "Three years makes her the other woman, don't you think?"

"Three years? Did Annabelle know?" Delia asked.

"Not until that last summer. But by then, she was such a wreck, I don't think she cared. I wish I'd been able to talk her out of going back that final summer and putting herself through that again."

"She mentioned that she'd started using drugs—"

"We were all doing drugs back then," Mitch said. "Everyone except Mel, or so I thought. That was the hardest thing to deal with—the idea that someone got him hooked. Such a waste. I was so upset, I didn't even go to the funeral."

"Goosebush must have had very painful memories for you," Lilly said gently. "I'm surprised you came back."

Mitch smiled and shrugged. "Leon called and invited me. He said he wanted to bring back a higher caliber of work to Goosebush. Something that would make Stanley proud. He wanted me to help him run the new theater company."

"And he invited Jerry and Annabelle to be part of it?" Ernie said. "I know he'd reached out to Jerry."

"He wanted Jerry to write a check. Which he did. He donated to the theater, and to the Goosebush Players, for old time's sake. Those pictures that Portia showed us?"

"They were great," Ernie said.

"Lots of memories in those pictures. Jerry took a picture of one of them, and kept asking me if I recognized one of the interns. He'd probably slept with her and was trying to remember her name. Or he was getting sentimental."

"Did he ever find out?" Lilly asked.

"Not that I know of. Anyway, I was channeling Leon when I had dinner with Jerry and Annabelle. That's why I invited him to do the part. That, and three bottles of wine with dinner."

"It wasn't a terrible idea," Roddy said. "He certainly helped fill the audience."

"The play could have used a smaller audience and a better Scrooge. No, I wish I hadn't asked Jerry to take part in the reading. It never would have worked—us working together after all these years. Jerry had turned into a hack, and there was way too much water under the bridge."

"Do you think Mitch killed him?" Ernie asked Lilly as they were loading the dishwasher.

"I don't know," Lilly said. "He certainly seems to hold some anger about the past."

"He does," Ernie said. "He's also a little, well, self-centered, don't you think? I hadn't noticed that before. I mean, Jerry died, for heaven's sake, and he's complaining about his performance?"

Lilly wiped her hands on a towel and then reached over to give Ernie a hug.

"He seemed to be a bit of a jerk," she said, letting go and stepping back toward the sink. "I hope you're not too disappointed."

Ernie shrugged and tossed the rest of the forks into the basket. "A little," he said. "It's been a long time since I was interested in someone. My jerk filter is rusty."

"Mine was never very good," Lilly said. "I dated a lot of toads before I met Alan."

"You married a toad named Pete," Ernie said.

"Hey now—" They both laughed and finished cleaning up the kitchen before joining Delia and Roddy back in the dining room. Roddy had brought the three cases back out, and Delia was working on the inventory sheets while Roddy was reading one of Stanley's diaries.

"Minh could help us archive all of this," Delia said.

"We're not archiving anything until we know what's in here," Lilly said. "I promised Fred that I'd use my discretion."

"But, Lilly, the facts—"

"Delia, don't. We've both moved quickly on the facts before without a lot of concern about who they might hurt. This time, let's make sure that no one suffers because we want the facts to be found out."

Delia nodded, remembering her close encounter five weeks ago. "I'll follow your lead on this one," she said.

"And I'll hear all about it at dinner tonight," Ernie said. "I've got some errands to run, and then I'll be at the Triple B later this afternoon until closing."

"Ernie, I emailed you and Mary the grid that Scooter was working on for the Alden Park event. Speaking of which, I'm working on a list of things we'll need for our Garden Sculpture and Lights entry," Roddy said.

"*Our* entry?" Ernie asked.

"We'll talk about it at dinner," Roddy said. "I'll call you later."

Ernie left, and the three of them went back to making lists and reading materials. They all seemed to be full of memorabilia more than anything. Clearly, Stanley had a point of view, and included that in what he kept and the notes he made.

"I wonder which picture Jerry took a picture of?" Delia said aloud. She was looking at the book she'd put together for him, comparing Portia's photos to some of Stanley's.

"Why don't I call Bash and ask him?" Lilly said. "He was supposed to stop by last night, but didn't."

Lilly stepped out to the porch and sat down on her rocking chair. Max hopped up from his bed and climbed on her lap, and Luna followed suit. "It's a good thing I have a large lap," she said to them both, petting their heads. "Why are you staying out here? It's cold. But I'll bet you like the views, don't you? I do, too. Now Luna, don't try and push Max off. You'll need to share."

Lilly took her phone and dialed Bash's cell.

"Lilly, I'm sorry I didn't come by. After I read the case files, I called Liz, and she came by to talk about them."

"I thought you were having dinner."

"It ended up being a working dinner with takeout from the Star, while we looked at crime scene photographs. All of the records were on paper, and she took the files with her. I did make copies of some of the reports. I'm reread-ing them now."

"What kind of drugs did Mel John die of?" Lilly asked.

"Funny you should ask," he said. "The syringe had co-caine in it, but there wasn't a lot in his system. He didn't have any other needle marks."

"They still ruled it an accidental overdose?" Lilly asked.

"No, the coroner called it inconclusive, but a heart at-tack was the actual cause."

"A heart attack?"

"Apparently."

"Why did everyone think it was a drug overdose?"

"That was the rumor that got started, and no one was able to stop it. According to the records, Stanley wanted a further investigation, but then he died and everything stopped. I called Ray Mancini about the case this morning. He said that he never felt good about it, but there was nothing to go on."

"A dead end, then."

"Except, I think I found something."

"What?"

"Mel John was injected in his left arm."

"And?"

"And he was left-handed. Not a big deal, but it would be awkward to inject yourself with your nondominant hand. Not impossible, mind you."

"Interesting. I've always thought that pieces that don't make sense should be paid attention to. And compared to other pieces. Bash, do you think you could have someone compare Mel John's blood work with Leon's? I assume they ran some tests."

"They did," Bash said. "They aren't as conclusive as the tests we run today, but they did run some. What are you thinking?"

"I'm not sure. It may be interesting to see if they share the same abnormalities, if there are abnormalities."

"Okay, I'll ask. Do you think Leon's death may have something to do with Mel John's?"

"I don't think anything, yet," Lilly said. "Only looking at the pieces. I have one more favor, though."

"Go ahead," Bash said.

"Jerry took a picture of a picture that Portia showed him. With his phone. Could you get a copy and send it to me? I have some of Stanley's photos here, and I may find another picture of the same person. I'd love to see what he was interested in."

"I'll have to call Liz, because they have the phone. But I'm sure they've downloaded everything. I'll email it to you. Anything else?"

"That's it for now. Perhaps you could come over for dinner?"

"I'd be happy to," Bash said. "I hope by then you've come up with an idea or two. I'd love to show Captain Flavia how cases are solved here in Goosebush."

"Mentioning me won't help, but I know what you mean. I'll see you tonight."

After Lilly updated them on her call with Bash, she and Roddy went outside to rinse off their beach findings again and do some more scouring for wreath materials in their yards. They were cutting back some of Lilly's grasses when Lilly felt her phone buzz. She'd gotten an email from Bash. They went inside to look at the attachments he'd sent.

Lilly grabbed her laptop from the library and brought it into the dining room. She found the email and opened up the picture. The close-up of a particular face in a production photo was hard to discern. Was the person in the front of the picture the person he was curious about, or was it the person behind her? She turned the computer to face both Roddy and Delia.

"This isn't very helpful," Lilly said. "How can we tell when this was from?"

"See that costume on the person standing? That was from a *Julius Caesar* they did in 1987. I just logged some pictures from that show," Delia said.

Lilly turned her computer back around. "They're wearing clown costumes," she said.

"Yeah, his idea seemed to be that he was doing a reflection of the political circus."

"Oh, I see," Lilly said, not seeing at all.

"Okay, here's the photo. Bless Stanley; he labeled everything. Huh, what do you know? The clown is Scooter. Wow, that doesn't look like her, does it?"

"No, it doesn't," Lilly said. "It's also terrible news for Scooter if Jerry was trying to remember her—"

"Hold on, let me see that picture," Roddy said. He looked at his phone, and started to play the video recording he'd made of Delores's Facebook post the night before. He froze the video and zoomed in on a moment. "This is Delores talking about the young girl who fell in love with theater. She's holding up a photo of the girl. See anyone who looks familiar?"

Lilly took the phone, and Delia stood up to look over her shoulder. Delia turned Lilly's laptop to face them both, and pushed Lilly's hand so that the phone and the computer were side by side.

"That looks like the girl in back of Scooter in Jerry's photo," Delia said. "You know, it sort of looks like *she's* who Jerry was focused on. She's the center of the picture. Here's another image of her from Stanley's photos. Let me see. Her name was Loli."

Delia walked back to where she was sitting and looked over her spreadsheets. She moved her hand to one of the piles she'd created and pulled out a program. "Loli Esteban was listed as one of the production interns that summer. She worked on *Julius Caesar*."

"Could she have been a friend of Delores's?" Roddy asked.

Delia looked at both images and started typing on her computer. "Hold on. According to Google, Loli is a nickname for Delores," she said.

"And Esteban means Steven," Lilly said. "If that picture is of Delores, then she knew Mel John."

Roddy stood up and looked at the piles Delia had created. He took Stanley's agenda out of one of the piles and flipped through it. "I seem to recall that Stanley had a lot of meetings with—yes, there we go. The six weeks before he died, he had a lot of dinner meetings with L.E."

"Dinner meetings?" Lilly asked.

"There are also a couple of references to ordering flowers for L.E."

CHAPTER 25

"All right, what have we got?" Roddy asked. They'd moved the white board from Delia's office in the dining room, and Roddy had started to make notes on it.

"Six people have died in the theater," Lilly said. "If Delores worked on Mel John shows, then she knew Mel and Stanley. That means she was around when all six of them died. That feels like a fact to me, given the picture."

"We don't know that the L.E. in Stanley's diary was Delores," Roddy said. "Was his wife still alive then?"

"She was," Lilly said. "So was Leon's wife. You're right. We don't know that she actually knew either of them. Maybe she'd volunteered at a show—"

"Or maybe her first husband went to college with Mel John," Delia said, looking up from the program she was reading.

"Wow, that was fast," Lilly said.

"Not really. See in the program? The scenic designer was Ricardo Esteban. He went to college with Mel John, according to his bio." Delia started to type into her computer. "Whoops."

"Whoops?" Lilly asked.

"He died in 1985. Car accident. He fell asleep at the wheel while he was on vacation with his wife in the mountains of Nevada." Delia tapped some more keys, and then she turned her computer around. "Here's his widow after they found the wreck of the car."

"It's the woman in the theater photo," Roddy said. "Presumably Delores."

"Wait a minute," Delia said. "We're forgetting that Jerry ordered the cupcakes for Delores. Maybe Delores and Jerry had an affair back in the day, and he wanted to reconnect? Remember, Mitch said he'd made a donation to the Goosebush Players as well as to the theater."

"He did," Lilly said. "But Mitch said that Jerry was asking questions about who the woman was."

"Right. Besides, Delores was in the theater when the cupcakes were delivered, right?" Delia asked.

"But she may have had time after the curtain came down—"

"Surely someone would have seen her. Unless . . ." Lilly took a deep breath and called one of her least favorite people in the world. She put the phone on speaker.

"Cupcake Castle!"

"Kitty, it's Lilly Jayne. I'm glad that you're open. I came by yesterday, and no one was in the shop."

"Oh, it's you. Yeah, we stayed closed for a couple of days. May as well have stayed closed today, too. No one's coming in."

"It's early yet," Lilly said. "Surely no one could blame you for what happened to Jeremy Nolan."

"Seems like they might. You should see my Facebook page. Full of hateful reviews. That stuff matters, you know."

"That's terrible," Lilly said. "You had no idea that Jerry would eat Delores's cupcakes."

"Right? I know. They weren't even that special. They were the same old red velvet I always made for her."

"You'd made them before?" Lilly asked.

"Twice a week. She insisted on the mini cupcakes because she thought they were more refined. Except she liked me to put a mixture of coffee syrup and almond syrup instead of the normal vanilla. I thought it tasted kind of gross, but she's a good customer. She likes what she likes, and they don't take any time to make."

"And Jerry ordered them for her? That was awfully nice of him."

"Could have blown me over with a feather. He specifically asked for them just like she liked them, too. Even the silver foil—she loves her bling. Of course, it would have been a lot more fun if he'd ordered them in person."

"He didn't?"

"No, he ordered them online. But they're saying Scooter ordered them for him. What a mess. I don't know what I'm going to do, Lilly. They've started calling my cakes Killer Cupcakes."

"Oh, I am sorry, Kitty. I'll tell you what. Could you box up a dozen cupcakes for me? I'll pick them up in a while. And I'll need another dozen for Saturday."

"Wow, thanks, Lilly. Any particular kind for today?"

"You choose. I know they'll all be delicious," Lilly said, and she hung up.

"We're going to eat a dozen cupcakes?" Delia said. "I don't think I can."

"We'll give them to Warwick to bring to school, or Ernie can bring them to work. One of the only good things Kitty Bouchard has done in her life is open that bakery. She doesn't deserve to go out of business because someone decided to use her cakes as a weapon."

"I find it interesting that these particular cupcakes were ordered," Roddy said. "One would need to know exactly what Delores ate, which seems fairly specific."

"Scooter made the order," Lilly said. "She said that Jerry had called and asked her to order them specifically. Unless—"

"Okay, wait. Delores's maiden name was Abbly," Delia said. "She graduated the same year as Ricardo and Mel. Guess what her major was?"

"Theater?" Lilly guessed.

"Chemistry," Delia answered.

"What would happen if Jerry's death had nothing to do with Leon or even Mel John?" Roddy said.

"Go on," Lilly said.

"What if it has to do with Delores? Not that she was the intended victim. But that she thought of herself as a victim."

"Explain," Delia said.

"We have here a series of deaths going back thirty or so years," Roddy said. "What would happen if, and this is a leap, Delores is responsible for them all?"

"What?" Delia said. "That makes no sense."

"Unless you consider that each of these deaths may

have gotten Delores what she wanted," Roddy said. "Her husband dies, and she goes to work for Mel John. Then she has an affair with Stanley. When James Jentry takes over, he brings Delores on as his assistant. Then she takes over for him. Seems like a reasonable life progression until you realize that in order for her to move forward a step, a person had to die."

The three of them stared at the list Roddy had written on the board. After a minute, he added one more name. Leon.

"What would happen to Delores if Leon was serious about taking the theater in a different direction. Maybe he'd become nostalgic for his father-in-law's vision."

"Or he'd figured out that she'd had an affair with Stanley."

"Another possibility. Killing Leon would mean that things would stay status quo."

"Except that Ernie would take over as president of the board—" Delia said.

"And he'd know what Leon had wanted, because they'd been working on the reading series together. Ernie was willing to talk to the rest of the board and make Leon's last wishes a reality," Roddy said. He stood up and dialed a number on his phone. Lilly heard ringing in the kitchen and went to check.

"Ernie left his phone here, charging," she said.

"Okay, you're both scaring me," Delia said. "If what you say is true, then the only person standing in Delores's way right now—"

"Is Ernie," Lilly said.

* * *

Lilly called Mary Mancini at the store. No, Ernie wasn't in. She didn't know where he was. Yes, she'd ask him to call her.

Roddy called Stan. No, he hadn't seen Ernie. Sure, he'd call.

"I'll go check the theater," Roddy said. "In case he went there for some reason."

"I'll go with you," Lilly said. "Delia, call Warwick and Tamara. And Bash."

"What should I tell them?"

"Tell them we think Delores is dangerous. And that we have to find Ernie."

They went out the back door and walked to Roddy's garage to get in his car. Lilly was just as happy to have Roddy drive. Her heart was beating quickly, and she was having trouble breathing.

"We'll find him," Roddy said, reaching over and squeezing her hand before slipping the car into gear and roaring out of the driveway. The normally twenty-minute drive took ten. The theater looked empty, but Roddy and Lilly got out of the car anyway, and ran around the outside of the building, pulling on doors.

"What next?" Lilly asked. She ran her palms down the front of her dress and looked up at Roddy.

His phone rang, and he answered without looking at the pad. "Oh, Minh. Yes. Yes, well. Oh, right. That's great—listen, dear, I'll need to call you back."

Roddy looked at Lilly. "She's just left Ernie at his house. Let's go."

Lilly clutched the side of the door as Roddy gingerly

made progress towards Ernie's house. When he saw the school bus, he sped up so that they could turn down Sparks Street without getting stuck when the bus stopped. They drove down the hill, mindful of the bumps and pot-holes as they headed towards Shipyard Lane. They were almost there when a car came barreling up the street.

"That's Delores," Lilly said.

"Go check on Ernie. I'll follow her," Roddy said.

Lilly nodded and stepped out of his car. He waited until she was out, but just barely. He backed up and did a quick turn in one of the driveways, moving quickly up the hill.

Lilly was always glad she wore sensible shoes, especially today. She did her best to run the rest of the way towards Shipyard Lane. She got a stitch in her side, but she didn't stop. Sure enough, Ernie's car was in the driveway.

Lilly ran up to the back door, but it was locked. She ran around to the front of the house and up the porch stairs. The French door was locked. Lilly looked in the windows but didn't see anything. With Gladys's boxes still piled high, it was impossible to see inside, but she tried. She knocked on the windows and called his name.

Ernie had set up a table and chairs to the right of the door, so Lilly walked over to see if he was there. It looked dusty inside the house, so she peered closer. What was that on the floor behind the table? A sneaker? She walked to the French door and tried to see to the right, behind the table. Looking down on the floor, she saw Ernie lying on the ground. She knocked on the window and called his name. He didn't move.

She looked around the room and saw orange sunlight

moving along some of the boxes. Wait, that wasn't sunlight. She peered in more closely, trying to see through the dust. Except, she realized, it wasn't dust.

She was seeing smoke.

She patted her pockets for her phone, but it wasn't there. She must have left it in Roddy's car. She took a deep breath and looked around. The pot. Ernie left a key under the pot. She picked it up and fumbled with the lock for what felt like hours. When she opened the door, she felt a vacuum of air and saw some flames leap up from the kitchen area.

"Ernie, Ernie," she shouted. The smoke was getting thick, but she moved forward, bending down, feeling for him. She finally found him, and looked back to where she'd come in. She could do this. She hooked her hands under his arms, but she could barely move him. She bent down and tried again. She moved him about a foot, but had to stop. The smoke was making it difficult to breathe, and she started to cry. That wouldn't help. She had to get him out of there. She wouldn't let herself look up, but she could feel the heat near her head.

She bent down again and grabbed his arms. She was pulling him when she felt a hand on her waist. She looked over her shoulder, and it was Warwick.

"I can't move him," Lilly shouted.

"We'll do it together," Warwick said. "Get his feet."

Lilly waited until Warwick had dragged him forward, and then she reached down and grabbed his feet. They moved quickly. Warwick paused at the top of the porch stairs and then carried Ernie down to the lawn. He walked for a few more yards and put him down. Lilly dropped his feet and fell on the ground.

"You okay?" Warwick said.

Lilly nodded. Warwick turned and ran toward the side of the house. He dragged the garden hose around and walked up the stairs. He turned it on and moved forward toward the door.

Lilly pulled herself over to Ernie and put her head on his chest. She felt his heart beating and heard him start to cough. Lilly fell back on the grass when she heard sirens coming down the hill.

CHAPTER 26

Lilly rode with Ernie to the hospital and waited with him while they checked him out and gave him some oxygen. The emergency room doctor asked Lilly what had happened, and when Lilly told her, the doctor insisted that Lilly be checked out as well. She tried to argue, but started to fall over when she stood up.

"Get some blood to test," Lilly said to the nurse as she was being taken out of the room. She refused to allow the doctor to treat her until she was able to use his phone and make a call. She called home and told Delia where she was. She also told her to call Bash and have them test Ernie's blood.

The next thing that Lilly knew, she was lying on a gurney, hooked up to an IV, and taking in oxygen. "We're waiting for a room," the nurse who was with her said.

"Absolutely not," Lilly said.

"You've had a shock, ma'am. You need to let us take care of you. At your age, this could have serious repercussions."

"Where's my friend?" Lilly asked.

"He's waiting for a room, as well," the nurse said. "Chief Haywood is with him."

"Tell the chief I'd like to see him," Lilly said. She turned her head to the wall and closed her eyes. After a few minutes, she felt someone take her hand, and she opened her eyes and looked at Bash.

"What am I going to do with you?" he said.

"What do you mean?" Lilly asked.

"Running into burning buildings. You could have been killed."

"First of all, I didn't run. And secondly, what should I have done? Time was of the essence, and I didn't have my phone."

"Thank God Warwick got there in time," Bash said.

"I thank God for Warwick all the time," Lilly said. "I'm fine, Bash. Did Roddy catch Delores?"

Bash shook his head.

"But you've arrested her."

"For what?"

"Trying to kill Ernie?"

"Ernie doesn't remember seeing her," he said. "He'd been showing Minh around the house, and then he helped her load some things into her car. He remembered going in and finishing his coffee, and then the next thing he remembered was waking up on the lawn next to you."

"But we saw her coming out of Shipyard Lane!" Lilly said.

"She said that she'd stopped by Ernie's house, but no

one was there, so she left a note for him in the back door. We found the note."

"She must have drugged his coffee," Lilly said. She'd tried the back door first. Had she seen a note? She couldn't remember.

"Yeah, well, we took the cup, but it was soaked, and all the coffee had leaked out. They're going to run some tests on Ernie's blood. But even if he was drugged—"

"We can't pin it on Delores," Lilly said.

"We can't pin anything on Delores," Bash said. "Listen, I'm not even sure I understand what Delia was trying to tell me on the phone."

"Get me out of here, and we'll discuss it at home."

"They want to keep you overnight for observation."

"Nonsense," Lilly said. "Delia can observe me at home. I hate hospitals. Get me out of here."

Bash nodded. He hadn't let go of Lilly's hand yet. He picked it up and held it against his forehead. "I don't know what I would have done if something happened to you."

"Bash, I'm fine. I really am. You're very dear to be so worried. Do you think Ernie can go home?"

"He's as stubborn as you are," Bash said. "He's insisting he be released."

"Excellent. You can take us both home."

When Bash drove up with Lilly and Ernie, the entire Garden Squad was waiting for them. Roddy came down the kitchen stairs first and helped Lilly out of the back seat of Bash's car.

"My darling Lilly, I am so, so sorry," Roddy said.

"It's all right. I know you tried to follow her," she said.

"I mean about leaving you alone," he said, smiling.

She leaned on his arm and let him help her by taking her waist and half lifting her up the stairs. Tamara was in the kitchen door and took Lilly's hands to help her into the house.

Lilly turned to look back at Roddy.

"Roddy, you couldn't have known. I'm fine, I really am. Now, go help Ernie. He's in worse shape than I am."

When they walked through the kitchen, Lilly started to walk to her right, but Tamara took her by the elbow and guided her towards the stairs.

"Let's talk first," Lilly said.

"Lil, you smell like smoke and antiseptic. You look worse. You're going upstairs and taking a bath or a shower, your choice. Then we'll see how you're doing."

"What time is it?"

"Eight-thirty."

"That late," Lilly said. "No wonder I'm so tired."

Lilly went in to take a shower, and when she came out of her bathroom, Tamara and Delia were both waiting for her.

"Oh, Lilly," Delia said, giving Lilly a tender hug.

"Now, now, I'm fine. I certainly hope someone is fussing over Ernie."

"He's still in the shower," Delia said. "I'm planning on fussing over him. I brought you up some soup and a cup of decaf tea. There's also a big glass of water. The doctor said you need to stay hydrated."

"I can have the soup downstairs," Lilly said.

"No can do," Tamara said. "You and Ernie need to rest up. Seriously, Lilly."

"But Delores—"

"We'll figure out how to deal with Delores tomorrow," Tamara said.

"Is Bash still here? I'll bet Roddy and Warwick are trying to figure it out right now."

"But they won't be able to, not without you, Lilly," Delia said. "Please rest tonight. Please."

Lilly looked at both women, and then at her bed. It looked very inviting. She climbed in and pulled her covers up.

"Tamara, stay and talk to me while I have this soup. Delia, go and help Ernie. You're right, what I need is a good night's sleep. After I tell Tamara what I'm thinking."

Lilly was sleeping on her side when she finally woke up on Thursday morning. She felt warm and cozy, and found out the reason why. Max had snuggled up right next to her, and she'd been hugging him all night. When she stirred, he looked up and started to purr.

"You are a sweetheart," Lilly said, kissing him on top of his head.

She rolled over carefully and sat up. She was a bit achy, but actually felt pretty good. Stretching here, bending there. All seemed to be in working order. Which was good, because there was work to be done.

Ernie was walking down the hall when she came out of her room.

"How are you this morning, Ernie?" Lilly said.

"I'm fine. Then I realize how close we both came, and I'm not fine." He'd gotten close enough that he reached out, and she took his hand. "How are you?"

"I'm focused. I want to stop Delores."

"Delia tried to explain what you thought happened, but I don't think I understand. Delores tried to kill me? Why?"

"Have you ever heard the term 'black widow'? Delores is a black widow from way back. Unfortunately, we have no proof of that. Yet."

When Lilly and Ernie finally got downstairs, they found Tamara and Delia in the dining room. Tamara had Lilly sit next to her, and Ernie sat next to Delia. Lilly heard Roddy talking to someone in the kitchen.

"Is Warwick here?" Lilly asked.

"No, but he's only working half a day. Bash took the day off. He's making us all pancakes."

"He is, is he?" Lilly said, smiling. She'd known Bash for his entire life. When his parents died and he'd had to give up art school to take care of his sisters, Lilly had done what she could do to help. That included inviting them all over for Sunday breakfasts, which included Bash's favorite, pancakes.

A few minutes later, Roddy stuck his head in the dining room. "We've made quite a feast. Might I suggest we eat in the kitchen or on the porch, and then we can get back to work?"

"Porch," Lilly and Ernie both said at the same time.

"Porch it is," Roddy said.

Feast was a good word for it. In addition to pancakes,

Bash had made scrambled eggs and bacon. He'd also fried up some of the leftover Thanksgiving ham.

"I hope you like hash browns," Liz Harris said, carrying in a large, steaming plate of potatoes.

"Love them," Ernie said.

"Trooper Harris, this is a nice surprise," Lilly said. "What brings you here?"

"Bash caught me up on what happened last night, and Delia told me what you'd all think it means." She heaped some hash browns onto her plate and passed them on to Roddy.

"And—" Bash prompted.

"Right, sorry. Captain Flavia isn't budging off the idea that Scooter McGee did it. So, I decided to take the morning off and have breakfast with all of you."

"Neither one of us is here in our official capacity," Bash said.

"More as advisors," Liz said, giving Lilly some bacon and then taking some herself.

"Because if Delores has gotten away with a half-dozen murders over thirty years, we need to be very careful about how we proceed," Bash said.

"Agreed," Lilly said. "Which is why the first thing we need to do is to put Ernie in a coma. And make me his healthcare proxy."

CHAPTER 27

Lilly drove up to Leon's house and parked her car. She looked at the house and sighed. Tamara was right; it needed updating. But still, those views. Lilly turned around and looked at the water in the distance. Water views always fueled her soul.

She let herself into the house and turned off the alarm. She took a deep breath. The house was still musty. She needed to get the cleaners in. She opened the front door and lowered the screen door a bit. She kept the front door open to air out the house, then walked back and opened a window in the kitchen for cross-ventilation. Not optimum in November, but the house needed fresh air desperately.

"Dammit," Lilly said out loud. "All right, Leon, where did you put the letter of intent you told Ernie about?" Lilly searched the office for a few minutes. Her phone buzzed, and she sat down to read the message. She sighed and looked around. She opened drawers, and as a last re-sort, she ran her hands inside and under the desk.

Finally, she grasped the piece of paper that was taped under the drawer. "Leon, bless you. Here it is," she said.

Lilly's phone rang, and she turned it on speaker.

"Fred, hello," she said.

"Lilly, oh my God, I just heard. How's Ernie?"

"Not good, I'm afraid. We took him home last night, and he had a major heart attack."

"But he'll be all right—"

"Too soon to tell, but it doesn't look good. He's in a coma," she said, her voice catching. "You know, he just made me his healthcare proxy. Little did I know I'd be put in a place to use it so soon." She put the phone down on Leon's desk and sat down, looking around the room.

"Are you his legal proxy as well?" Fred asked.

"I suppose I am—"

"What about the board meeting this weekend? Can you run the meeting in his place?"

"Oh, Fred, there must be someone else who can do it."

"I'm counting on you, Lilly," Fred said. "You heard the lawyer. Dad said he had a new will that left every-thing to the theater alone, but unless we find it, Delores gets most of it."

"But he sent all of those memos?"

"We can try to use them to show intent, but they wouldn't hold up if Delores sues."

"Surely we can wait a little while—"

"No, we really can't. The accountant says we should try and settle this by the end of the year, and since the will is so cut and dry, it should be easy. We'll go with what he planned, unless you can find more recent instructions that had been witnessed."

"I'm at the house now, so I'll keep looking," Lilly said. "What about the Goosebush Players' lease?"

"It will get renewed for ten years," Fred said. "No choice. Please call me if you find anything."

She heard a knock and then the screen door open and close. "Hello?" a voice called out.

"Delores, what are you doing here?" Lilly asked, walking toward the front hall. Delores was standing in the living room. How much had she heard?

"I'd loaned dear Leon a book of plays, and I was hoping to retrieve it," she said. "It's only a book. Sentimental value only. Surely you'll let me take it."

"How did you know I'd be here?"

"Fred called me to tell me about the issues with the will. He said you were coming by to try and find a letter of intent that Leon supposedly left."

"No 'supposedly.' He'd told Ernie all about his plans, and he wrote them down. It seems to be pretty clear—"

"Except that Ernie can't testify to that, and you won't find the letter. Oh look, there's my book." Delores walked into Leon's office and made her way over to the bookcase. She glanced over at the desk and then at Lilly. "Or perhaps you have found the letter after all? That's a shame, Lilly. That's a real shame."

Delores moved quickly and picked up the letter on the desk.

"Delores, put that down. Right now. It doesn't belong to you."

"Oh, I think it does," Delores said. "It's about my life. It should belong to me. It all should belong to me."

"Give me the letter, Delores," Lilly said again, slowly.

"Let's see what it says, shall we?" Delores said. Lilly

tried to move toward her, but she dipped out of the way. Delores ripped open the letter and read it.

"That imbecile," she said. "Did he really think that he could do this? After all I've done? He thought he could take it all away from me? What sentimental drivel."

"Delores, give me the letter," Lilly said.

"Poor Leon. So, he wanted to be true to Stanley's vision. Stanley's vision. If only he hadn't decided to go through Saint Stanley's personal papers. It's been almost thirty years, and now he decides to turn over the rocks in his father-in-law's memory garden."

"Delores, what are you talking about? What papers of Stanley's?"

"You haven't found them either?" Delores said. "Good, that means they're still here. Though where, I have no idea. I've looked all over this house—"

"When did you look all over the house?"

"Afterwards," Delores said.

"After what?"

"After Leon and I talked."

"You killed him," Lilly said. She was trying to back her way into the kitchen, but she tripped over a wastepaper basket and sat down hard on a box. She struggled to get up, but Delores walked over and pushed her back. Then she moved and sat behind Leon's desk.

"Stop, please. I mean it, Lilly, stop." Delores put her purse on the desk and patted it. "It's no good; really, it isn't. I can outrun you easily. You're not in very good shape, but I suspect you know that. Honestly, given the stress of the past few weeks, would it be any sort of surprise that you keeled over?"

"Keeled over—"

"It is a little awkward, but give me a minute to think about how to handle the situation. I've always been good at improvisation. Lilly, I told you not to move. A burglar could come by any minute and bash you over the head if you're not careful."

"Are you threatening me?" Lilly said.

"Just pointing out another way this scene could turn out," Delores said. "But there's not a lot you can do about that, is there?"

"Oh, well, actually there is," Bash Haywood said. "Hands in the air, Delores. Delores Stevens, I'm arresting you for the murder of Leon Tompkin, and the attempted murder of Lilly Jayne."

"You were supposed to say 'Miranda' when things started to go sideways," Delia said to Lilly. She'd waited until Lilly was done writing, but not a moment more. They were in Bash's office with Roddy, waiting to see what happened in Delores's interview.

"I wanted to get her to confess to killing Leon," Lilly said. She handed her statement to Officer Polleys, who was stationed at the door to Bash's office.

"While she was threatening to kill you!" Delia said, once they were alone and the door was closed. "Honestly, Lilly. You're worse than a teenager. You just do what you want to do without thinking about how it might impact anyone else."

"What are you talking about?" Lilly said. "I knew you were all out there, watching my back. I waited until I got your signal to find the letter, and then I made sure she could overhear my conversation with Fred. I only hope there's enough to get her to confess."

"I do, too," Roddy said. "She didn't even seem flustered when she came into the station, even when she saw us all sitting there."

"She was as cool as a cucumber the whole time," Lilly said. "She's probably used to getting away with things. But she did mention Stanley, so there's that connection."

"True. She seemed to have reinvented herself when James Jentry took over, but she connected herself to Stanley," Roddy said. "They can at least arrest her for threatening to kill you. Perhaps there can be a case made for killing Leon."

"Doubtful," Lilly said. "She only said they'd met. Maybe there's enough information so that Bash can search her house. I wonder what was in her purse?"

"I asked Bash. Nothing," Delia said. "Nothing she could have killed you with."

"Darn it," Lilly said. "Maybe she *was* going to hit me over the head and act like it was a break-in. I thought this plan would work."

"Scooter's going to stay under suspicion," Roddy said. "Even though Delores killed Jerry."

"Oh, Delores didn't kill Jerry," Lilly said. She took out her phone and selected a contact. After a minute, she hung up and sent a text. *Scooter, pick up the phone.* She waited a minute and dialed again.

"Scooter, thank you for reading my text. I have a question—could you tell me what happened when Jerry called to ask you to order cupcakes for Delores? Yes, I know. I know. Calm down, and tell me everything you remember."

CHAPTER 28

"I heard that Delores was being questioned regarding Jerry's death?" Annabelle asked. She and Mitch were sitting at the dining room table, looking at Stanley's pictures.

"She was being held because she tried to kill me—" Ernie said.

"And she threatened Lilly," Delia said.

"But she's been released. Lack of sufficient evidence," Lilly said.

"So Scooter killed Jerry?" Annabelle asked. She flipped through the pictures and found one of Scooter back in those days. "It's so hard to believe. I mean, after all this time."

"I talked to her earlier today," Lilly said. "One of the pieces of evidence against her is that she ordered the cupcakes for Delores. The ones Jerry asked her to order."

"She did?" Mitch asked. He was sorting through the pictures absently.

"It's a bit complicated, actually. You see, someone called and said he was Jerry. He asked her to order Delores's favorite cupcakes with the credit card he'd used to do his donation. He even gave her the details—the ones with the silver foil, things like that."

"She should have said no," Delia said. "Using his credit card like that isn't good business." She took the pile of pictures from Mitch and handed them to Annabelle. She took Annabelle's and handed them to Mitch.

"She should have, but apparently, Jerry sweet-talked her into it. Flattered her, told her how much he was looking forward to seeing her on Sunday. She said he was very convincing. He even remembered what she used to drink back then: gin and Tab. A dreadful-sounding concoction, but then again, she was very young. The problem is, they haven't found proof that Jerry made that call."

"What do you mean?" Annabelle said.

"I asked Bash to check. He didn't call using his cell phone, or from his hotel. He didn't even use the phone from here," Lilly said.

"Maybe he borrowed a phone," Mitch said.

"That could be, I supposed. Though I did ask Bash to check on another phone number. He found a record that you called the box office on Saturday, Mitch. Around the time Scooter said she got the call."

"I didn't call the box office," Mitch said. "Maybe Jerry used my phone—"

"There were several calls to the theater using your phone," Lilly said. "Over the past month, four in total."

"You can't—"

"But back to that phone call. The one on Saturday,"

Lilly said. "I remembered how you'd imitate Jerry when you talked about him chewing up the scenery. I started to wonder if it was you who placed the call."

"Why would I? What a convoluted idea. I called Scooter to order red velvet cupcakes with coffee almond syrup for Delores but said they were from Jerry?"

"How did you know about the coffee almond syrup?" Ernie asked.

"What do you mean?"

"The syrup was a particular order from Delores. Usually Kitty would use vanilla or chocolate syrup for red velvet cupcakes," Lilly said. "The only way to know what Delores's favorite cupcakes were was if you'd eaten them. When you'd visited with Delores."

"This is preposterous. Annabelle, let's go. She's obviously delusional, desperate to get her friend off the hook."

"I think I want to hear this story," Annabelle said.

"Well, I'm going—" Mitch said.

"Sit down, Mitch," Ernie said. "Hear the lady out. Lilly, tell him what you think happened to the cupcakes."

"The thing about syrup on cupcakes is, it keeps them moist. Delores would order herself a dozen every few days. It was one of the things she'd share with people during meetings, so she always had some on hand."

"So what?" Mitch said.

"You'd been to her office, so you knew the routine," Lilly said. "Here's what I think. You meant to poison Delores, Mitch. You ordered the cupcakes pretending to be Jerry so he'd get blamed. But the cupcakes Kitty delivered weren't the cupcakes that killed Delores. You'd poisoned the cupcakes in her office earlier in the day, during tech."

"Her office was locked," Mitch said.

"She kept a key in the box office," Ernie said.

"And Scooter said that you were very nice that day, and came to visit her a couple of times," Lilly said. "So, you poisoned the ones in her office. Then when the delivery came, you took the box you'd ordered for her and got rid of them."

"How did I do that?" he asked.

"You went backstage to visit Annabelle, and you used her bathroom. You probably flushed them down the toilet. They were mini cupcakes. It could be done. The boxes could go in the dumpster. If anyone found them, they'd assume they came with the order for the party."

Annabelle looked at Mitch and then at Lilly. "He did use my bathroom. Right before curtain time. He was in there a while, but I thought it was just nerves. I remember he came out with a trash bag. He said mine was full, so he changed it for me. He offered to put it in the dumpster. He went out the back door, and walked around the theater." Annabelle moved her chair away from Mitch, and then she stood up.

"Annabelle, come on. You know I could never—"

"But then how did Jerry get the poisoned cupcake?" Annabelle said. She was leaning against the dining room window, staring at Mitch.

Lilly wished she'd stayed sitting down, because she wanted to look at both their faces. "Delores loved her special treats. She brought her cupcakes out, and put them in the box office so that she could have a couple during the reception. There's a picture of her putting two on Annabelle's plate, and two on Jerry's plate."

"Which means she poisoned them—" Mitch said.

"No. Believe it or not, I think she was being nice. She also put two cupcakes on her plate," Lilly said. "But she hadn't eaten them yet. Here, let me show you the picture." Lilly pulled a number of 11-by-17-inch pieces of paper out of the folder in front of her and unfolded them. They were blown-up pictures of the reception. The first showed Delores with the box of cupcakes. The next showed her putting two on her plate. The final picture showed her putting them on Jerry and Annabelle's plates.

"I could have been killed," Annabelle said, looking at Mitch.

"Why were you so worried about the vitamin pouch the other day?" Lilly asked.

"The vitamin pouch? Oh, that," Annabelle said.

"Yes, that."

"It's where I keep the things that help me get through the day," Annabelle said. "Cigarettes, a joint, some tranquilizers. Nothing too heavy. It would be bad if it got into the wrong hands, is all. I was worried about that, so Mitch told me I should come back and look for it."

"Do you remember that night, leaving the theater? You climbed into the back of my car to avoid the reporters," Lilly said. "You must have had it in your pocket. It got stuck in the wheel well back there. Bash found it this afternoon."

"Bash? The chief of police, that Bash? Why was he looking for it?" Annabelle asked.

"It occurred to me that if Mitch intended to kill Delores and have Jerry blamed for it, he needed a backup plan. When he came back to see you, he brought the poison with him. And he put it in your pouch."

"Why?"

"So that the poison would be found in your possession," Lilly said.

Annabelle walked behind Ernie and picked the pictures up off the table. She examined them closely.

"Look at your face, Mitch. You knew," Annabelle said. "You knew he was going to eat that cupcake. But you didn't say anything? How could you? What if I'd eaten it?"

"I thought you were off gluten," he said. "If you'd tried to eat it, I would have stopped you. Honestly, you have to believe me."

"What about Jerry?" Annabelle asked.

"Jerry? Jerry the star? Jerry the chosen one? Did he take any of us with him, Annabelle? No. He ruined our lives and left us."

Annabelle started to cry, and Ernie stood up and put his arms around her.

"Why did you want to kill Delores?" Lilly asked Mitch.

He looked around the room, and then he hung his head for a minute and looked up at her. "Leon wanted me to take over the theater," he said. "That's why I agreed to let my play be in the reading series. So that he and I could work together. She must have gotten wind of it. She called me in for a meeting. She'd found out about a deal that Stanley and I had back in the day. It cut Leon out of the theater. I have no idea how she found out. But she had the letters I'd written to Stanley, saying some unkind things about Leon. She threatened to tell Leon unless I paid her off. Which I did. Then she wanted more money, so I told Leon myself."

"Then what happened?" Lilly asked.

"He was furious. Not happy with me, but furious with her. He and I were supposed to have a meeting, but he died that morning. She texted me and told me I still owed her. I couldn't—you went to bed early Thanksgiving night, Annabelle, but Jerry and I stayed up drinking and talking. We started talking about Mel, and Stanley. I told him about Delores." Mitch looked over at Annabelle, who was still crying.

"Then Jerry found the picture of Delores in the show," Ernie said. "He must have started putting it all together."

"He told me right after the show that I wouldn't have to worry about Delores anymore. By then, it was too late. I am sorry about Jerry, Annabelle," he said. "I'd give anything if Delores had died like she was supposed to."

CHAPTER 29

"Do you need help with that, Lilly?" Minh Vann ran up to Lilly as she walked into the front of the library.

"No, thank you," Lilly said. "We're here with our wreaths."

Minh looked around and then looked back at Lilly. "We're?"

"Roddy and Delia are parking the car," Lilly said. "It's windy outside, and my wreath is a bit tenuous."

"I can't wait to see it. Here, let me look at the chart to see where yours is going to hang. Oh, of course. In the Alan Macmillan Room. Outside it, actually. Let's go up and get your wreath hung; what do you think?"

Lilly and Minh took the elevator up to the second floor. Minh ran to the closet to get a short ladder, which she climbed up. Lilly carefully moved her hands so that she could expose the back of the wreath by moving the sheet she'd wrapped around it. Minh found the handhold that Lilly had created out of wire, and she held tight while Lilly extricated the wreath from the sheet. Minh lifted it onto the hook that they'd installed to hang in front of the room's center window.

Once Minh was sure the wreath was secure, Lilly stepped back so that she could climb down. Then Lilly climbed up and futzed with the decorations, making them 3-D again.

"That is wonderful," Minh said. "Look at that train! It looks like it's going around the wreath, but it's disappearing in the white—what are those?"

"Spray painted bits and pieces. Some ferns, a bit of ivy, some branches. I wanted it to look like a snow drift."

"So cool. Look at all the details. Wow, the handkerchief with an 'H' embroidered on it. The dagger, the police badge, the mustache. Are those burned photographs? How wonderful! There are a million things to look at, but it still looks like a festive wreath."

"Delia talked me out of spattering blood on it," Lilly said, looking up at her creation with a smile. "I really enjoyed working on it these past two days. It's gotten my mind off other things."

"I heard about those other things—well, some of them," Minh said. "Mitch Layton. I've got to say, I was surprised. But I'm glad that the killer was found."

"One of them, at least."

"One of them?"

"A long story. Minh, thank you again for your help with all of those theater materials," Lilly said. "They were very interesting. The summary sheet was so helpful."

"Roddy told me that you used them to show how the scanning procedures worked. I'm glad that the meeting went well last night, and the Historical Society board was happy with the process."

"Happy? They're thrilled. I'm so glad that you're coming on board. Promise me one thing, though."

"What?"

"That you'll only work the number of hours we're paying you for."

"I don't mind—"

"I'd like to show the board that part-time is not sufficient, and that we need to make this a full-time position. I can only do that if you and Delia slow down and help me make the case." Lilly stepped up the ladder and tweaked a few more things.

"I'll do my best," Minh said. "I really do appreciate the opportunity. Working with the Historical Society is my dream job."

"The perfect woman for her dream job. That's the kind of synergy I like."

"Did this really only take you two days? I'm impressed that you got your wreath done so fast," Minh said.

"To tell you the truth, we all worked on our wreaths together last night," Lilly said.

"We?"

"Roddy, Delia, and I. Ernie helped, of course. And Warwick and Tamara. We had a lot to discuss. I also hoped that getting ours done early might encourage other people to draw a title."

"It will definitely help," Minh said, taking a picture of the wreath with her phone. "Do you know if Ernie is coming by tonight?"

"No, he's at the store. They're pretty busy over there."

"Oh, I was hoping to talk to him," Minh said. She looked at Lilly and paused. "I'm not sure how to, though."

"What do you mean?"

"He gave me some boxes of Albert Preston's things when I went over. I've been looking them over. I found a picture of my mother in one of them. It was in with his documentation from the Army. The Army stuff was on top, but there was a cigar box of other stuff underneath."

"Was there just one picture of your mother?"

"There were other pictures of them together. One done in one of those photo booths; you know, the ones where you get four pictures on a strip. She looked so young, and so happy. I don't ever remember her looking like that. I also found some letters she wrote him."

"Did you find anything like that in your mother's things?"

"No, she told me she burned everything."

"Do you think that Albert's—"

"My father, yes."

"I'm surprised—"

"I'm not making things up—"

"No, no. I didn't mean that. I'm surprised that Albert didn't do the right thing by your mother," Lilly said. "He was a very gentle man."

"I think I found the reason she didn't hear from him," Minh said. "He was in a training accident, and hospitalized for months."

"So, by the time he got out of the hospital—"

"My mother was married, and I was already born."

"Why didn't he tell his family about her so that they could let her know what happened?" Lilly asked.

"Maybe his family didn't like the idea of a daughter-in-law who wasn't white?" Minh said. "It's okay, don't look so sad. Some of the letters my mother wrote him said that neither family was happy. She did love him. The letters showed that."

"I wish he'd known about you," Lilly said. "I think he would have been thrilled."

"Thank you, that means a lot. I'm going to ask Ernie if he'd mind me taking Albert's papers and trying to get to know him better."

"I'm sure he wouldn't mind that at all," Lilly said.

When Lilly and Minh got back downstairs, Roddy was just finishing hanging his wreath behind the circulation desk.

"Now that's a place of honor," Lilly said, joining the group who had assembled to the side of the foyer.

"Well-deserved," Dot said. She was beaming. "A wreath that looks like a whale tail. In two days. Amazing."

"Only possible because Delia and Ernie helped," Roddy said, walking over to the three women.

"I like the peg leg looking like a harpoon that missed," Delia said. "See it? It's sort of melded into the drift-wood."

"I do see it," she said, looking closely. "There's a lot to see. I love all the detail on your *Great Expectations* wreath. The wedding dress as a ribbon was an especially nice touch."

"It was fun to work on," Delia said. "I was mostly done, which is why I could help Roddy. Wait till you see Ernie's. It should be done next week."

A man brushed by them and walked over to the librarian who was organizing the book return.

"Excuse me, could you tell me where the Historical Society is?"

"I'm sorry, it's closed."

"Hello, sorry, he's here for me," Delia said. "Hello, Captain Flavia. Trooper Harris. Thank you both for meeting me here."

"Miss Greenway," Captain Flavia said. "Trooper Harris mentioned that you were going to explain a few things to me."

"We all are," Delia said, sweeping her arm towards Roddy and Lilly.

"I might have known," he said to Lilly.

Bash Haywood walked in and looked around with a confused look on his face. "I got an email to meet you here?"

Lilly plastered on her best smile and stepped forward. "Right this way, Captain Flavia. Bash, I'm glad you're able to join us. This seemed more appropriate for a presentation. Why don't we head downstairs?"

Delia and Roddy were hooking up the large projection screen to Delia's computer. Lilly had the three officers sit at the table facing it.

"Thank you all for being here," Lilly said.

"Since you solved our case, I figured we owed you one," the captain said.

"But I didn't solve the case that I wanted to solve," Lilly said. "I'd like to lay it out for all of you, hoping that your minds can help put mine at ease."

"Which case did you want to solve?" Liz Harris asked.

"The death of my friend, Leon Tompkin," she said.

"Haywood told me about that case," Captain Flavia said. "I looked at it. Heart attack."

"Heart attacks have played an important part of Delores Stevens's life," Lilly said. "Would you mind if I explain?"

Captain Flavia made a grunting noise, so Lilly spent the next ten minutes doing the presentation she and the Garden Squad had worked on last night and this morning. Wreath making had helped them keep busy while they were going over the same material several times. Lilly started with Delores's first husband, who fell asleep at the wheel and died. She connected her to everyone else involved with the case, ending with Leon's death.

"So, as you can see, there have been seven unexpected deaths that have touched Delores Stevens's life. Her husband. Mel John. Stanley Sayers. Jefferson St. John, a donor to the theater. Bruce Webb, a set designer. James Jentry. Leon Tompkin."

"That could be bad luck," Captain Flavia said.

"It could be. Except for two things. First, there's the deaths themselves. As I said, they were all unexpected. But they also follow a pattern. Mel, Jefferson, James Jentry, and Leon all seemed to have heart attacks. Her husband Ricardo, Stanley, and Bruce Webb all looked like suicides, but if they were unconscious, they could have been murdered."

"Murdered? That's—"

"I looked at the crime scene photos from Stanley Sayers's death," Trooper Harris said.

"Oh, you did, did you?" the captain asked.

"He was supposed to have killed himself, but the gunshot wound and the way the body fell don't look like that could be true. They ran a tox screen, and he had high levels of a sedative in his system."

"A lot of people use a sedative before they kill themselves—"

"The same sedative was in Ricardo's blood. And Bruce Webb's blood. It's a powerful sedative. Used in animal hospitals mostly, for large animals. They're running tests on Ernie Johnson's blood to see if he had it, as well. He didn't drink his entire cup of coffee, which is probably what saved him," Bash said.

"The other four men all died of a heart attack," Lilly said.

"I asked the medical examiner to compare Mel John's blood tests and Leon Tompkin's blood tests. There's nothing conclusive, but a couple of markers are present in both. I'm trying to see if Jefferson St. John and James Jentry had the same markers," Bash said.

"That would mean?" Captain Flavia asked.

"Possibly the same toxin was used to induce a heart attack," Bash said.

"Possibly." Captain Flavia looked around. "That's all you've got?"

"There's the second part," Lilly said. "There's the benefit each of these deaths had for clearing the path for Delores to move forward in her career. Can I explain?"

"Go ahead," he said gruffly.

Lilly used the clicker to advance to the next part of their presentation. "Delores's husband worked for Mel. We found some letters in Stanley Sayers's papers that indicated he wasn't being hired back for the next season. They might have meant that Delores wasn't coming back, either, but then Ricardo died. Mel John hired Delores as an intern after he died. At one point, Delores applied for a job as an administrator, but she wasn't hired."

"How do you know that?"

"James Jentry emptied Mel's desk and donated the contents to the Historical Society. Delia recently found the box, and Minh has been going through it. She found a list of names in Mel's files, and Delores's married name was on the list."

"So, she didn't get the job she wanted."

"Right. Mel John died a few weeks later. After he died, she got close to Stanley Sayers."

"Who also didn't hire her," Roddy said.

"By then, she'd become friends with James Jentry. Shortly after Stanley decided not to hire James, he died. James was hired."

"Did Delores get a job then?" the captain asked. He'd taken out his notebook and was writing things down.

"She did. She was his assistant, and ran the front of the house," Delia said.

"What happened to Jentry?"

Lilly moved to the next slide, which included the newspaper articles about his death. "James Jentry had a heart attack during a tech rehearsal."

"Delores was sitting next to him, according to the newspapers," Roddy said.

"After his death, Delores took over running the the-ater. Bruce Webb was appointed artistic director. He was a scenic designer—he'd taken over from Delores's hus-band. He killed himself in the scene shop. He'd locked himself in the paint booth and then combined bleach and ammonia."

"Interesting," Captain Flavia said. "We can pull that report."

"Then Jefferson St. John threatened to pull funding from the theater for some reason," Delia said. "I asked Portia Asher about it. She said he called an emergency meeting of the theater board, but he had a heart attack before the meeting. He didn't leave any records behind."

"He was the treasurer for the theater, so I can guess the reason," Lilly said. "This is an aside, but I do think a financial audit of the Goosebush Players would be interesting."

Lilly clicked to the final slide. "And then there's Leon. He was dying, and trying to put things in place before it was too late. From what I can see in going through his papers and talking to his lawyer, he'd changed his mind about how much to leave the Goosebush Players and was going to leave most of his money to the theater instead. That would have left Delores out of a job."

Captain Flavia stood up and looked at the board. He looked at Lilly and then at Trooper Harris.

"You think this idea has legs?" he asked her.

"I do," she said.

"You?" he asked Bash.

"It sounded far-fetched at first, but the more I think about it, the more it makes sense. It's scary as hell to think about, having a killer in our midst—"

"A serial killer," Captain Flavia said.

"A black widow," Delia said.

"A black widow," Bash said. "But something didn't feel right about Leon's death. Reading the reports on these other deaths, I wondered if the investigating officers at the time felt the same way. I reached out to Ray Mancini, and he verified that the cases felt off, but they didn't have proof. Or motive, for that matter."

"Proof is the problem. Okay, run this by me again. Slowly. Is that a pad of paper I can borrow? Thanks. I need more room to write. Start it again, then fill me in on the rest of what you've got."

"It's all in the presentation—" Lilly said.

"Don't even start with me," the captain said. "I know there's more. If you can get me to believe there's a case here, I'll see what we can do."

CHAPTER 30

"Are you sure they're both safe?" Lilly asked again.

"We're sure," Bash said. "Now Lilly, you need to focus. If Delores says something that Virginia doesn't know, she's going to say something about coffee. You tell me the answer, and then I can let Virginia know, all right?"

"All right—"

"The feed works? Your earpieces are in?"

"Yes to all of that," Lilly said. She looked around the dining room table at Roddy and Delia. Roddy gave her a thumbs-up, and she smiled at him.

"All right. Here we go," Bash said.

Lilly, Delia, and Roddy saw the front door of the theater being opened and held for Virginia Blossom. Ernie was wearing a body camera that was hidden in a lapel pin on his coat. Virginia Blossom was also wearing a body cam, but they didn't have her feed. Lilly could hear her in the earpiece, however.

"And this is the lobby," Ernie said, gesturing to the space. "The box office is over there. The management office is right behind it. The bathrooms were redone three years ago, and the dressing rooms all have a—"

"What on earth do you think you're doing?" Delores came storming out of her office. "I told you that a tour was not possible today."

"And I told you that it wasn't up to you," Ernie said. "I have to go to rehearsal this afternoon, and this is the only time that worked for Virginia and me."

"You're still doing that ridiculous reading?" Delores said. "I would have thought you would have taken a week off, considering your boyfriend tried to kill me."

"He wasn't my—oh, never mind that. Delores, we have a board meeting tonight, and Virginia is going to put in a proposal to run this space as of April first."

"I thought the board hadn't voted on my lease yet," Delores said.

"They haven't. That will happen at the board meeting, as well."

"From what I've heard, you don't have the votes to pull this coup off," Delores said.

"Then you've heard wrong," Ernie said. "I've been on the phone all morning. People are excited about a new vision for the theater. As long as Virginia shows up—"

"Are you kidding me? I've been waiting for this opportunity," Virginia said. "I'll be there."

"I thought you were taking over the Star," Delores said.

"Not if I can get my hands on this place," Virginia said. "I'm heading over there to meet Stan at two. I'll let him down easy."

"Let's take a look at the space," Ernie said. "It's bigger, but the Star is more state-of-the-art. Come this way."

They watched Ernie open the door, and Virginia walk in, followed by Delores.

"Why is it so dark in here?" Virginia asked.

"Theaters are dark. And electricity is expensive," Delores said.

"Electricity you don't pay for. I told you I was coming by," Ernie said. "I'll go backstage and turn on the house lights. Hold on for a second."

They watched Ernie walk to the edge of the stage. He turned on the flashlight on his cell phone and went through the stage left doors to find the lighting panel. Meanwhile, Delores had started to talk to Virginia.

"Listen, I don't know who you think you are—" she said.

"I think I'm you thirty years ago, but cuter and smarter," Virginia said. "Put me in front of the board tonight, and this is a done deal."

"You have no idea how hard I've worked for this place. What I've sacrificed. All these years I've toiled just so you can sashay in and take over? If you think for one minute, I'm going to let you—"

"You're not going to let me do anything, Delores. Or should I say Loli? Loli. Oh, the stories Jerry told me about you. He'd figured out that you and Loli were the same person. Did he have a chance to mention that to you?"

"How did you know Jerry?"

"Please, a movie star in town, and you don't think I'd

make it my business to get to, um, know him?" Roddy and Lilly looked at each other, and Roddy raised his eyebrow. "I'd heard of you before that, though. Remember, my folks own a summer place here. I've been hanging around for years."

"So, you've seen my work," Delores said.

"Jeff St. John—do you remember Jeff? Jeff and I were good friends. *Really* good friends. He's the one that told me that you were a crook."

"Why, you—"

"Delores, honey, you look ill." The lights in the theater came on, and they all saw Ernie walk back to the two women. The image was blurry, but Virginia was right; Delores did look ill.

Virginia started to ask specific questions about the theater, and Ernie answered them. After a minute, Delores left them, but Ernie and Virginia kept up the conversation. After a few minutes, Ernie went back and turned the house lights back off.

"Let's head over to the Star to talk about it some more," Ernie said while they were in the lobby, outside Delores's office door. "I could use a cup of coffee."

"It's done," Bash said when he called Lilly later that afternoon.

"What do you mean?" she asked.

"We kept a tail on Ernie and Virginia after they left the theater. They went to the Star to get a cup of coffee and talk. Then Ernie left and went back to the Triple B. Virginia went upstairs to look at the theater, and brought her coffee with her."

"Did you follow her up?"

"We had the cameras all set up, and an officer in the theater. A couple of minutes later, Delores came into the Star with her own cup of coffee and went upstairs."

"Her own cup?" Lilly asked.

"Coffee in a Star Café cup. She'd bought one earlier in the morning. She went up to the theater lobby. Virginia's back was turned, and she switched cups with her. Then Virginia turned around. Delores said she wanted to talk about the theater, but Virginia told her to get lost. Then she took a sip of her coffee and started to choke. Delores switched the cups back as Virginia fell down."

"She took a sip—"

"Not really. We told her to be careful. She's a great actress. She helped us catch Delores in the act. The coffee cups are being tested now."

"What do you think she was going to do? Delores, I mean?"

"Who knows? Maybe take Virginia into the theater and stage her suicide?"

"Dear heaven," Lilly said.

"Listen, I've got to go. Captain Flavia is letting me sit in on the interview. We were just taking a break."

"Has Delores confessed?"

"Not yet. I've got to hand it to the captain, though. He's pretty smooth," Bash said. "He kept making mistakes while he was talking to her, and she started correcting him. Then he started asking inane questions. She thinks he's an idiot."

"She's trying to show him how smart she is," Lilly said.

"Exactly. That's starting to trip her up. She's saying things that contradict what she'd said before. Then she tries to backtrack. Her lawyer's here, but she won't stop talking."

"I'm glad that Captain Flavia is taking the lead," Lilly said. "She knows she couldn't trip you up."

"Thanks, Lilly."

"I appreciate the update. And Bash?"

"Yeah?"

"Nail her," Lilly said.

"Yes, ma'am."

CHAPTER 31

"All right, to your left. Your other left, Lilly," Delia said as they navigated the fifth and last piece of their garden sculpture into Alden Park.

"We're at the end of the park," Delia said. "You okay?"

"I'm fine," Lilly said between gritted teeth. "Are we having fun yet?"

Delia took the turn and walked backwards, looking over her shoulder to make sure they weren't going to crash into someone. It was a legitimate concern. All entries in the Goosebush Garden Sculpture and Lights event had five hours to get their sculpture installed and lit. There were three more hours to go. Since Ernie was helping run the event, he didn't feel as though helping the Garden Squad would be fair, so it was up to the rest of them.

Warwick, Roddy, and Delia had planned their installation. Lilly and Tamara were helping put it together.
Roddy's idea took several days to frame, two days to decorate, and three hours to disassemble and get in the cars.
Lilly had no faith it was going to work, but she was trying
to get a better attitude.

They finally got to the other end of the park, where
Roddy and Warwick were tying the pieces back together,
and Tamara was holding a piece up with one hand and a
tube of pink lights with another.

"How's it going?" Lilly asked.

"You were right," Warwick said. "We're going to need
to fill in some spaces on the piece."

"Good thing I brought a bag of leftover flora and fauna
then, isn't it?" Lilly said.

"You're a brick, Lilly," Roddy said. "Tamara, could
you feed me a bit more of that tube lighting? Thank you;
the edging is almost done. Let's get that last piece in
here."

The five of them spent the next two hours on the
sculpture. The entire park was full of people working on
their projects. Even though it was very cold out, the work
kept people warm, as did the volunteers, who were handing out hot cider.

"Your project looks great, Lilly," a voice said. Lilly
looked over and saw Scooter McGee standing there with
a new clipboard.

"Scooter, how lovely to see you! I'm glad you're
here."

"Ernie insisted I show up," she said. "He gave me a
pretty good pep talk."

"He's good at those pep talks," Lilly said. "Hold on,
our corner is tilting. I'm sorry, I have to help."

"Of course. It looks beautiful," Scooter said as she moved to the next sculpture to check on progress.

Lilly looked up. Only the Garden Squad would try and put a six-foot heart on a pedestal so that it appeared to be floating. She stepped in to hold it while Roddy laid down on the ground to plug in the lights.

"All right," he said, standing up slowly. "Delia, what do you think of the stability?"

"Warwick and I just added more zip ties to the stabilizing poles, so I think we're pretty good."

"Let's take a step back. We have forty minutes to embellish," he said.

Each of them let go slowly, and they stepped back. The heart didn't move. In fact, from here, it just looked like a big decorated heart. Lilly hoped that all of the details worked. They spent the rest of their time closing gaps and adding the exterior lights. Delia got down and plugged those in. They cleaned up their space and stepped back just as Ernie gave the five-minute warning.

Lilly looked around at the other sculptures. She saw Portia and her grandson putting the finishing touches on what looked like a martini glass and olive. The Girl Scouts had created a rainbow. From where she stood, Lilly saw a menorah and fish and hashtags and smiley faces and sharks and wreaths and more.

Ernie blew a horn, and everyone started to count down. "Ten, nine, eight, seven, six, five, four, three, two, one!" Lilly saw lights go on all over the park. Successfully, in most cases. Other teams rushed to figure out what wasn't plugged in or to rearrange lights. Lilly slowly turned around and looked at their sculpture.

She needn't have worried. Roddy's precise design ensured that the heart looked exactly as they wanted it to.

Pink lights lit up the edging from inside, so it glowed. GOOSEBUSH was written in cursive in ivy that had been spray-painted gold. Lilly also saw the initials they'd all woven into the piece. She knew that the plants were all carefully chosen to represent each one of the Garden Squad. From the outside, it looked simple, but the piece took a lot of thought.

All of a sudden, people began to cheer and clap. Roddy walked over to Lilly and put his arm around her shoulder.

"Thank you for being a good sport, and for indulging me," he said, giving her a quick kiss on the temple.

"Thank you for getting me out of my rut," Lilly said, putting her arm around his waist and giving him a quick hug. "Life would be far more boring if you hadn't moved in next door."

"I'm glad I can help. Do you want to take a stroll?" Roddy turned around to invite the rest of the team.

"I'm going to stay here and talk to people who come by," Delia said.

Warwick and Tamara went over to talk to Ty, who had been drafted by the football team to help make a football. It looked more like a pancake, but Warwick started helping them reshape the piece.

Lilly and Roddy took their time walking through. Roddy took out his phone and started snapping pictures. Lilly kept walking; he'd catch up with her after a while. They kept moving like that until they got to the end of the park and saw Ernie. Roddy wanted to keep moving, so Lilly walked over to her friend.

"Congratulations, Ernie, this is a huge success," Lilly said. "I hope people are buying lots of wreaths and trees."

"We're having a banner day," Ernie said. "It's been a

great couple of weeks, due in no small part to the 'made in Goosebush' hashtag."

"Which I had nothing to do with," Lilly said. "But I am glad it worked."

"I love the heart," he said, looking down at the end of the park. "It's stunning."

"Again, not me, but thanks. It is lovely from a distance, isn't it? I wasn't sure if the 'Goosebush' would read, but it does. Oh, hello, Minh," Lilly said, waving to Minh, who made a loop gesture, and Lilly nodded, assuming she'd see her when she finished walking through.

"Are those her children?"

"They are," Ernie said. "Hey, Lilly, now's not really the time, but I wanted to let you know about a decision I've made. I'm going to sell the Preston house to Minh."

Lilly stepped back and stared at Ernie. "Are you sure?"

He nodded. "There's so much Preston history in that house, and Minh is thirsty for it."

"You could just give her all the contents."

"I could. But honestly, almost getting killed in there? Not sure I'd ever be able to sit in the front room without remembering."

"Okay, that one I can't help you with," Lilly said. "How much fire damage was there?"

"Not much, thanks to Warwick. But it will take some work. Minh and her family are up to it."

"How fast are you going to sell?"

"Pretty fast. She's offering what I bought it for, plus all of the costs I've put in. Tamara's handling the sale without taking a commission, which is nice of her."

"When did all this happen?"

"Just the last couple of days. I've been thinking about

it for a while, though. It's a big house, and the thought of rambling around it by myself wasn't fun."

"I know what you mean," Lilly said. "Having you and Delia living with me has made a world of difference."

"And the cats," Ernie said.

"Oh yes, the cats," Lilly said. "You know you're welcome to stay for as long as you'd like."

"Thanks, Lilly. I'm going to take you up on that. I thought about renting a condo, but the thought of being alone for the holidays—"

"Say no more. You're not going to be alone for anything."

"You're the best," Ernie said. "By the way, thanks for everything you've done for the theater so far."

"I'm just trying to live up to Leon's expectations," she said. "It will take a while to sort through all of his papers, but we're figuring it out."

"Having Delores gone helps in a lot of ways," Ernie said. "I still can't believe she confessed."

"I think she wanted everyone to know how smart she was," Lilly said. "Bash says that Captain Flavia played her like a fiddle. Obviously, she's nuts. I'm thrilled that she's in jail, though."

Roddy and Delia walked back toward Ernie and Lilly. They arrived at the same time as Warwick and Tamara. All six of them stood in a semicircle and looked around.

"To the Garden Squad," Ernie said quietly. "Long may we reign."

Arms intertwined, they laughed. Lilly looked around, feeling a contentment she hadn't felt in a long time. Life was certainly better with friends.

Acknowledgments

I love writing the Garden Squad series, and am delighted that their adventure continues. Thank you to John Scognamiglio, Michele Addo, Larissa Ackerman, the wonderful cover artist, and the rest of the team at Kensington.

Thank you to my agent, John Talbot, for your support.

I blog with five amazing women, the Wicked Authors (www.WickedAuthors.com): Barbara Ross, Sherry Harris, Edith Maxwell, Liz Mugavero, and Jessie Crockett. For readers who'd like to become writers, here's my best advice. Find people who act as advisors, confidants, cheerleaders, and dear friends. The Wickeds are all that and more to me.

Huge thank you to Jennifer McKee for all of her help on the business side of my writing life.

Thank you to Kim Ten Eyck for helping me name Scooter McGee.

A special thank-you to Jason Allen-Forrest, my first reader. I wish I could explain how helpful his comments are.

Thank you to Scott Forrest-Allen, who always is there for title help.

Thank you to Deb Brown, John Montgomery, Scott Sinclair, Megan Keeliher, Tracy Stewart, Stephanie Troisi, Marianna Troisi, Ruth Polleys, Craig Coogan, and all my other friends who cheer me on.

A special thank you to Sisters in Crime, particularly the New England chapter. If I hadn't joined that organization, I don't think you'd be holding this book in your hand. I'm proud to be part of a group that does such good work in the writing community.

Thank you to Edith, Kay Garrett, Judy Parks, Gale Shanahan, Janet Graham, Kay Bennett, Renee Wiswell, Ginny Crouse, and Abby Fabian for their gardening tips.

I have a wonderful family who I adore. A special shout-out to my strong, fierce, funny, kind, loving sisters, Kristen and Caroline. I'm blessed that you are my sisters, and my friends.

And finally, a huge thank-you to my wonderful readers. I love meeting you at events and conferences or hearing from you on social media. Please stay in touch with @JHAuthors and make sure to say hello. Your reading support means the world.

Gardening Tips

- Fall is a great time to take care of your gardening tools. Make sure they are free from dirt. Pour a bit of old motor oil on a rag and rub down the metal and wood to preserve them. You'll be glad you took the time next spring.
- Put mulch around your carrots and parsnips in the fall so the soil doesn't freeze. These root crops sweeten up with the cold, and the mulch lets you harvest them for your holiday feast and later.
- Interested in growing garlic? Fall is a good time to plant. In a sunny bed full of loose compost, plant cloves of garlic root side down. Press them beneath the surface, and then cover them with 6 inches of mulch for winter protection.
- Are you having trouble getting your annuals to self-seed successfully? Don't open the beds and weed too early. Wait until two weeks after the last frost before you start.
- The best way to tie up tomatoes or plants that have running vines is panty hose strips. Just take old, torn-up, about-to-be-discarded panty hose and make cuts straight across the leg—about ¼- to ½-inch strips. Then just tie around the vine to some form of support, like the tomato cage or post. The strips hold and support but give enough when the wind blows to keep the plant vine from getting cut, nicked, or damaged by the support of a regular tie.
- Do you have a favorite coffee shop? Ask them if you can take their grounds and add them to your compost.

You'll have to take out the coffee filters, and make sure to fork the grounds through the compost.

- Do you have trouble with aphids? Here are a couple of ideas that may help. Build a trap. Get some yellow plastic cups. Put 16-inch sticks in the ground about a foot from the plant, and turn a cup upside down on the stick. Use a thumbtack to keep it in place, and then coat the cup in petroleum jelly. You can also spray your plants every other day with a mild solution of water and a few drops of dishwashing detergent. Keep this up for a couple of weeks, and it should help.
- When you deadhead flowers, consider throwing them into a wildflower bed or tossing them down to reseed.
- If you trim back mums and asters twice before fall, you'll have a nice, round, compact plant.
- If you don't want to use as much mulch, consider ivy or succulents to fill the spaces in your garden. Do make sure they aren't invasive.
- Fill up an empty wine bottle with water. Turn it over and put it in a pot or in the ground. The water will slowly seep out, helping keep your plant watered. This is a great tip if you're going away for a few days or have plants that need more TLC in the summer. Here's an idea for the wine corks—chop them up and add them to your soil.
- Do you have trouble with birds and deer bothering your plants? Try using pinwheels. Yes, pinwheels. One suggestion says that reflective surfaces work best.

Grab These Cozy Mysteries
from
Kensington Books

Available Wherever Books Are Sold!
All available as e-books, too!
Visit our website at **www.kensingtonbooks.com**